KATE GRENVILLE

*THE SECRET RIVER*

COMMONWEALTH WRITERS' PRIZE
SHORTLISTED FOR THE MAN BOOKER PRIZE

'Beautifully written and compelling from start to finish, this is a marvellous novel' *The Times*

'In *The Secret River*, Kate Grenville has written a book that will satisfy her critics' craving for more action. Grenville, as ever, describes an Australia so overwhelmingly beautiful that readers will lust after its sunbaked soul' *Daily Telegraph*

'Reading *The Secret River* may put you off reading anything less accomplished for a while' *Daily Express*

'Ambitious . . . Grenville writes prose which is immediately engaging. There are overtones of Macbeth in this study in how a man, not inherently evil, can be corrupted by circumstances. Grenville's skill is to turn what could have been too obviously a representative moral fable into a rich novel of character' *Sunday Telegraph*

'A vivid and moving portrayal of poverty, struggle and the search for peace' *Independent*

'This wonderful story about ownership and identity is filled with imagery that transports you immediately to its heart' *Marie Claire*

'Elegantly calibrated prose . . . a lovely, watchful stillness: a sort of astronomy of the human heart' *Sunday Telegraph*

'This engrossing story evokes the excitement of discovery and the beauty of an unspoilt land' *Irish Mail on Sunday*

'In lucid prose and perfectly measured strides, Grenville lays down her riveting tale. A novel aglow with empathy, its author's capacious visions still deliver an elemental thrill' *Daily Mail*

'This novel is a triumph. Read it at once' *The Times*

'An original, inviting tale' Lionel Shriver, *Daily Telegraph*

'A particular kind of stillness marks Kate Grenville's characters out as uniquely hers . . . Between the words and among them, this is a profoundly uplifting novel' *Independent*

'Compelling . . . intelligent, spare, always engrossing' *Times Literary Supplement*

'Grenville inhabits characters with a rare completeness . . . She occupies the mind of Rooke with a kind of vivid insistence, and his isolation – and moral dilemmas – become ours' *Guardian*

## ALSO BY KATE GRENVILLE

# Sarah Thornhill

## KATE GRENVILLE

CANONGATE

Edinburgh · London

This paperback edition first published in 2012 by Canongate Books
First published in Great Britain in 2012 by
Canongate Books Ltd, 14 High Street, Edinburgh EH1 1TE

1

First published in Australia in 2011 by the Text Publishing Company,
Swann House, 22 William Street, Melbourne, Victoria 3000

www.canongate.tv

*British Library Cataloguing-in-Publication Data*
A catalogue record for this book is available on
request from the British Library

ISBN 978 0 85786 256 3
Export ISBN 978 0 85786 534 2

Page design by Susan Miller
Typeset by J&M Typesetters

Printed and bound in Great Britain by Clays Ltd, St Ives plc

*This novel is dedicated to the memory of Sophia Wiseman and Maryanne Wiseman, and their mother, 'Rugig'.*

It does not follow that because a mountain appears to take on different shapes from different angles of vision, it has objectively no shape at all or an infinity of shapes.

E. H. CARR

# PART ONE

THE HAWKESBURY was a lovely river, wide and calm, the water dimply green, the cliffs golden in the sun, and white birds roosting in the trees like so much washing. It was a sweet thing of a still morning, the river-oaks whispering and the land standing upside down in the water.

They called us the Colony of New South Wales. I never liked that. We wasn't new anything. We was ourselves.

The Hawkesbury was where the ones come that was sent out. Soon's they got their freedom, this was where they headed. Fifty miles out of Sydney and not a magistrate or a police to be seen. A man could pick out a bit of ground, get a hut up, never look back.

You heard that a lot. *Never looked back.*

That made it a place with no grannies and no grandpas. No aunties, no uncles. No past.

Pa started a boatman on the Thames. Then he was sent out, what for I never knew. *Eighteen-oh-six, Alexander transport.* I was a pestering sort of child but that was all he'd ever say, sitting in the armchair smiling away at nothing and smoothing the nap of the velvet.

Thornhills was in a big way. Three hundred acres of good riverfront land and you had to go all the way up the river to Windsor before you saw a house grand as ours. Pa had got his start in the old *Hope*, carrying other men's grain and meat down the river to Sydney. Given that away, now he had his own corn and wheat, beef and hogs, and let other men do the carting of them.

But still a boatman at heart. Always a couple of skiffs down at the jetty, and when they put in the new road to the north he saw an opening, got a punt going. A shilling for a man, half a crown for a man on a horse, sixpence a head for cattle. Where you had people you needed an inn, so he built the Ferryman's Arms, had George Wheeler run it for him.

I never saw Pa lift an axe or carry a stick of firewood and he had other men now to do the rowing for him. Done enough work for any man's lifetime, he'd say. Of a morning he'd eat his breakfast, light his pipe, go out to where the men were standing with their hoes and spades. Jemmy Katter, Bob Dodd, Dickie Parson, three or four others. Assigned from Government, serving their time like he'd done. Sent out from London the most of them, never seen a spade in their lives before.

He'd set them to chipping between the corn rows, mucking out the hog-pens. Fill his pipe and stand watching them work. Point and call out if he thought they wasn't doing it right.

He made them call him *sir*. A flogging if they forgot.

When you done as well as Pa had, no one said *sent out* or *worn the broad arrow*. Now he was what they called an *old colonist*. Still plenty of folk who wouldn't put their feet under the same table as an emancipist or invite him into their house. As far as some people went, *sent out* meant tainted for all time. You and your children and your children's children. But for other folk, money had a way of blunting the hard shapes of the past. Dressing it up in different words.

Pa was Mr Thornhill of Thornhill's Point now, but he had some habits that were from before. Of an afternoon he'd get a bit of bread and go out on the verandah. Sit on a hard bench beside the window—didn't want a cushion—with the bread and a glass of rum-and-water beside him on the sill. He'd put his telescope up to his eye and look down the river where you'd see the boats from Sydney come round the last spur into Thornhill's Reach. Sliding up fast if the tide was with them, or having to get out the oars if it was sucking back out to sea. Other times he'd swing it round the other way, to the reedy place where the First Branch wound down from among the hills. But mostly he'd look straight across the river up at the line of bush along the top of the cliffs. Nothing up there, only rocks and trees and sky, but he'd sit by the hour watching, the leather worn through to the brass where his hand clamped round it.

~

I was born in the year eighteen-sixteen, Sarah Thornhill, named after my mother. She was Sarah but always called Sal. I was the baby of the family, why I was called Dolly.

Never liked *Dolly*. Never wanted to be a doll.

Next above me was Mary, nearly three years older and never let me forget it. Got the side of the bed near the fire. Pushed ahead when we went up the stairs. You know, silly things, but they matter when you're little.

I had three brothers too, all of them older.

Johnny was two years above Mary. Always with a scheme in his head. Got a lot of lemons once and rigged up a thing to get the juice. Begged some sugar from Ma, set up a stall down at the punt, made a shilling or two.

Bub was two years again above him. Even as a boy Bub was like an old man, sober and slow. Never went anywhere without a hoe and if he saw a thistle he'd stop and grub it out. It was him got the lemons for Johnny. Him got the hiding for it, too.

The oldest of us was Will. Fifteen when I was born and already out on the boats doing a man's work. Will was away more than he was home. Up and down the coast with the cedar. Over to New Zealand for the seals. Be away so long I'd think he was never coming back, half a year or more.

Captain Thornhill, people called him, though he was really only Will Thornhill who'd worked his way up. Never got his papers, nothing like that. Didn't read, see. None of us did.

Pa had no time for learning. Could sign his name but often said how a few acres and a flock of sheep was a better gift to your children than anything you'd get out of a book. When he needed something on paper he got old Loveday at Beckett's Reach to do it for him. Loveday had come free, could of done all right, but drank it all away in his miserable leaky hut. See, Pa would say. Old Loveday's not got the taint, but tell me this, you rather have his life or mine?

It was never spoke of, but Ma was not really our mother.

I had a few memories, sharp little pictures, of another mother. Will in the kitchen doorway and me sitting on the edge of the table working away at the peas in a pod while this other mother magicked them open down their backbone one by one with her thumbnail, the peas popping out into the blue-striped bowl with the grey chip on the edge. She sat puffing away on her pipe, doing the peas without having to look. The picture was so sharp it even had a smell, baccy and peas together. She'd take the pipe out of her mouth and sing, tuneless and wavery. *Oranges and lemons, say the bells of Saint Clement's,* she'd sing. *You owe me five farthings, say the bells of Saint Martin's.*

Will with his hands under my armpits, hoisting me in the air, the underside of the shingles swinging round, the pod clutched tight in my fist while the kitchen rolled up and down and under and over, and then I was back on the table with my mouth open, would I cry or laugh I didn't know, and Will was clattering at the stove, shouting and joking, head way up near the beams, and my mother with the peas all fallen in her pinny lap and not caring.

Then they brought me into a dark room, summer outside but all the curtains drawn across and the shutters closed, someone leading me by the hand over to the high bed where

7

my mother lay, but I was frightened and shy, she was sweaty, her hair in strings, her cheeks sunk in, and her hand on the coverlet waxy and bony.

Whoever was with me, I could feel their hand at my back, pushing, they wanted me to kiss the yellow face on the pillow. Her eyes slid sideways at me, she was smiling, but her lips were so white and dry and her face nothing but wrinkled skin sliding over the bone. I pulled back, how could I kiss such a thing! Her hand crawled towards me over the coverlet and she touched me on the shoulder, top of the head, shoulder again, then the hand fell back and they let me go away.

Like a dream, that first mother melted away and there was another person we called Ma.

Pa had no stories but Ma had enough for the both of them. Turned over the places and names and dates like coins in her hand, counted and re-counted them for the pleasure of it. Her Daddy was in the sugar trade and she grew up in a house at Brixton-Hill, *on the north side, that's the superior side.* A husband something in the army, she was Margaret Grant. *Come free* to New South Wales along with him. Then he died.

I come up the river to help your pa, she'd say. Your mother too sick to care for a houseful of children. Then by and by we was wed.

I loved how neat it was, the way she told it, then and now stitched up tight.

Ma had a scurrying way with her, tilting forward from the waist like a hen in a hurry. Always putting something to rights. She never forgot the stain Pa carried. But the way she saw it, it was a wife's job to hide it, even if she couldn't wash it out.

She had a headful of all the things you did so no one would know you had the taint. Elbows off the table, remember Dolly, she'd say, and a well-bred person leaves a scrap on their plate. She'd be running after us with our bonnets when we went outside, did we want to look like blackfellows? Church, rain or shine, every Sunday, that fog of mothballs. *We have left undone those things which we ought to have done and we have done those things which we ought not to have done.* Church was full of hard words, but those were plain small ones mortared together into something that nothing could get into or out of.

Pa did his best, but he'd forget. Eat off his knife, or say *victuals*, when Ma thought that was vulgar.

It's food, William, she'd say. Or comestibles.

By God Meg, he'd say. Combustibles is it?

He'd laugh, but then he'd reach over and touch her arm.

Oh, I'm an ignorant feller, he'd say. Lucky she took me, your ma.

Humour not Ma's long suit, but she'd smile then, and when she did that you could see what they shared. The two of them, no one else in the room.

I'd seen Pa drink out of the teapot spout, but when Ma was watching he cramped up his thick fingers into the silly little teacup handle. At table he'd work the silverware the way Ma liked, squash the peas onto the fork and line it up with the knife when he'd finished.

If we'd go to him about something he'd say, *Best see what your Ma says.* Not that he was a weak man, Pa. Not by any manner of means. But he'd done his bit. Got us the house, the land, the money. Found us a good mother. Now he could sit back. Knew Ma would see to it his children had a clean break with the past. Leave it behind the way he had.

Pa enjoyed his money. You once gone without, he'd say, you know it's better to have than not. The best if you can get it. *The best* meant meat every day. All the potatoes you could eat, with sweet fresh butter.

And oranges. Never seen an orange before I were twelve year old, he'd say, not to eat. It was a bit of joke between me and Mary, one of the things we did share. Every time Anne brought in a dish of oranges Pa would force his great square thumb into one and lever up a piece of peel. *Never seen an orange before I were twelve year old*, he'd say. *Not to eat.*

Mary and me would slip each other a look. She'd suck her lips into a fishmouth and I'd have to make out I was snorting because of my tea going down the wrong way.

Ma would give us the rounds of the kitchen later. Your pa known some hard times, she'd say. You silly girls don't know the half of it.

~

There was Mrs Devlin in the kitchen and Anne the maid-of-all-work. A woman once a week for the washing and a native boy for the wood. Still, girls of our class, well-off but not gentry, we learned all the household things. Mrs Devlin showed us how to do the bread and keep the yeast bottle going, the basic things like that, and Ma taught us *the finer points*, how to slice the bacon thin and the way to fold the flour into a sponge cake so it stayed light. Mary liked working in the kitchen, but I got sick of Mrs Devlin forever on about Mr Devlin that died, and Ma saying oh yes, how hard life was for a poor widder. I didn't want to spend my time sweating away at the stove, everything eaten by half past twelve and not a thing to show for it.

I learned how to make a loaf and pickle a brisket of beef and all the rest of it, because that's what a girl was supposed to know. But I'd get away soon's I could. I had a place of my own, a cave in the bush up behind the house. It was a steep scramble but not far. Close enough so I could be back if Ma called, she'd never know I was gone. Far enough, it was my own world. That country was full of overhangs where the soft yellow rock was worn away underneath, but this one was big enough to stand in and full of light the colour of honey. The floor level, soft with dry sand fallen from the roof, never wet by rain, not since the world began.

I set up house there, the way a child likes to do. Had a chipped teacup and a milk-jug with no handle and a dipper, because on top of the cave was a hole, made by man or nature I didn't know, that filled with sweet water after rain. The lip of the cave was on a level with the treetops. You could sit there and watch the breeze shivering through the leaves and the river beyond, a band of colour like a muscle. When you sat in the cave the bush sounds come to you sharper. It was like a big ear, listening.

Mary never wanted to go up there. Said she couldn't see why you'd want to climb up there and get all over prickles just to sit on the hard ground. That suited me. The birds were company enough. One I called the What Bird, it had a call like a question. *Dit dit dit dit dit?* it would go, and I'd screw my mouth round to answer, *Dit dit dit dit?*

I thought about flying, stood sometimes on the edge of the rock and wondered. But much as I'd of liked to, and young as I was, I had the sense to know I'd have to wait for some other way to fly.

NONE OF us Thornhills had our letters, but you didn't need a book to work out how to count, at least what you had the fingers for.

One day, I'd of been five or six, I went out to Pa on the verandah. A shiny morning, the river with a brush of wind on it that sent a handful of sparkles across the water.

I got three brothers, I said. See, Pa? I know how to count!

His face always seemed bigger than other people's. Big chin, big nose, big cheeks. And his eyes, the way one was a different shape from the other, that you only saw when he looked at you straight on. Which he did that time. Those blue eyes, and his mouth a funny shape.

No, Dolly, he said. You got four brothers.

Took a gulp of his rum-and-water so I could hear it go down

his gullet as if it was having to find its way round something in there.

No, Pa, look, I got three, I said.

Showed him on my fingers.

Will, Bub, Johnny, I said. See?

You got four brothers, Dolly, he said. Only Dick's gone away for a time.

How come, I said. How come he went away? Where'd he go?

His face hardened down. I knew that meant trouble, told myself *let it go!*

When's he coming back, Pa? I said. When's Dick coming back?

Then he was on his feet, the glass knocked over, the bench clattering on the boards so the dust flew up and he was above me, his big face shouting down into mine. A dizzy ringing when his hand caught me across the side of the head, my ear making a high thin noise like something screaming a long way off.

That's enough, he said. Get away out of my sight, damn your eyes.

Pushed me, hard, so I stumbled through the doorway into the hall. Crept upstairs to the bedroom, Mary still dead asleep. Got in the bed, coiled myself up small as I could go, pulled the blanket over my head. In the stuffy dark I folded my fingers over one by one. Johnny, Bub, Will. One, two, three.

The rest of the day I kept out of Pa's way but after lunch I went looking for Will. He was in the old blue skiff, spokeshave in his hand and a bit of wood on his knees, making a new oar-blade.

Pa told me I got four brothers, I said. But I only got three.

Ready to show him on my fingers, but the spokeshave never paused, Will not looking up. All I could see was the top of his old cabbage-tree hat and his shoulders moving with each draw of the spokeshave, the white curls falling away around his feet.

Oh, well, he said. There was Dick. Between me and Bub. That'd be what Pa had in mind.

He dead? I said. Did he die?

Will lifted up the oar-blade, ran his finger over the edge, blew at it.

Not dead, he said. Went off.

Went off, I said. How's that, went off? Went off how?

Dick was always a funny one, Will said. Had some funny ideas. Never knew which way he'd jump.

Didn't you like him, I said.

That made him look up. His eyes like Pa's, cold blue in his sunburnt face.

Not a matter of not like, he said. Dick and me never had too much to say to each other, all there is to it. Him and Pa, they didn't get on.

How's that, I said. Not get on?

Will put down the spokeshave, laid the oar-blade aside. Stood up in the boat so it rocked on the water.

Come down in here, he said.

Lifted me into the boat, sat me on the seat at the stern, his knees nearly touching mine. It was still and hot, a thick smell of pitch coming out from the planks. Like the two of us gone into a room on our own.

Now Dolly, he said. Listen to me. I never known what went on or what didn't go on. I asked Pa one time. Keep your damned nose out of it, he told me. Belted me. Matter of fact near broke my arm.

For once I sat quiet.

Never asked again, he said. Never thought it was worth another belting. My guess is, Pa had a bust-up with Dick, sent him packing. You know the way Pa is.

Put his hand on my shoulders.

Dolly, we got a brother, he said. Lives somewhere up the Branch so I've heard. But I put him out of my mind and tell you what, Dolly, if I was you I'd do the same. Honest to God I would.

All right, Will, I said, because I was a bit frightened, never seen Will so grave.

But I was thinking who could I ask.

~

Iris Herring lived up the river at Cat-Eye Creek, fowls pecking round outside her hut and a few goats watching you sideways. A patch of potatoes and a bed of the same blood-red geraniums we had at home. A plain woman like a boulder, getting on in years, always with an old pipe in her mouth. But if a baby was on the way or you cut your leg open and needed stitching up, she was the person you got.

Mrs Herring knew everything that went on along the river.

Didn't always tell, but she always knew.

Next time Jemmy Katter rowed Ma up to Mrs Herring's with a flitch of bacon and a basket of oranges, I come along with her. Sat on Mrs Herring's lap, on the pinny with all the stains, and leaned my head against her cushiony bosom. They drank their tea and talked about little pitchers having long ears, then Ma went outside to pull a bunch of Mrs Herring's special scallions and I got in quick.

Did you know my brother, I said. My brother Dick?

Course I did, Mrs Herring said. Heaven's sakes, I borned the whole lot of you!

Held out her hands, brown and swollen round the joints, shiny bulges on the knuckles, the skin wrinkled as crepe merino.

You was a good handful of bub, Dolly, she said. Come out looking round like you owned the place. And yell! My word you had a good pair of lungs.

Did he die? I said. Dick? Did he die?

Course not, silly goose, she said. Went away for a time, that's all. Now hop down quicksticks, we get them taters done for tea.

Ma was back then, we could hear her knocking the dirt off the scallions on the wall outside. Mrs Herring touched my cheek with her finger.

Best look forward, lovey, she said. I don't never look back. Never ever.

That was how it was on the Hawkesbury. Everything hidden away and those everlasting cliffs and ridges blocking us into the narrow valley. Would of liked to push them back, get a clear look at all the things people knew but wouldn't say.

THOSE DAYS there was blacks all round. People talked about the wild blacks that lived further out where the whites hadn't got to yet. Went about stark naked and ate their babies, they said. Killed any white man they saw, cut his heart out.

I didn't believe it. Only ones I ever saw had clothes like us, but more raggedy, and you couldn't see them killing anyone.

They'd come to our back door sometimes and wait, one or two women in rags of clothes, a couple of little ones with snotty lips. Didn't knock, didn't ask, didn't look at us.

Here you are back again, Mrs Devlin would shout. Come to cadge again are you?

They might of been deaf. Never answered.

Mrs Devlin would go to the cupboard, get out a loaf

and some bacon, yesterday's leg of mutton. Eggs, oranges. Grumbling as she put the stuff in their billies.

Up to me or your ma, we'd send them packing, she said. It's your pa. Said to me, when they ask, Mrs Devlin, you be sure and give. Now Dolly, you get right away or you'll get their fleas off of them.

When Jemmy rowed Ma up to Windsor with Mary and me, we'd see the smoke drifting up from places away off in the bush. That'll be the blacks, Ma would say. I'd look, but I never saw anyone, just the smoke, and that sometimes so faint you couldn't be sure.

At Windsor there'd be groups of them on the edge of town, under the trees or sitting round a few smouldering sticks. So dark and still you had to look twice.

Ma would grab our hands, hurry us along.

One time a man got up, joint by joint, walked over to us with his hand out. Close up I could see how his palm was pale as mine, only threaded with dark lines. His hair stuck out like feathers, his face all rough from the smallpox.

Ma had a hold of me so tight it hurt. Panting, she was pulling us along that fast.

Who's that, Ma, I said. Who was that man?

She bent down to us so we'd listen.

Now girls, she said. I got nothing against the blacks. I pity them, truly I do, hardly better than beasts of the field. God in his wisdom put us above them.

He smelled, Mary said. I smelled him, pooh!

Not civilised, see, Ma said. Can't help it, poor things. We

give, you've seen them at the house, we're forever giving out. Our Christian duty, do right by them. But this begging in the street, that I can't abide.

I looked back at where the man was sitting with the others. The smoke from their little fire whipped around in the wind.

Where are their houses, I said. Why don't they go home?

I wouldn't know, Ma said. But I wish they'd take themselves off and not go bothering respectable folk.

~

We had some blacks near us, only I never knew for a long time. Bub and Johnny was mostly off on their own boys' things, but now and then they let us girls tag along. Up in the bush behind the house, or out on the river in one of the skiffs. Pa made sure we could all handle an oar. One morning the four of us took it into our heads to go along the riverbank further than we'd ever been. I loved to see a new place, couldn't wait, ran on ahead.

At the start it was a sweet sandy track under the she-oaks, a breeze coming and going with that dry whistle through the leaves and the water shining in the sun. A pair of wallabies hopped up the ridge, an emu stalked along. A fat lizard made me jump, sliding through the grass like a snake.

I waited for the others at the end of Thornhill's. No fence there, but a stony spine of ridge coming down into a jumble of rocks. The end of the good land, nothing past that but prickly bush.

Mary wanted to go back, but I had my heart set on seeing what was further on. There was still a track, rougher and not as clear as before. I started off along it and the others came after.

Pretty soon it stopped being a novelty. No shade, the sun hot, and we hadn't thought to bring any water. Mary got a blister and cried to go back and Johnny called for me to stop, but I made out I didn't hear.

The track did a turn and suddenly I came out in a flat part with shady trees and a little stream. And a couple of bark humpies round a smoky fire. Three old black women turning their faces towards me. A couple of pot-bellied children and an old man by the fire with a blanket over his shoulders. All of them so skinny you could see the knobs on their joints.

And leaning hard on a pole, a tall crooked man. One side of his head was shiny stretched skin where something bad had happened and never mended. The stick was mostly what was holding him up.

Stood watching me. Didn't as much as blink.

One of the children coughing, on and on, that was the only sound. The women turned away. One of them reached forward and moved something in the ashes. The man never moved, never took his eyes off me.

The others caught up to me. I heard Bub go *Oooh!*

Come away, Dolly, Johnny said. Quick, we best go back.

Bold as I was, something about this place, the man staring, made me glad to leave. We started back, Mary running, blister or no blister, and none of us looking behind.

Back on our place we all got brave again.

What was you running for Mary? Johnny said. Think he'd eat you? God, that old feller?

Bub and I laughed along with him, but all of us avoiding each others' eyes.

We never told Ma or Pa. Never talked about it among ourselves. But never went along that track again.

The only blacks we knew to speak to was the two fellers worked in our stables. Pa learned to ride late in life, it was like oranges, something else he hadn't grown up with. But riding was what gentry did, so he'd got a stableful of horses, and Jingles and Phillip to look after them. Been with us since I could remember, lived in the stables along with the darkie boy who did the firewood.

Jingles was very big, very black. A thick beard with threads of grey and his eyes set deep. Don't think I ever heard more than six words together from him, and those few mumbled in his throat. Kindly enough, but I never saw him smile. Nothing jingly about him that I ever saw.

Phillip was a different make altogether. Younger than Jingles and nowhere near as dark. Must of had one parent white. A tall sinewy feller, amazing the weight he could move round with those skinny arms. Lift a saddle as if it was nothing. His face long and clever in the shade of his hat, the skin yellow, with black freckles the size of farthings.

He was a charmer, Phillip. Thin as a lizard, with a smile that could melt stone.

My word Phillip had a good way with the horses. I watched him with one just come in, never had as much as a halter on, that big eyeball swivelling and the scared poor thing tittupping around all left-footed with fright, and Phillip so patient. Walking him in the horse-yard talking softly to him by the hour. Next thing I knew he had the halter on and the horse pacing beside him as nice as ever you saw.

Pa rode now and then, but he was never at ease. He was frightened of his big thoroughbred Star, you could see it in the way he mounted, needed Phillip to hold the horse beside a stump so he could get up in the saddle. Once he was astride he was awkward, perched up like a cherry on a cake.

Will didn't get on a horse if he could be on a boat, said he got seasick in a saddle, but Bub and Johnny rode. Riding meant they could come and go as they pleased, Bub off to the end paddocks with his hoe and Johnny up the hill on the Sydney road, he'd go as far as Martin's Corner, work the horse too hard on the hill and get in strife from Pa when he brought it back all of a lather.

I couldn't wait for the day I was old enough to ride. Knew the world would be a bigger place once I had legs under me longer than my own. I'd go down the stables, talk to the horses, feed them bits of apple off my hand, the way Phillip showed me.

Ma didn't like that. No place for you girls, she'd say. I catch you in the yard with them blacks, you'll get a hiding you won't forget.

Why, Ma? I'd say. Why can't we? But she wouldn't say, just press her lips together.

When Pa thought we was old enough—I'd of been around eight, Mary ten or eleven—he got us a couple of ponies. I'd never seen a sidesaddle before. That funny bent post sticking out of it, and the stirrups on the same side.

What's this thing for, Jingles, I said. I want a proper saddle.

How ladies ride, Phillip said. Hook your knee round, see? Legs together. More polite.

Damn that for a lark, I said, something I'd heard Pa say, and Mary looked at me as if the lightning would come down and strike me dead.

I'll ride the way the boys do, I said. Or I damn well won't ride!

Plonked myself down on the stones of the yard. Mary was already up on Belle with a knee bent round the post on the saddle but I wouldn't get on Queenie, wouldn't go near her, never mind how Phillip coaxed me, and never mind how I wanted more than anything in the world to ride.

Phillip went up to the house. Stood at the back door tapping until Mrs Devlin stuck her head out the kitchen window and called what did he want. Then Ma come and talked to him through the window.

She walked down to me very brisk.

Get up this minute, Dolly Thornhill, she said. Making an exhibit of yourself in front of the blacks!

Grabbed at my wrist, but I leaned my weight back against her. Phillip and Jingles watching, and Ma getting red in the face.

Your pa's the one to settle this, she said. You come along with me, my girl, that's if you don't want me to fetch him down here.

Pa cranky was one thing. Pa cranky and hauled away from his bench would be another, so I went with her. He laughed when he saw me.

My word Dolly, he said. You could sit on that bottom lip!

Ma put it to him, it wasn't ladylike for a girl to ride astride.

But Pa, I said, I don't want to be a lady!

For a little thing, I had a good dose of cunning.

Old Loveday's a gentleman, I said, but you always say, who'd you rather be?

No doubt about you, Dolly, he said. Got all the answers. Look, Meg, way I see it, what's the odds how they ride? Long as they got the best bloodstock under them. Hold their own with anyone if they got that.

Ma knew how to choose her battles. Grumbled about me being a hobbledehoy, but let me have a pair of Bub's old trousers to wear under my skirt.

Heaven knows what kind of end you'll come to, Dolly, you're that wilful, she said. All's I can do is make sure you're decent.

That first day we went out on the horses, Pa rode along with us. Star rolled his eyes and trampled and Pa shouted out, Steady! Whoa! Steady now Star! so the horse got even more flighty. Jingles led us out on Lightning, then Mary on Belle and me on Queenie, then Pa, and Phillip coming along behind on Valiant.

When we got to the rocks where Thornhill's finished, Jingles kept going, the horses picking their way along the stony track. Thought I'd hear Pa call for us to stop, but he didn't.

Hoy, Jingles, I said, where are we going?

Didn't answer.

When we got to the clearing it seemed no one was about.

Then a woman crouched out of one of the humpies, her skinny legs and arms like sticks poking out of the dress. Didn't seem surprised to see us. Spoke sharp and quick back into the humpy and out come the crooked feller. Hung on the stick, watching the ground. The woman bent and went back into the humpy. Watched us through the opening.

Pa got down off Star, gave the reins to Jingles. Had something wrapped in a cloth from the kitchen. Stood with the fire between him and the man.

Good-day to you my old friend, he called.

His voice too loud for the place. I thought, how come he knows that man?

Wish you a mighty good day of it, he said, and here's your bite to eat.

Held the bundle out but the man took no notice. Seemed he could lean on his stick all day while Pa watched him across the fire, the smoke rising into the still air. Pa put the bundle on the ground, unwrapped it, laid the things out. Bread, meat. Potatoes. A twist of baccy. They lay on the ground like so much rubbish.

Pa looked up at Jingles on the horse.

I've asked you before and I'm asking you again, he said. You talk this feller's tongue. Tell him I mean well.

You'd of thought Jingles didn't hear.

Pa turned to Phillip.

Come now, lad, Pa said. Tell him good-day, no more than that.

Phillip coughed, rubbed his neck as if it was bothering him.

Damn your eyes, Pa shouted. What does a man have to do!

Sorry Mr Thornhill, Phillip said. Begging your pardon.

The steam went out of Pa quick as it had come.

Never mind, lad, he said. Never you mind. Take the girls back now, and Star along with you.

Up on the horse, it might of been the first time I was ever taller than my Pa.

No, Pa, I called, it's too far! Come with us!

Get along, lass, Pa called. Get away off home now. I'll be along directly.

As we left the clearing I looked back. Pa standing by the fire, the man on the other side. I watched the man turn and bend, showing his skinny backside in the sad old trousers, and get himself into the humpy. Last I saw, Pa was alone, with the smoke swirling round him and the victuals lying on the ground.

What's that, Jingles, I said. What's that he give them?

Jingles didn't turn, didn't answer.

Few victuals, Miss, Phillip said from behind me.

Yes, I said. But why'd he bring it?

That was the wrong question. You didn't need to ask why you'd bring bread and beef for those skinny folk.

Who are they, I said. They kin to you?

Kin to Jingles, Phillip said, but not in his usual bouncy way. Through his auntie up the Branch.

Oh, I said.

Your pa takes victuals regular, he said. Or sends them along of us. Rain or shine.

Just to give, like, I said.

That's it, Phillip said. Just to give.

Part of Christian duty, I supposed. Never known Pa bother with anything churchy before, but what else could it be?

Why'd they leave it on the ground? I said.

That was only the start of the questions I had, but Phillip come in like he hadn't heard me.

Poor old things, your pa don't like to see them wanting, he said. Told me once, knows what an empty belly's like. Reckon you young ladies never been hungry, eh? Reckon you'll be having a nice leg of mutton today?

Turning the subject, of course, and Mary chimed in then about the crown of lamb she was going to help Mrs Devlin with. The rosemary and the onions and the new potatoes.

When we got back I sat in the yard on the woodchop stump, waited for Pa. He trudged up as if he was tired, bent to scrape the mud off his boots without seeing me, his face so heavy I thought better of saying anything. He went to the back door and took his boots off so he was just in his socks. Made to go in, but saw me.

You been a long time, Pa, I said.

He walked over across the flagstones, crouched down in front of me.

They're poor souls, Dolly, he said. Poor helpless souls. Dying out like all their race.

That blue stare of his.

I'd give, Dolly, he said. Ease their passing. Only they won't take. Oh, they take when I'm gone. Take and eat. If not they'd of starved long since. Only not from me. Not from my hand.

Something twisted his face out of shape and I thought he was laughing, but he caught his breath in a sob.

Your mother took their part, Dolly, he said. Made me promise. Why you seen me down there. Why I'll stand there and beg them.

His voice was strangling round the words. He'd gone an old man suddenly, eyes blank and dark.

Stand and beg them, he said. Come again the week after, do it again. Because of your mother.

On the last word I could hear the feeling come up his throat and stop him.

By God Dolly, he said, voice just a raspy whisper. By God but I wish that day back again, and have it come out different.

What day? I thought. What different?

Is it cadging, Pa? I said. When you give them? Or Christian duty?

He cleared his throat with a great cough. Took a breath I could hear going all the way down. Stood up and touched the top of my head, a brush of his fingers.

Yes, well, he said. Your ma's of a different view, you know, Dolly.

His voice was ordinary again.

If you wasn't here in them days you wouldn't know, he said. Your ma weren't here, she don't know. In this one thing I got to go against her.

Stood up, lifted a foot to see the bottom of his sock, where he'd walked on the stones.

Your ma wouldn't like it, he said. You girls being down

there. Shouldn't of taken you. No need to say where you was today, Dolly. I'll tell Jingles, take you down the other track when you go out on the ponies.

Went over to the back door, took his socks off and laid them on his boots, walked into the house with his big white feet bare.

What he'd told me was nothing more than commonsense. You couldn't see people go hungry.

So what was that terrible twisting across his face? That thing that was like an animal eating away at him from the inside?

MA WAS a great one for visiting. Not gentry, we wasn't on visiting terms with the quality. Not the folk from along the Branch either, scrabblers with not a boot to their name. The ones we visited with were *the better families*. Folk on the up-and-up like we were, mostly emancipists. Cobbs from Milkmaid Reach, and the Lewises from Ebenezer, Fletchers from Portland Head. Old Mr Loveday if he was sober. The Langlands. They'd row down of a Sunday afternoon, the river a highway for the families along it. Mrs Devlin would cook up a big batch of cakes and scones, Anne busy all afternoon keeping the cake-stand full.

Ma knew everyone's stories, which ones were *come free* and which ones was *sent out*, and if they was *sent out*, what they'd done. Different from Mrs Herring, she didn't mind telling what she knew. Mr Chapman stole a sheep at Burleigh Fair, lucky not to of hanged. Mr Fletcher knocked a man down, took his watch and two half-crowns out of his pocket.

What about Mrs Fletcher, I said.

Can you keep a secret, Dolly? she said, and before I'd said yes she told me. Mrs Fletcher was one of those women sells themselves to men, she said. Got caught when she stole the purse of a man come to take his pleasure.

How did she know all the secrets, I wondered.

Langlands come often, Ma and Mrs Langland out of the same mould, very genteel in their view of themselves. She was a stout woman bursting out of her clothes but dainty in her ways like a doll. Had a shawl, paisley pattern, soft and light as duck down. She'd leave it on the back of a chair and then ask you to give it to her. Be waiting for you to say, goodness that's soft, and so light! because then she could tell you it was Indian kashmir, a bit unusual, which was her way of saying it was better than anyone else's.

No secrets stood behind Mrs Langland. From a good family back Home, if you believed what she said. Not too high up to marry an emancipist, mind. Long as he'd made good. My people were in a comfortable situation, she'd say, and settle the shawl on her shoulders. *My people.* After she said it, I noticed Ma started saying it too, about her *people* in Brixton Rise.

She liked to lord it over everyone, Mrs Langland. Very pleased with herself, and thought it was all her own cleverness.

Old Mr Langland, he'd worked for a silk-weaver in Spitalfields, Ma told me. Caught running off with twenty-seven silk handkerchiefs under his coat. He was in the first lot sent out forty years before, when the Colony was just a few tents in among the bush and not too many rules about anything. Him and Pa would rather of been out in the yard with their pipes going, spitting on the stones. But they was trying to latch on to being respectable now, so they sat with the teacups and the scones and listened while Mrs Langland went on about her joints.

Langlands had a string of children. Took after Mrs Langland, pale and soft like cakes not given a hot enough oven. Charlie was a chubby fellow the apple of his mother's eye. Next down was Sophia, not much older than me so everyone thought we'd be friends, but I couldn't be bothered with her. All she could think about was what her dress was like, and if the ribbons on her bonnet matched her gloves, and how a girl should fix her hair to *make the most of herself*. Her lacy handkerchief peeked up out her bosom so it *drew the eye*, and she was forever dropping it to *put some colour in her cheeks*.

Knew all those tricks. Told me and Mary, only to make us feel like fools that we didn't know.

Sophia was taller than she thought a girl should be so she never wore anything but flat slippers. Sat down when she could. If she had to stand, she'd kink one hip sideways. Mary said Ma had her eye on Sophia Langland for Will, but I pooh-poohed her. Why would he fancy a dull girl like Sophia Langland, when my handsome favourite brother could have his pick?

Then there was Jack. The oldest of the Langland children by six or seven years, and as different from the others as night from day. Jack's mother was not Mrs Langland. She was a darkie, long dead. Ma told me, but it was no secret. Everyone knew that Jack was half darkie.

When Mr Langland went with Jack's ma, New South Wales by all accounts was a rough place. Not much between a man and starvation and not too many women other than the native ones. A man did what was natural. As for the children that come along, the old hands like Pa and Mr Langland thought it nothing so very terrible. What counted was not if you were half darkie, so much as if you could handle an oar or split a log.

But things had changed. The ones that come later, and come free, drew the lines strict. *Sent out* and *come free*, white and black. Mr Langland was a churchy sort of feller now and had got himself a respectable wife. Wouldn't like to be reminded he'd been happy enough once upon a time to bed a native woman.

Everyone knew about Jack's mother, but no one said. It was like stealing a sheep or knocking a man down for the coins in his pocket. You didn't mortify anyone by saying it.

Easy in Jack's case because you wouldn't pick him straight away. Dark in the face, yes, but the men who worked the ships all got dark. A heaviness round the brow. That might tell you. And the colour of his eyes. A greeny colour, very bright against his skin.

But he was no different from the rest of us. Talked about *the blacks* the same way everyone did. They were strange to him the same way they were strange to us. He knew Mrs Langland wasn't his real ma. But he'd never known the native woman. She died when he was too young.

He was on the outer in that family, though. Called Mrs Langland *Ma*, but she had no warmth for him, and there was no love lost between Jack and his half-brothers and sisters. Didn't know them that well, because he'd been away on the ships since he was a lad, didn't have the easy life they'd had.

Jack was younger than Will by a good few years, he'd of been around fifteen when I first got to know him, and Will into his twenties. I was only a girl still, seven or eight. The two of them like brothers, everything about them on a grand scale. Both of them deep in the chest and wide across the shoulder. Black beards, and faces burnt from the sun and the salt. Worked side by side on *Industry*, Jack a match for many an older man.

When *Industry* put in to Sydney they'd stop with us till she sailed again. Come up the river on someone's boat if they could, or on the new road, catch rides off the wagons. Jack would be with us for a night or two, then he'd borrow one of Pa's skiffs.

Off to Langlands now, he'd say. Back in a few days.

That's what he called it, Langlands.

Don't think anyone at Langlands cared if Jack visited or not. But it was the right thing to do, visit your kin, so that's what he did. Be back from Langlands a few days later, with us the rest of the time.

Pa and Jack sat by the hour with their pipes. Will with them sometimes, but more often away up and down the river visiting, a sociable feller our Will.

Jack knew as much about the weather and boats as Pa, but clever enough to make out he didn't.

In for a bit of a blow, Pa would say and whether Jack agreed or not he'd say, Yes, Mr Thornhill, looks that way.

A rough unlettered man, but had a natural courtesy.

Pa thought Jack Langland was near as good as a son of his own. That Jack Langland, he'd say, good a man as ever you'd find. Honest as three men.

Ma not so warm.

Well Jack, here you are again, she'd say when he first arrived with Will. Be off to see your pa and Mrs Langland directly I expect.

Pa would come in very hearty. Your ma and pa can do without you for a time, he'd say. Stop with us long as you like, Jack lad.

We had a dog, white with dark speckles all over and silky black ears. Jack was always a soft touch for a dog. Now get away off! he'd say when it lay on his feet, and it'd stand up and turn round, but next thing it'd be lying closer than before. Wherever Jack was, that speckled dog would have its paws one over the other, grinning up at him with its black lips as if he was the best thing in the world.

~

Will and Jack kept us entertained of an evening, the fire flickering shadows about the parlour. The ship's biscuits so full of maggots they was rich as a Welsh rabbit when you roasted them. The weather so hard the trees grew on a slant.

Get away, Johnny said. Pull the other one!

So Will and Jack stood on the hearthrug leaning sideways

together being the trees of windy New Zealand, but we still didn't know if they was having a lend of us.

Now what about the seals, Pa said. How would you go about the killing?

They'll be on the rocks with a flipper in the air, Will said. Like they're waving good-day. Get your stick, one good whack on the nose. Not spoil the skin, see.

Then what, Bub said. Peg them out or salt them down or what?

Peg them out, salt them down, the both, Jack said. Got to peg them out perfect to get the good price.

What would a skin be worth, Johnny said. Three shillings, four?

Five, Will said. What they pay for them in China. That's with no marks on it.

You know they do got a pretty face, Jack said. Like a dog, only not so long in the snout.

Pretty face! Will said. What, you reckon it's a pretty face do you Jack?

Not a thing I like doing, Jack said. When they fix you with that eye of theirs.

I pictured one of the dogs, only not so long in the snout. Whacking it on the nose hard enough to kill it.

Whyn't you do another trade? I said.

Five shillings a skin, that's why, Jack said. Man got to put something by.

That made us go quiet. There'd be plenty of money for the Thornhill boys down the track, but Jack would have to make his own way.

There was natives in New Zealand, but to hear it they was different as could be from the ones in New South Wales. Mad for fighting. Set against each other, tribe against tribe, the winners sitting down after and eating the losers. Tattoos on their faces all over, chin, cheeks, nose, everything.

Special clever man does it, Jack said. Gets a little chisel, little mallet. First time cut the skin. Second time put the ink in. Saw it done to a feller once. Tight as a bowstring, not to cry out with the pain of it.

Are they black? Ma said.

Not like our natives are black, Mrs Thornhill, Jack said. More a brown.

Like your kind of colour skin? she said.

Oh, he said. I suppose similar, Mrs Thornhill.

Will threw a log on the fire and thrust his boot in to settle it so the sparks flew up.

Get yourself one of them damn tattoos, Jack, he said. Pass for a New Zealander!

Everyone laughed, but when you thought about it, what was so funny?

Only don't eat me, there's a lad, Will said. Make a damn tough meal. Now get up, Jack, we show them that dance.

The two of them yelled and slapped their arms and stuck out their tongues and stamped on the floor so hard the windows rattled, what they claimed was the New Zealand way of saying how d'you do.

~

From the beginning Jack and me liked each other. Somehow we saw eye to eye on things. He never called me Dolly, only my full and proper name. How did he know I didn't care to be a doll?

When they come back from sea Jack always had some little thing for me, a shell shining rainbow colours inside, a pebble with a hole in it. The sort of thing a child takes a fancy to. But one time when I was older, ten or eleven, he brought me a slip of green stone, polished smooth, with a hole in the end to take a cord.

Made by a New Zealander, that one, he said soft and private. So's you won't forget your friend Jack.

The stone sat in the curve of my palm like a jewel. It was the loveliest thing, even though it was nothing but its unadorned self, soft in your hand as green water would be if you could hold it. I wrapped my fingers round it tight. Didn't know how to say *I couldn't never forget you, Jack.*

But Mary saw.

Oh, Dolly! she said. Going to marry Jack Langland, are you?

She was laughing, Johnny too, everyone watching me.

I was shamed at my feelings so easy to mock. Could feel the blood pounding in my cheeks. That got them laughing harder. Even Will smirking.

Jack took hold of my hand.

That's all right, he said. Question is, what finger's the ring going on?

Touched my fingers one by one.

This one, he said. Reckon it's this one. Got to get the money first. Get the gold ring. Put it on that finger there. Then we'll be right.

His steadiness shamed the others.

He always had something for Mary after that, a shell necklace or scrimshaw he'd done, *Industry* under sail. And for me, nothing that would make trouble.

It got to be always good for a laugh between us. When he and Will come back from New Zealand he'd wait for a quiet moment with no one about. Still want to marry me, Sarah Thornhill? he'd say. I'd come right back at him. Course I want to marry you, Jack Langland!

THOSE YEARS split up into the times Will and Jack was away, and the times they was back. Another kind of day and night, only months long. I turned twelve and Jack gave me twelve shells in a box, the whole thing small enough to fit in my palm. *Want to marry me, Sarah Thornhill?*

I turned thirteen while they was away again. Wondered if he'd bring back another box, thirteen shells this time, but he never brought the same thing twice. That year it was an eggshell, creamy with green specks, that he'd blown out and kept in a box full of feathers. Then they went off again.

It got to be so every trip was longer. The seals running out, Pa said. Had to go further to find them and when they did, not so many as before. Where it might of taken two months to fill the hold, now they might be gone the best part of a year.

By and by I started to get a womanly shape, and my month-lies come. Ma was too genteel to talk about anything that went on in your insides, but Mary was fifteen going on sixteen, had her monthlies for a few years. She was making eyes at Billy Cobb from up the river. He was a lump of a boy and I couldn't see that Mary liked him much, she was just practising on him. He'd row down from Cobb's now and then and the two of them would go off by themselves. When I got my monthlies she was kind about it. Not children anymore, we got on better.

You can have babies now, Dolly, she said. That's what it means.

I must of looked blank.

With a man, you know, she said. You seen how the horses let down that tube thing they've got. Get up on the mare if you let them, put it inside. Same with people, only a bit nicer about it.

I'd seen the poor old mares, and the cows too, and I wasn't going to have anything like that done to me. But I was ready to stop being a child. Had a feeling Mary might not know every-thing about what men and women did together.

With Will and Jack gone so long it was a dull old time. I'd wake up early but wish I hadn't, the day stretching out too long. So many people in the house, but empty too. I'd go up to the cave, the way I always had, and sit in the honey-coloured light listening to the What Bird. The bird was the same and the light was the same, but somehow they'd lost their flavour. I wondered at the child I'd been not so long before, who thought a morning answering the What Bird was a morning well spent.

My body was becoming someone else's, and my self too, but body and self neither settled yet into their shapes. I was out of sorts, waiting to catch up with myself.

Have you got worms, Dolly, Ma said. You're restless as a cat.

Came at me with the opening medicine. I made myself sit still after that. *Commend thy soul to patience*, I said to myself, like I'd heard the parson say. *Commend thy soul to patience*.

Every day and every week much like the last. We'd have the visits from the Langlands and the rest of them, Sophia always on at Pa, when would Will be back? Me and Mary went riding, as far as the rocks where Thornhill's finished, or down the other way towards Payne's Mill. Might go with Johnny up out of the valley along the Sydney road as far as Martin's Corner, he was sweet on Judith Martin, her father had the place there. Once or twice we took the horses across on the punt and up the new road on the other side of the river. Stop at the top and look at the view down over the valley, turn round again.

Never far enough to get anywhere, and back home a few hours later.

A trip to Sydney one time, that was a big thing. I'd just turned fourteen. Down the river on Trevarrow's *Emily*, then out to sea for the run down the coast to Port Jackson, lucky to have a fair wind and a calm sea. A public house in Bridge Street wanted a man to train up, and Johnny was nineteen, wanted to do it. Couldn't wait, he was that keen to get away from old Dead-and-Alive, by which he meant our valley.

I didn't fancy Sydney, loud and people rude and quick, and the gentry running you down on the street prancing along on their horses. Caught a glimpse of the governor, all gold braid and a cocked hat with a feather, that was exciting for two girls from the Hawkesbury, but a few days later and we was back home and the damn bread and mutton having to be done over and over and the same old dishes washed and put away morning noon and night.

That speckled dog was a smart creature. Didn't care one way or the other about Dolly Thornhill. But knew that wherever she was, Jack would be there too, sooner or later. If I went to the cave, the dog pushed through the bushes and sat up with me on the sandy floor so I'd feel its warm breath on my ear. If I went down to the jetty it lay on the boards watching down the river the way I was doing, one black ear cocked up.

I'd sit with Pa on the verandah, he let me have the telescope if I didn't ask too often. Black shiny mangroves, wet rocks, water. You could see every ripple through the glass. If there'd of been a boat you'd of seen all the faces on deck.

Every day that passed was a day I was waiting for Will and Jack to be home.

I was sitting on the front steps one afternoon, the dog nosing up and down the gravel path and Pa behind me on the bench. I was staring out at nothing, wishing but not knowing what I was wishing, when I heard the bench fall over, Pa jumping up so quick.

Will! Will's home! he shouted.

Pushed past me, took the steps two at a time, out the gate and down the road with that funny crooked run he had and the telescope still in his hand. Didn't care that the men were staring at Mr Thornhill with his boots flapping from where he hadn't taken the time to lace them up.

I was halfway down the track after him when the dog ran past and when I got to the jetty it was standing out on the end, straining towards the boat, but it was still way off down the end of the reach. The sail hanging slack from the yard, the people on board no bigger than ants. One of them must be Will. And one of the others would be Jack.

That thought—Jack!—brought something into my throat, as if I'd run too hard. I knew then what I hadn't known all those months of mooning about. It was Jack I was waiting for.

There was a crowd on the jetty now, Mary and Ma and Bub, all telling each other how long Will and Jack had been gone and how slow they was coming up the reach, and was the tide on the turn or would they have to get out the oars. On and on they went, and the boat not seeming to move.

Give us the glass, Pa, I said. So's I can see.

The eyepiece full of sky, then bush. I slanted down too fast, missed the boat. Tracked along those blue ripples and there was the old grey wood of *Emily*, and up on the bow, leaning forward as if to get to us quicker, there he was. Jack. Black hair glistening in the sun, beard so thick it hid most of his face. Looking straight at me. I waved and he waved back, even though I must of been nothing more than a shape with an arm coming out of it.

When *Emily* got up to us at last, Jack jumped across the last yard of water, didn't wait for them to tie the boat up. So light on his feet for such a big man. Landed next to me neat as a cat.

Well, he said. It's Sarah Thornhill, I do believe.

The same as I'd remembered, his eyes crinkled up with smiling.

Dolly Thornhill, stuck for words! That was a new one.

The speckled dog ran in circles with its tail going like a carpet-beater. Pa slapping Will's shoulders, Will slapping Pa's, the two of them shouting at each other.

*Still want to marry me, Sarah Thornhill?* The humour of it was on Jack's face, he took a breath, his mouth started the words. But then he saw the new shape of me, changed his mind. The words hung between us.

It was nothing. A silence the length of a heartbeat, and Jack's eyes looking into mine. But it said *everything is different now*.

When the others walked up to the house the two of us hung back. We'd walked up that track together a hundred times but I'd never had to think before how you walked beside someone. How much space did you leave between you? Did you touch them as you walked, did your hand brush against theirs as it swung backwards and forwards, and how did you breathe?

Pa stoked up the fire in the parlour and splashed out his best madeira into the good glasses. His hand shaking, he was that pleased to see Will back. Anne brought in cake but Pa said, none of that stuff, Anne, these fellers need some of that meat from last night. Pickle with it and plenty on the plate, mind!

I made sure I ended up next to Jack on the sofa. Took a leaf out of Sophia's book, working it that way as we come into the room, but making it look like chance.

Pa wanted to know everything. How many storms and how

many skins, was the first mate any good and did they give you enough victuals. Couldn't get enough of their tales of hardship, sitting in his cosy parlour with his rich acres round him.

An ember flew from the grate and I put out my foot to snuff it. New boots from Abercrombie's, buttons up the side, made my feet very small. Took my time with the ember and when I sat back I saw Jack was smiling to himself.

They'd had a dangerous time of it. Not enough seals, so they had to stay too long, past the good season, and the storms caught up with them. Went way down south, some island too far and too cold for anyone to live on. Took the risk rather than come home with the boat half empty.

Hard to find as a damn flea, Will said. Wasn't it Jack?

But Jack was smiling at the fire, and I was the only one who knew why he wasn't listening, because my hip was jammed up tight against his and where we touched something was running from his body into mine and from mine into his.

Wake up, Jack! Will said. Good living sending you to sleep!

So you find it? Bub said. Or what?

Found it right enough, Jack said. And these fellers on it, been there three years. Left behind to get the seals, some bugger of a captain forgot to come back for them.

Three years, I said. They'd be dead!

Well and they near was, Jack said. Ever think what a seal might taste like, Sarah Thornhill?

His face very close, I could see how the hairs of his beard sprang away from his red lips.

What does it, Jack, I said. Taste like.

He was watching my mouth, my eyes. His were flecked, green and brown. The eyelashes very black.

Bloody awful! Will shouted from across the room. Rank like fish, that right Jack?

So these fellers, Pa said. No boat to get away?

That's right, Mr Thornhill, Jack said. No boat, so it was make one or stop there till they died. A few trees on this place, but no saw with them, only an axe.

What, cut the tree down, chip it away to a plank! I said. One plank out of a whole tree!

You're a quick study, Sarah Thornhill, Jack said. That's it. One tree, one plank.

God in heaven save us, Pa said.

How many they done when you got there, I said. How far off a boat?

Eight done, Jack said. Long ways off a boat. By God they was pleased to see us.

Kissed us, Will said. Bloody kissed us!

Pooh! Bub said. What, on the mouth?

Get away with you, lad, Pa said. They never.

Reckon you'd find it in yourself, Sarah Thornhill, Jack asked me under everyone laughing. Set in to cut that first tree?

I would, I said. Got a stubborn streak, Jack, and not as dainty as you might think. What I want, I don't stop till I got it.

JACK ALWAYS sang for his supper when he was with us. Carried in wood for the parlour till the box was full, always the one to tend the fire till it blazed up bright. Got out the yard broom, had the verandah and the front steps swept before anyone was up.

That first morning he was back I woke up early. Lay for a moment, then I remembered. Jack's home! Got dressed and went downstairs where Mrs Devlin was in the kitchen, saw Jack in the yard splitting kindling. The hatchet never missing, the wood falling away clean from the blade. His body moving so smooth and easy, him and the wood and the hatchet like a dance.

Well, it's Sarah Thornhill, he said. Bright as a bird.

How did I pass those months without him? Now he was here, it felt like I'd been half dead.

Come to stack for me, have you, he said. Just mind them splinters. Them soft fingers of yours.

Our valley was that deep, the sun came into it late. Gold on the hills all round before it reached down to us. A lovely time. That soft light, and knowing the sun would soon shine warm on you. Me and Jack. Nothing said because nothing needed to be.

Then Ma was bustling out from the house.

Jack, leave that, she said. And Dolly, look at you all over splinters!

Happy to do it, Mrs Thornhill, Jack said. You and Mr Thornhill good to me, least I can do.

Well, Jack, she said. Glad you're not a cadger like some. But we got the boy to do the firewood, rather you left it to him.

All right Mrs Thornhill, he said.

Ma went back into the house. The kitchen door banged behind her.

Why's she cranky? I said. Always nagging how there's no kindling.

Won't be beholden to me, Jack said. Doesn't want to have to say thank you. Her way of telling me she don't want me here.

Some of us do, I said. Want you here every minute of every day.

We might of gone on smiling at each other all morning, except for Mrs Devlin calling out the window for Jack to bring her some kindling.

He took an armload in, dropped it in the basket.

Do the knives for you, he said. Mrs Thornhill told me she likes a good sharp knife.

It was true Ma liked a sharp knife, but far as I knew she'd never said so to Jack. Mrs Devlin didn't argue, got the knives out of the drawer and found the whetstone and the oil. I followed him through the house to the verandah.

Can't get her one way I'll get her the other, he said. Want to hear her say it, thank you Jack.

He sat on Pa's bench, the whetstone on his knee, a bit of rag underneath to save his trousers, dripped the oil on the stone. Picked up one of the knives, an old one with the point broken off.

Wouldn't cut butter, he said. No one in this house got any idea of putting an edge on a blade.

Smoothed the knife against the stone, turning his hand one way, then the other. That sweet stropping sound.

Pa come out with his pipe and a drink of tea, sat watching.

Your mother fetched that out from London when we come, he said. In her bundle. Little enough we had by then, but you had to have a knife. Got it off a man in End Lane, broken like that when we got it, but your mother said, it'll see us out, and here it is, on the other side of the world, still good.

Sat watching Jack's hands, back in End Lane, in that past he never talked about.

I see that knife, I think about the bit broke off, he said. Out there somewhere in this wide world. Nothing ever gone, just you got to know where to look.

He drank down his tea and picked up the telescope, the

end of it tracing the shape of his watching. Jack winked at me, turned the wink into the kind of one-eyed squint that was Pa with the telescope. No one but Jack would laugh at Pa, even behind his back.

A boat was sliding up the river. Sail up, man with a blue cap on the stern.

There's Dick, Pa said. There he goes.

Hundreds of Dicks in the world. Still, I asked.

Dick who, Pa? I said.

Seemed he didn't hear. The man in the cap leaned on the steering-oar and the boat swung round to where the First Branch joined the river.

Going up to Blackwood's, Pa said. Away aways up. Ever been up the Branch, Jack?

Watching where the boat had gone, as if it might come back.

Never had reason to, Jack said. Was that Dick Blackwood, Mr Thornhill?

Pa glanced at him, blue eyes like chips of glass.

That's what they call him, lad, he said. Dick Blackwood.

Gave the name a scornful weight.

What they call him, he said. But not who he is.

Then he was gone, down the steps and out the gate towards the river as if he couldn't sit still.

Who's Dick Blackwood? I said.

Lives up the Branch, Jack said. Got a still, cooks up brew. Pa gets it off him. That raw it'll strip the lining out of your guts.

Got a brother Dick, I said. Wonder is that him.

No one ever looked at me as straight as Jack or listened so well.

Dick Blackwood your brother, he said. Think so?

Mightn't be, I said. Only, you know, the name.

Jack picked up another knife and stroked the steel against the stone, this way, that way.

Will told me, I said. Some kind of bust-up with Pa, this brother sent off. Name of Dick, see.

Never heard anyone say Dick Blackwood might be a Thornhill, Jack said. Then again, he's a feller keeps himself to himself.

Thought you'd laugh at me, I said. You know, what a silly idea.

Never that, Sarah Thornhill, he said. Never laugh at you.

Touched his thumb to the blade, laid it with the others.

Only I'd like to know, I said. One way or the other.

Now look, he said. There's plenty of mights and might-nots in this world. Leave them alone till they come out and bite you. That's my view, Sarah Thornhill. For what it's worth.

He gathered the knives, stood up.

We get these back in the drawer, he said. Want to see her face when she does the bacon.

So I let it go. But knew there'd be a chance, one of these days. Find out one way or the other.

We stood innocent as the dawn when Ma started on the bacon. She made the first slice, stopped and looked at the knife, turned with it in her hand.

You done this, Jack, she said. Sharpened this?

Yes, Mrs Thornhill, Jack said.

She cut another slice. The meat fell away from the knife so thin you could see through it.

Well I'll say this for you, Jack, Ma said. You do know how to put an edge on a blade.

Yes, Mrs Thornhill, Jack said.

Meek as meek, but when she turned away he gave me a grin like a tiger.

~

That afternoon Langlands paid a visit. No one else, and Ma most particular for Will to put on his good new coat. No seven-guinea coat from Deane's for Jack, just his blue shirt and a bandana at his neck, his black hair combed through with water. But to my eyes, the handsomest man in the world.

I missed my moment to get him beside me on the sofa again, and he went to sit on a chair where Mrs Langland had her shawl. Picked it up to give it to her, somehow got his fingernail caught in it and pulled a thread. My word, the way Mrs Langland carried on. He stood with the bit of fluff in his fingers, head bowed under her scolding. The shame came off him like heat.

That's ruined now, Sophia said. No putting that right.

Yes there is, Mary said. Give it here, Jack. I'll have it fixed, never see where I done it.

Mrs Langland wasn't sure she wanted to trust anyone with her precious kashmir, but Mary took it out of Jack's hand, picked the thread off where it was caught in his nail, went away to the sewing room. I thought, if she makes it worse, Jack will be the one pays.

But I could see by her bounce when she come back in that she'd fixed it. Mrs Langland looked and Ma looked but blessed if they could see the mend. Sophia took the shawl over to the lamp, pored over every inch.

Think you'll find it's as I promised, Mary said. Never see where I done it.

Oh well, Sophia said. I best not try too hard then, had I?

That's all right then, Pa said. I'll have another of them scones, Meg, and Jack, you got nothing to eat lad, get yourself one of them cakes going begging. And a fill of your cup.

Mrs Langland started on about her joints again.

Dr Mitchell said I had the loosest joints he'd ever seen, she said. I put my foot down, it's flat on the floor, I got no arch at all.

Goodness, Ma said. Fancy that now.

Pa took a bite out of his scone so the crumbs rained down on his lap. Ma frowned and shook her head at him. He must of thought she was frowning because when people visited you were supposed to speak up and *make yourself pleasant*.

Why Sophia, he said, you're near as tall as me. Course you got your height off your pa. Funny the way a child will favour their Ma or their Pa. See Dolly there. Spit image of her mother, God rest her soul.

Pleased with himself. Thought he'd done well.

Now that's plain silly, William, Ma said. Sophia's nothing like as tall as you are. Nothing like. Just the angle, isn't it, Mrs

Langland? And Sophia dear, that's a lovely way you done your hair today.

Pa got the hint, didn't say any more. But it made me think. I'd never known I was the spit image of my mother. It meant she was still alive, in a way, in me. Must be the same with everyone, carrying the people that had gone before them, their ma and pa and their grannies and grandpas, all the way back to Adam and Eve.

It made the room interesting, to look at all the faces. Mary took after Pa, easy to see that, the big face with the round cheekbones and the blue eyes not quite the same. Will too, he had Pa's square chin, the wide mouth. Sophia was like her mother, only not so fat. But there was Jack, side by side with Mr Langland, and there was no likeness whatsoever.

You can see how Jack don't look like you, Mr Langland, I said. Must favour his mother same as I favour mine.

Soon as I heard the words I wanted them back. Mr Langland's teacup stopped in mid-air, Pa took his fingers out of his waistcoat pocket, Mrs Langland's hand went up to her cheek like she'd seen a snake under the table. There was a terrible quiet. Ma put the teapot down as if it was glass. You could hear it click on the table.

Jack had taken a bite of his cake, but when he saw everyone go like statues he went still with it in his mouth. His eyes went to Mr Langland, but Mr Langland was looking nowhere at all.

Twenty years ago Mr Langland had lain with a native woman. That was why Jack was in the world. But who she'd been and how they'd come to lie together was known only to

Mr Langland now. No one asked, no one spoke of it. As if that woman had never been. Except that Jack carried her blood in his veins and something of her features in his face.

This tea's cold as a stone, Ma said. Will you call Anne for a kettle of hot water, William.

So everything got going again, Pa went to the door and called, Mr Langland drank his tea and wiped his lips, Mrs Langland got interested in a fleck of something on her skirt.

Jack was looking down at his knees. To have that moment again and keep my thoughts to myself! The clock chimed out the hour and I hated it because it only went forwards, never back.

When Langlands finally got up to go, Jack and me hung back.

Jack, I whispered. Could cut my tongue out. Saying, you know.

Well, he said. That's it. Everyone knows, Jack Langland's mother a darkie. But not a word said. Not ever.

Not your pa? I said.

Pa won't have it spoke of, Jack said. What he says is, you can pass for Portugee. You can pass, so do it.

Mrs Langland was making heavy weather of the steps outside. I heard Ma calling, Take Mrs Langland's hand, William! No, the other one, for heaven's sake! There was the crunch of feet on the gravel and the squeak of the gates.

Truth is, Jack said, be easier in my mind if I knew. Her name, who she was. How she come to be my mother. Did she know me, did I know her, even for a week. All I know is, she was a native woman. And died.

This was a Jack I'd never seen before. Not the cheery Jack we all knew, but a man with a shadow of sadness going along with him through his days.

Even that lad does the firewood, he said. Or that feller Jingles. Never be any more than doing the wood, mucking out the horse shit. But know what name their ma had, where they come from.

You'd be no different if you knew, I said. Still be Jack Langland. What's it matter?

But I knew it did matter. The peas and the pipe, *oranges and lemons, say the bells of St Clement's*. I had those few pictures of my mother that I'd go over and over. Why would I do that if it didn't matter?

You know them New Zealanders, Jack said, and I thought he wanted to get off this tender ground. The tattoos on their faces. Every one of them lines is a story, you know how to read it. Who's the feller's kin. Back through the fathers and grand-fathers, all the way back down the line. Who you come from, where you fit. Out there plain on your face. Why they sit through the pain of it.

The gate squeaked, gravel crunched.

William, will you oil that blessed hinge! Ma called.

I see what you're saying, Jack, I said. Knowing what's made you.

Put a hand on his arm, the words nowhere near what I wanted them to say, but hoped my touch would tell him.

You're a good soul, Jack said.

Pulled me to him, put his face in among my hair.

Sharing my troubles with me, he whispered. I thank you for your good heart, Sarah Thornhill.

Then footsteps on the verandah, we got ourselves apart. The feel of his arms round me and his words in my hair stayed with me all the rest of the day. The softness in his eyes when he looked at me, in among the talk of all the others, told me it stayed with him too.

NEXT MORNING Jack said he'd be off to Mrs Herring's, cut her some backlogs for the winter. I was casting around for a reason to go with him but Ma made it easy.

Dolly, you go with Jack, she said. I got a nice smoked hock for Mrs Herring and one of the cheeses, poor old thing be glad of them.

All right, Ma, I said, some sly streak in me making out it was a burden.

Jack rowed, I sat in the stern. He'd taken his jacket off and I put it round my shoulders. Heavy, and the warmth of Jack still in it. His face with each stroke coming in close to mine, then away.

Mrs Herring was on the bench outside her door, pipe in her mouth, fowls round her feet where she'd sliced the kernels off some cobs. Watched us come up from the jetty, jostling each other as if the track was too narrow, for the secret pleasure of touching.

Well, she said. Jack Langland and Dolly Thornhill.

Her shrewd old eyes, hidden in a web of creases, they missed not a thing.

I thank you kindly for the victuals, Dolly, she said. Thank your ma for me. Now I wouldn't be trusting Jack on his own, you best go up there along with him, make sure he does it right. Wouldn't you say, Dolly?

Jack sawed the wood the way he did everything, strong and steady. Got the log up in the cradle and never took his eyes off the line of cut, never stopped till the length fell off. I stacked each one, watched him start on the next. He'd taken off his shirt to work and I could see his arms roped with sinew, browner where they got the sun, his back and shoulders with the muscles moving under the skin. I was sorry when he was done.

Going back down to the hut, we saw another skiff at the jetty.

That's Dick Blackwood, Jack said. Tough old bird if she can take Blackwood's liquor.

Dick Blackwood! I said.

Now I see what you're thinking, he said. But leave it alone, I would.

We'll see, I said, but I had my mind made up.

Dick Blackwood was sitting with his hand round a mug of tea. A tall strong-looking feller not much older than Jack. A shaggy head of hair could do with cutting, and a beard hiding half his face.

Dick, you'll know Jack Langland, Mrs Herring said. And this is Dolly Thornhill.

Dolly Thornhill, Dick said.

Gave me a stare, the kind takes in a lot. But not much warmth in it.

Dick Blackwood, I said. Seen you up and down on the river.

Have you now, he said. Spying out from up there at the house.

Heard you could be kin to me, I said.

Something in his face made me stop short of saying *brother*.

You heard that, have you, he said. Well, Dolly, go back far enough, you could say every man and woman on this earth is kin to every other. That right, Iris?

Wished I could make him out better among the beard. Might of been smiling or might not.

Sent off, I said. Sent off, that's what I heard.

Sent off! he said. Listen to this, Iris! Says I was sent off!

Smiling all right now, but not a nice smile. I was wishing I'd listened to Jack, kept my mouth shut.

I never known for sure, I said. No one said, just I thought.

Listen, Dolly Thornhill, he said, and he wasn't smiling any more. I never been sent off from nowhere. Anywhere I gone, I gone of my own free will. You hear different from that, by God you heard wrong.

Then he was standing up, pulling his blue cap on.

I'll be off now, Iris, he said. You ready for another quart, send me word.

I stood at the door of the hut, watching him get into his boat and row away. He might of been watching me under his cap, pulling back on the oars, same way I was watching him. When he was out of sight I tried to catch Mrs Herring's eye.

Is that Dick Thornhill? I said.

But she was making a to-do of getting the fire hot again. Bent down blowing at the coals.

Let it be! Jack said. Let it be, now!

Never said I was wrong, did he? I said. Never said he wasn't Dick Thornhill.

But I was talking to Mrs Herring's back. Getting those coals to flame was all she was going to do. When they flared up she stood and wiped her hands on her pinny.

Jack got the right idea, Dolly, she said. Some things best you let them be.

I took a breath, my blood was up.

Now that's enough of that, Dolly, she said. What I want to know is, you two sweet on each other or what?

Jack looked at me, I looked at Jack.

No or what about it, Mrs Herring said and laughed so you could see the dark gaps in her mouth.

Never met a girl like Sarah Thornhill, Jack said. Never in all my life.

Put his arm round my shoulders.

Who in the world wouldn't be sweet on Jack Langland? I said and put my arm around him. Could feel the skin behind the cloth of his shirt.

What a funny old world it is, Mrs Herring said. And tell me

this, Dolly, what do they say about it at home? You and your good-looking sweetheart here?

Offhand, but I could feel her listening for the answer.

Oh, I said. That'll be all right.

That's good, she said. Glad to hear that, Dolly.

~

The tide was with us on the way home, running strong down the river. Jack sat in the stern, no need to row, just that lovely surge and bubble when he shifted the steering-oar and the water broke up round it. Our wake left a pale line with kinks along it where he'd pushed the oar.

So, Sarah Thornhill, he said. Sweet on me, are you?

Sweet as honey, Jack, I said.

Leaned forward and he leaned in to meet me, his hand along my cheek. My first proper kiss.

Come here alongside of me, he said after a while. Where I've got you close.

There was something in his voice as he said it, tender and a bit wavery, that told me what he felt.

We sat side by side, Jack's arm around me and mine around him, watching the farms slide past. Doyle's, with the skiff pulled up on the sand, then on the other bank, Fletcher's corn, yellow straws scratching against each other in the breeze, and a kooka-burra in a tree telling the world he'd got his lizard, and wasn't it the funniest thing you ever heard. At Cobb's, the children down at the river, Kathleen the big girl had a rod and line and the little one that wasn't right in the head mooning around. Waved when they saw us and we waved back, but not letting go of each other.

It was the same old river I'd known all my life, the same mud on the banks, the same people. But coloured through with happiness because I loved Jack Langland and Jack Langland loved me.

When we come in sight of where the Branch went off to the left I craned past Jack to look up it. It rankled, the way Dick laughed at me.

Now listen, I see what you're thinking, Jack said. But best leave well alone. You saw how he was.

He wouldn't answer, I said. And did you see his eyes, Jack? Pa's eyes!

Grabbed the steering-oar, pushed it hard over.

We find out once and for all, I said. Get an answer out of him. Do it for me, Jack.

He shook his head but did it, had us heading up the Branch in a stroke or two. Past Devine's, past Matthew's, past Maunder's. Maunder's was far as I'd ever gone, the last of the farms. The Branch narrowed after that, the hills closed in.

*Way up the Branch.* All I knew about where Dick lived. And there'd be a lagoon.

Beyond Maunder's it was quiet. Just the bush falling down steep into the water, reeds and rocks along the bank, and the glossy mangroves pressing in dark over the stream.

Jack rested on the oars.

You sure, he said. Sure this is what you want?

I wasn't. Not any more. The stillness of that tight valley, and the way the bush was holding its breath, watching us. If you'd been sent away, how would you feel about the ones allowed to stay?

We come this far, I said. Can't be too much further.

Jack gave me a look but bent to the oars again. Then we come round one last bend and there was a jetty, half hidden in the mangroves, with Dick Blackwood's boat. An open patch of ground and beyond that, water glinting. Back on some rising ground, a house.

And dogs racing towards the boat barking, big ugly brutes.

Someone come out of the house, hand up against the sun. A woman, you could see the dress blowing round her legs.

Thought the dogs would stop when they got to the water but not a bit of it, two of them jumped straight in off the bank and the other one raced along the jetty. Close enough you could see the slaver hanging off its mouth, and the sharp teeth bare. Judging the distance, could it jump into the boat. The two in the water swimming strong. One of them bit the oar, nearly pulled it out of Jack's hand.

God save us! he said.

He swung the boat round so hard it nearly went over. Rowed like a mad thing, the dogs coming after, barking with their mouths full of water, the noise ringing back from the hills, echoing in that slit of a valley like a dozen dogs. Then we got past the bend, the barking faded.

By God Sarah Thornhill, Jack said. You do get a man in a pickle!

He laughed, but shakily.

I'd say Dick Blackwood likes his privacy, he said. He'd have his still there, see. Feller in that line of business won't be wanting folk snooping round.

I was all a-tremble. Never been in fear of my life from an animal before.

You're white as a sheet, he said. Dick Blackwood, Dick Thornhill, God almighty, what's it matter?

Well, I said. A brother. You know.

Look, every family got something, he said. Not a family doesn't have its secrets big or small. No business of anyone else. That's my view, Sarah Thornhill.

Put his hand along my cheek, kissed me again.

Now this, he said. This is our business.

GEORGE WHEELER was the gloomiest soul in the world but even so the Ferryman's Arms was full every day. The country opening up to the north, men taking their flocks and herds to the good country there.

Which is how it came about that Archibald Campbell and John Daunt stood in our parlour next day. The inn full up, George was explaining, but these two gentlemen on their way to Sydney, needed lodgings for the night.

Gentlemen, you see. You didn't turn gentlemen away.

They were youngish fellers, Archibald Campbell a cheerful chap, broad face, blond beard and hair the colour of honey. A man like a rosy cake.

John Daunt was a different make of man altogether. Stood leaning backwards and sideways a little, as if not sure of his welcome. He was no oil painting. An awkwardly-put-together feller, as if his arms and legs not out of the same set. No older than Jack, but his hair thinning, you could see he was set to go bald.

Pa had come off Star and hurt his wrist and his foot, so he couldn't get up to greet them.

Good-day to you sirs, he said. Very welcome here in my house and owing to my recent mishap I'm sorry I'm not able to stand for you.

Too much, and too hearty. That was because of having *worn the broad arrow*. Ma come over and stood beside him. Had her chin up ready in case of insult.

Daunt stepped forward and put out his hand. Pa not sure then what to do, his right hand being bandaged, so Daunt had to more or less seize the left and shake it.

Very pleased, Mr Thornhill, he said. Very pleased indeed to make your acquaintance.

You could hear the Irish in his voice.

I assure you, sir, how grateful I am, he said. Mr Campbell and myself both. To be your guests. We thank you heartily for your hospitality.

In brief, *I know you are an emancipist and it makes no odds to me.*

Campbell smiled, but blank. I thought, out of this pair Daunt is the brains.

Ma started in on a lot of flummery about how the horse that threw Pa was thoroughbred and inclined to be skittish. I saw Campbell sliding his eyes at Daunt. They'd laugh later. The colonials skiting about their bloodstock. Then it was bowing to us ladies. Mary was *Miss Thornhill* but I was *Miss Sarah*. I was ready to take offence. Not far off fifteen, no child! Then remembered Ma said it was the right way of doing things if you was *well bred*. Only the oldest girl got the surname.

Will and Jack and Bub come in, the parlour full of men stepping forward, a tangle of hands going out to be shook. Beside the gentlemen in their fine suits our men looked rough. Beards bushy, faces sunburnt, and all feet in among the chairs and little tables.

While we waited for dinner, or *luncheon* as Ma called it today, we made ourselves pleasant. Archibald Campbell was Scotch and my word at the start I could barely make him out, the way he seemed to put a few turns extra in every word. Ma asked him about his family and he said his father had an estate near Aberdeen. A big family, as many brothers and sisters as would *thick a kirk*. That took some sorting out.

Never seen Mary put on the fancy before. Sitting up straight the way Ma nagged us to do, spine not touching the back of the chair. Dropped her handkerchief and when she picked it up, sure enough, her cheeks had the prettiest flush.

Whereabouts would your place be, Mr Campbell? she said. Is it what you might call remote?

No distance at all, Miss Thornhill, he said. A day's ride, no more.

She did look well with a bit of colour in her cheeks.

Up to the north is it then? Mary said.

A wee step the far side of the range, he said. As pretty a spot as you could wish. Finer land you never beheld.

Garlogie I've called the place.

Mary was nodding away. If she wasn't following, you'd never of guessed.

Best watch out, Billy Cobb!

I was on the sofa next to John Daunt, Will and Jack on the hard chairs across the room. Gave Jack a wink but with Daunt beside me he couldn't very well wink back. I started to feel a bit of a fool, me and Daunt with our heads turning from Mary to Campbell and back again.

And Mr Daunt, I said, whereabouts would your holding be, is it near Mr Campbell?

He caught on, shifted his backside so we were more facing each other. Close up, I thought I'd never seen an uglier man. Heavy brow, thick eyebrows, jaw like a bulldog. One eyebrow grew crooked and quirked up, gave him something of a mocking look.

Now to be honest with you, he said, in County Cork it would be the outside of it if you were two days on the road. But here in this grand country of yours it could be the most part of a week, owing to the land being not so developed.

You couldn't mistake the Irish in his voice but I had no trouble making him out. Half gentry, half Irish. I had the best of it, not like poor Mary puzzling away.

Mind you, he said, I'm not near as advanced as Mr Campbell. A man coming to this country is nothing but a fool for the first year. You'd agree with that, would you, Mr Thornhill? Mr Langland?

Oh yes, Will said, but not in a voice that said he was

sure what Daunt was talking about.

I'm here only this six months past, Daunt said. Have nothing up as yet grander than a hut.

Oh, Ma said, a hut.

I make no doubt of having a good house up before the year is out, he said. But as you'd understand, Mrs Thornhill, these things take a weary time to bring about.

That's so, Pa said. Nothing happens quick, on land or sea.

Now Mr Daunt, Ma said, whereabouts in Ireland would your people be from?

What she meant was, *Are you a Papist.*

A place by the name of Glenmire, he said. Close by the city of Cork. Did you go to Cork ever, Mrs Thornhill?

Ma shook her head, but still waiting for the answer.

We Daunts, he said, we're what you call the Anglo-Irish. We have the real Irish on the place, tenants. But to be honest with you, I'd not know a hundred words of the Irish tongue.

You're nobody's fool, John Daunt, I thought. Telling her, not Papist. And not poor.

~

Then Anne was ringing the bell for us to go into the dining room. Pa hobbled along between Will and Jack.

Now Mrs Thornhill, Daunt said, I'm wondering will there be *placement* at all?

He said it the French way and soon as the word was out he saw his mistake.

Or will we seat ourselves where we please, he said.

He'd given her the opening, so she got everyone to sit where she wanted. Pa at the head, of course, and Ma next to him. Campbell next to Mary, Daunt next to me. Will and Bub. And right along at the bottom end, Jack.

There was an empty chair opposite Jack, as if there was someone missing. If Dick was here, that would be his chair. I watched Pa at the head of the table and wondered if he ever thought about that empty chair.

Anne brought in the roast fowls and went to set them in front of Pa.

Now Mr Thornhill, Campbell said, since your wrist is a burden to you, would you permit me to do the honours?

Had the platter in front of him and the carving knife in his hand before anyone had worked him out.

And perhaps you would allow me to say Grace, Daunt said.

We never had Grace at our table before. I caught Mary's eye, but she was acting like it was the most usual thing in the world.

Grace was such a lot of words, I had to wait for the Amen to know it was done. Campbell got to work on the fowls with a fine old flourish. That knife had never had such a time of it, setting the meat separate so he could say, Dark meat or white, Mrs Thornhill, or will you take a wee taste of each?

My word but don't you do that well, Mr Campbell, Ma kept saying. I do like a man can carve a fowl neat.

She said it so many times, in the end Pa said, Yes, Meg, Mr Campbell not the only man in the world knows how to joint up a fowl.

Ma flushed. The muscle jumped in her cheek from having to keep the smile going.

Having been at sea since a lad, Jack didn't have all the right manners. Didn't ask for things to be passed, reached across for them. Turned his fork over to scoop up the peas. Got a bit of bread, mopped up the juice. By the time he'd finished, quicker than the rest of us, the plate was clean, the bone on the side, sucked white. He smoothed down his beard, wiped his hand on the table napkin.

Nothing he didn't do the rest of the time. But Ma was watching. Caught Daunt's eye, next to me. I saw her mouth do a little turned-down thing and her eyes roll up for a moment.

Oh, Jack, she said, loud enough to make everyone turn, looks like the girl gave you too small a serving, you best have some more.

We all heard it. Not that she thought Jack might still be hungry, but wanting to make him feel small. It was the gentlemen being here, and her having to show she knew good manners. Always been a snob. But up until now it had just been one of Ma's little ways.

You could see Jack think about saying yes, but he glanced at her and saw the smile was false. Looked at everyone else's plates, where they'd left that scrap of food you were supposed to. We all watched him see that he was the only one who'd applied himself so well that his plate gleamed.

Oh no, Mrs Thornhill, he said. I'm all right.

I'd never thought he could sound like that, uncomfortable, uncertain.

Jack, lad, Pa said, loud down the table. You're among friends here, we got plenty of victuals. Anne, bring some more fowl for Jack, and a good spill of gravy with it.

Anne came over and doled Jack out some more fowl and a ladle of gravy, another potato. We all watched, no one said anything. Pa saw he'd made it worse.

Over here now, Anne, he said. Give us a bit of that dark meat, and a potato.

Yes, me too, I said.

Daunt glanced at my plate where there was still half a potato and a piece of meat.

You can go to billy-oh, John Daunt, I thought. I'll not see Jack made a fool of.

The three of us set to labouring through our plates of food.

Now Mrs Thornhill, Daunt said. I couldn't help admiring your grand roses. Splendid blooms. The climate here.

Casting around, you could hear, for something to put into the silence, and then his voice changed, he'd thought of what to say.

Now I have to tell you I never liked a rose bush, he said. Not since I was a boy. My mother had a fine bed of them and I had a hoop, you know the kind of thing, and this particular day I'm spinning it along and it gets into the middle of those roses. Well, I went in after it and you'll not believe but I got pinned by those thorns as fast as a rabbit in a trap. Oh, I set up a cry. Just a lad, you see, thought I'd be there for the rest of my life. Thought they'd have to poke my dinner through to me on a stick.

He paused for a laugh and we all obliged.

The gardener came along and plucked me out, he said. Which was all well and good, only I left my breeches behind on a bush and never from that day to this could I have a rose in the room with me.

I saw that being ugly, Daunt had made himself handsome in this way, that he could tell a story, and didn't mind if it was at his own expense.

But not everyone was listening. Mary and Campbell had their heads together, having a conversation quiet enough to be private, and at the end of the meal she took me aside.

Mr Campbell told me, he's most interested to see along the river, Dolly, she said. Him and Mr Daunt. I told him we'd take them out on the horses.

Along the river, I said, but what's interesting?

Open your eyes, Dolly, she hissed. For God's sake.

I woke up then to how the land lay. Happy enough to have a ride, and good luck to her if she had plans.

PHILLIP HAD the horses saddled up out in the yard. Daunt was beside me, saw it was just the four.

Well now, he said. I'm wondering, Miss Sarah, if one of your brothers might not want to join us. Or Mr Langland.

He'd picked up what Mary and Campbell was up to, I could see, and didn't care to be paired off with me. Nearly laughed in his face, the idea I might want to set my cap at him! Went back through the house to where Jack and Pa had got settled on the verandah, puffing away on their pipes. It looked like Will and Bub had already made themselves scarce.

Mr Langland, you'll come with us riding, I hope? Daunt said. And Mr Thornhill, I mean your son, sir, if he can spare the time? Show us the lie of the land?

I thank you, Mr Daunt, Jack said. Thank you kindly. But

Will's gone up the river on a visit and I'm happy here along with Mr Thornhill.

I did a thing with my mouth behind Daunt's back, to say *Rather be here with you*, but he wasn't looking. Smarting still, I thought, from Ma making a monkey of him in front of everyone.

You're a proud man, Jack Langland, I thought, and I love you for it.

Mary looked sideways at me when I pulled on the old pair of Bub's trousers.

Dolly! she said. Won't you be mortified?

You go for your life, Mary, I said. But damned if I'm going to act the lady.

Daunt led the way out along the track, his back swaying with the horse but his head as still as if he was balancing a glass of water. Had a riding master grander than Jingles the darkie, you could see that.

Some devil got into me and I touched my heels to Queenie so she took off. Past Daunt, along under the trees. Going at it like a feller, the wind in my hair. Only stopped when I got to the rocks where our place ended. Hadn't been past there, not since that day riding with Pa, but I could see the stain of smoke still hanging over the trees.

Daunt pulled up alongside, smiling, easy on the horse.

My word Miss Sarah, he said. You do have a good seat on that mare. And more sense than the majority of the ladies, if I might say so. The sidesaddle I've never thought had much to recommend it from the point of safety or sense.

His words were all right, though who needed so many to get

a thing said? But I thought his smile had a flavour of mockery, was sorry I'd showed off.

Did you ride a great deal back in Ireland? I said. Or are you from the town?

No, a farm, he said. Though the tenants did the working of it. My father is a surgeon and it was thought I might follow in his path. But I was in earshot of an amputation at one time and it quite spoiled me for the scheme.

Might of been for the best, I said. I have heard say, New South Wales is so healthy a place it would starve a doctor.

Ah! he said. Now if I'd but known that, I'd have saved my father some heavy labour trying to talk me round!

I looked back along the track for Mary and Campbell. Wished I'd made Jack come with us, pride or no pride. We could of ridden along behind Daunt and had a high old time of it laughing at the way he rode so lovely with the glass of water on his head.

Daunt looked back too and met my eye for a glance.

And whereabouts would your place be, Mr Daunt? I said. Maitland way, did I hear you say?

In that general direction, he said. Gammaroy, that's the village not so far from my place.

Gammaroy, I said. Not heard of any place by that name.

A small place, he said. You'd not know it.

Still no sign of my sister and Campbell.

Gammaroy, he said. You know it's some distant cousin of the word the black natives have for the place. The closest that our English can get. As we've done in Ireland, you know.

Well, I didn't know, had not an idea in the wide world what he was talking about.

Take the Irish name for a place, he said. Mangle it into English. Glenmire you see as an example. We call it Glenmire but in the Irish it's—and then he said a word that did sound a little like *Glenmire*, but with more on the end, and a sort of hawk-and-cough thing in the middle.

Easier for us English, you see, he said. Make it something we know. As we did with Gammaroy.

He glanced to see if I was interested.

Now that I'd caught on to what he meant, I was. In all my fifteen years I'd never wondered where the name of a place might come from, nor ever met the kind of person who thought about such things. Made me ashamed, as Bub's old trousers didn't. The narrow ignorant life I'd led. Never been further than Sydney, never done anything grander than go to the Caledonian Hotel for dinner and catch a glimpse of the governor in a crowd, never learnt to read or write, not as much as my own name, or given a thought to why the things around me were the way they were.

My old friend the What Bird spoke from somewhere near and out of habit I pursed up my lips. *Dit dit dit dit dit?* Felt Daunt watching me. Think what you please, Mr Daunt! It was of a piece with the trousers and the galloping. A way of saying, this is who I am, an ignorant hobbledehoy colonial, like it or lump it. The bird asked the question again and Daunt cocked his bent eyebrow at me.

I'd say it's waiting for an answer, Miss Sarah, he said.

So I did it again, *Dit dit dit dit dit?* Daunt laughed and that made me laugh too so I couldn't say it, and every time the bird asked the question, *dit dit dit dit dit?* and I tried to answer, it set us off again. When Mary and Archibald Campbell come round the turn in the track, the horses hardly moving, we'd set up such a racket that our horses were turning in circles under us, wondering what the devil was going on.

Mary's cheeks were pink, her eyes lively.

What a fine step along through the way, Campbell said. A perfect paradise!

His face spoke for the pleasure he was taking in where he was and who was with him.

We'll go a step further? he said, letting the horse walk towards the rocks and the start of the rough track.

Oh no, Mary said. Nothing to see further along, is there, Dolly.

Campbell decided not to insist and I saw that these two were going to be all right. Mary sure of what she wanted, Campbell not a man to go against her.

Daunt led the way back, only not so sedate this time. Put the horse into a gallop, the way I'd done on the way out. I started Queenie after him but then thought better of it. It wasn't John Daunt I wanted to play any games with.

When we got back, somehow I couldn't find the chance to have a word with Jack alone. A scratchy feeling seemed to have started. As if what had been straight between us had gone crooked. But all through the cups of tea and the evening meal, he didn't meet my eye and one way and another he was always on the other side of the room.

Campbell and Daunt wanted to be on the road by dawn, and I yawned and carried on like I was worn out, so we all had an early night of it. I got into bed and made out I was asleep straight away, even though I had the feeling Mary would of liked to talk. Waited to hear her breathing change. When she was asleep, she breathed hard like she was indignant.

I slipped out of bed and went out into the hall. Daunt and Campbell were in the room across from me and Mary. Not a sound from there. Not a sound as I tiptoed past Pa and Ma's room. Rumbly snoring behind Will and Bub's door. At the end of the hall, the little cupboard of a room where Jack slept. I knew the door of that room, it squeaked if you opened it slow. I pushed it quick and got in and closed it behind me. The room dark as blindness. Heard a rustle from the bed.

Jack, I said, and groped my way through the air. Squeezed in tight with him.

Sarah Thornhill, he whispered, a warm puff of sound in my ear. What the devil you think you're doing?

Come here Jack, I whispered. Come right over here.

Even though in that narrow bed we couldn't of got any closer.

Laid my palm on his chest. Could feel his heart beating.

You're the only feller for me, I said. Know that don't you. Jack Langland, the only one.

What happened between me and Jack then was the most natural and lovely thing. The two of us melting into each other as if we'd always been the one. The bed was inclined to creak so we had to keep things small and tight. That and the dark made the feeling stronger. Nothing but skin and bits of arm and leg and the warmth that rises out of two bodies.

I knew all along Mary had it wrong. It was nothing like what the horses did. Not just *a bit nicer about it*. This was something different altogether.

Afterwards we lay wedged against each other, my head on his arm where the meaty part was, the muscle making a pillow for me. I could feel his skin moving against mine with every breath we took. It seemed I had more blood than I ever had before, roaring through my veins, the flesh pressing out against the skin.

I'd been only half awake all my life, only half alive. My body belonged to me now, joined up with me in a way it never had been before. I'd never imagined that a person could blaze like this, with bliss. Thought, I can die now. Nothing better will ever happen.

When I woke up it was still early but there was light enough to see. Propped myself on an elbow and watched Jack. His eyes were closed but I knew by the shape of his mouth, his smile, that he felt me watching him. There were the black eyelashes against the skin. The thick hair springing away from his brow. The fine hairs of his eyebrow, lying beside each other, tapering away to one. How did an eyebrow know to do that curve and lay that last hair exactly right?

I'd never need any other face but his.

His eyelids trembled and he looked at me. Touched my cheek with a finger as if I might be the tail end of a dream. That smile of Jack's, the way it made the skin round his eyes crease up. I couldn't leave off looking. All I could think was, this can be the rest of our lives. Together, all the years to come.

Never done anything harder than leave that bed. Like cutting away part of myself. Opened the door, remembering to do it quick. The hall was dim, but not so dark that I didn't see Daunt in a brown nightshirt at the door of his room at the other end. Coming or going, seen me or not seen me, I couldn't tell. It was only the blink of an eye. Then he stepped into the room and shut the door. I heard the click of the latch.

So quick, I wondered if I'd imagined him there. When I tiptoed past the door, it was as closed as if it had never in its life been open.

In our world of ordinary river folk, having a bit of experience with a man was no great crime. Not too many, man or woman, would have been new to the business when they got married. But I knew gentry had funny ideas about things. Be shocked, probably, at a young girl slipping out of a man's room.

That was all right by me. Made things simple with Daunt, if there'd been any thought of them getting complicated.

I went to sleep beside Mary and by the time I got dressed and went downstairs the gentlemen had gone. Good, I thought. Never have to meet you again, John Daunt.

I was sure you could see it in the room like smoke, the way Jack and me wanted to be near each other. That everyone would notice the difference in me. Wouldn't be the end of the world. Hurry things along, bring the future to us quicker.

But Ma glanced at me beside Jack and she didn't see. Pa had

a way of watching Jack. He might of guessed. But behind his big seamed face who knew what he might be thinking. Whatever it was, he kept it to himself.

None of anyone's business. Just between me and Jack, and the privateness of it was part of the pleasure.

WE HAD a few weeks before Jack sailed again. If I had a bit of life to live again, it'd be that time.

I took him up to the cave, it had been my private place and now it could be ours. First time we went there he looked at the dipper, the teacup, the dusty things from my childhood.

Good as a parlour, he said. No doubt about you, Sarah Thornhill. One of a kind.

We sat on the edge of the rock, below us the roof of the house, the dark shingles, the whitewashed chimneys. Pa in the horse paddock with his pipe puffing smoke and his hands behind his back, watching the men heaving a fence post into a hole. The boy in the yard splitting the kindling, the *tock tock* of the hatchet coming up to us small and slow, as if through water. Someone called out, something clattered that we couldn't see, the bucket in the well that would be. Then everything quiet, and the gold light all around us.

Just the two of us together. The wind in the treetops, and the rock warm under our backsides. I'd watch the shadow of a branch move across my boot and over the sand until it bent down where the rock fell away. That was how long we sat. No room I've ever been in, in any house, anywhere, was half as lovely as that cave, looking out into the valley.

The waiting was nearly as good as what came after. Our bodies touching and the soft light moving round us. I'd turn my head and he'd be smiling sideways at me fond and soft, the way he did—oh, I can see it now, that tender look! Then he'd stretch out on the sand.

Good as a feather bed, he'd say, the same every time. Try it, Sarah Thornhill, tell me I'm not wrong.

I'd lie beside him and we'd spin out the moment, looking up at the roof of the cave. The stone there was frayed away into a sponge of holes and grooves that you could follow till you were lost in the soft tangle. After a bit, the back of his hand would slide up against the back of mine and we'd lie hip to hip and hand to hand. It was like a hunger or a thirst, what I felt for Jack. Not anything in your power to say no to.

Afterwards we'd sit, twined up one into another. Didn't talk much, but Jack would sing. Just softly, so they wouldn't hear us down at the house. They'd be the kinds of songs sailors knew, a jiggy sort of tune and the words all about ships and faraway places and lovely ladies left behind. I didn't have much of a voice but he loved to hear me sing too, or so he said. Did my best to oblige, finding things floating up out of my memory.

*Oranges and lemons, say the bells of Saint Clement's.* The words coming out of my mouth so easy, it was like my mother in there singing for me. *You owe me five farthings, say the bells of Saint Martin's.* She was with us, the silly song like a blessing from her.

It was enough for me to live as if every day was the only day. I had no thoughts of what might follow. But one day in that time of closeness, Jack looked ahead.

My roaming years pretty well done, he said. Be time to settle down by and by.

What, no more sealing, I said.

Know Sullivan's, do you, he said. That old place down the river a piece?

Yes, I knew Sullivan's. An overgrown paddock and a half-ruined hut tumbling off the side of the hill. Someone had got a farm going there long ago, but must of walked off. No one there, all the years I'd known it.

Man has to think what he might do, Jack said.

And what might he do, Jack, I said.

Soon get that hut patched, he said. Man with a sharp axe get that patched up in a day. Patch it up, clear the paddock, grow whatever it is you grow.

What, be a farmer! I said. Jack Langland a farmer!

Don't give me much credit, do you Sarah Thornhill, he said. Be surprised what Jack Langland can turn his hand to.

Now I was racing after him, had a future mapped out for us in a moment, the two of us in the patched-up hut, growing whatever it was you grew.

Couple more trips for the seals, he said. Get a bit more put by. Keeping Sullivan's to myself till I'm ready. Not give anyone else ideas.

Took my hand, traced the lines on my palm, touched all the fingers one by one as he had once before.

Might be lonely in that old hut, he said. Be wanting company. A certain person who might join me. If she was that way inclined. But a certain person could do better than Jack Langland. I know that. Could do a lot better.

I'd never heard Jack shy before.

You tell me, he said. Tell me straight. If you seen something you like better, say the word. Jack Langland always be a friend to Sarah Thornhill no matter what.

Never seen anything I liked better, I said. Told you once before, you're the only feller for me.

Did I kiss him, or was it him kissed me? The wind in the leaves, the twittering of the little creatures in the bushes, a bird singing. I heard it all, felt every touch of the air on my skin, every bit of me never more part of the life of the world.

~

We had those few weeks, then word come from Sydney, *Industry* ready to sail, Will and Jack to go to Sydney on Trevarrow's boat that afternoon.

It was all a bustle and fluster, Will and Jack putting their things together, Ma fussing up and down the stairs, Pa in doorways getting out his gold watch and clicking it open. It was as much as me and Jack could do to find a moment alone together in the upstairs hall. Got our arms round each other, he hugged me so hard he squeezed the air out of me.

Will you wait for me, he whispered.

Till Kingdom Come, I whispered back.

Then Ma was at the end of the hall but we was quick, she didn't see.

Take care of yourself, Sarah Thornhill, Jack said in a voice anyone was free to hear. No mischief while I'm gone.

Come along now Jack, Ma said, Trevarrow's waiting! And Dolly, don't get in his way, there's a girl.

We all walked down to the jetty in the yellow afternoon light. Will striding with his bundle bouncing on his back and Pa walking beside him, two men with long legs and longer shadows. Mary and Ma going zig-zag down the steep part so they didn't slip. Last was Jack and me, and the speckled dog coming along beside us. Knew something was up, kept looking at Jack. At the jetty it got under everyone's feet, trying to stay beside him.

Off you go, Jack said, pointed up to the house. Home now! Off with you!

The dog panted up at Jack with its tongue hanging out, making out it was stupid. It was on the edge of the jetty when Will and Jack got on board and the man flipped the bowline up on deck.

I watched the boat slide out into the stream, Jack in the stern getting smaller every second. I waved with my shawl and he took off his cap and pulled it through the air over his head. Then the boat slid round the point behind the mangroves. That empty water.

Me and the dog trailed up to the house together. I gave it a pat, it looked up into my face, licked my chin. All the spring gone out of that dog's step. The dog didn't want me and I didn't want the dog, but we made do with each other.

Never you mind, I said. He'll be back. Then we'll see.

ARCHIBALD CAMPBELL made sure Mary didn't forget him. Every couple of weeks he rode down from Garlogie, and always with something for her, a lace handkerchief or a pretty pair of combs.

Back in Aberdeen he might of looked askance at a woman who couldn't read or write and with her father an emancipist. But in New South Wales there was a good deal more men than women, and if a feller was overly choosy he'd miss out. Mary was clever and knew how to manage a household, and she was pretty enough. None of the airs and graces of a woman of his own class, but up-country didn't call for airs and graces.

He'd stay a few days. Go round the paddocks with Pa, keen as if he never saw a cow before. Went on carving at the meal table even when Pa's wrist was mended, like the son-in-law already.

You've a good table here, Mrs Thornhill, he said. Mrs Devlin a fine hand with a joint or a pie. I've a fair cook at Garlogie but it's a throng place, eleven government men, the poor woman run off her feet. Does her best but it's the plain cooking. You might say alarmingly plain.

Except we didn't get *alarmingly*, it had such a Scotch twist to it.

Now her pies, he said, I don't tell a lie to say I broke a tooth once on her pastry. The one thing I hanker for, a pie like my dear mother made. The pastry to melt in your mouth, and the filling so succulent. Never had its like.

Mary took it as a challenge. Went up to Langland's one day, they had a woman did a lovely pie, to learn how to get the pastry light. Mix it with a knife and hardly touch it when you rolled it, make a rosebud for the top and brush it all with egg to bring up a good colour.

Presented her pie to Campbell that night and you'd of thought she'd given him the Crown jewels. One night not too long after that, Pa stood up in his place at the head of the table and said he had some good news, it was going to come as a surprise for everyone, Mr Campbell and Mary was betrothed.

We all laughed, oh yes what a surprise! All of us pleased. I liked Archibald, a mild sort of gent, and amiable without making too big a thing of it.

But Mary, I said later, he's a good feller all right, only thing is, how will you make out what he's saying?

Oh, I don't have to make him out, Dolly, she said. Just so long as he can make me out!

~

John Daunt come down for the wedding. Best man, smart in his top hat and grey swallowtail coat. Never in his life be handsome, but the clothes made the most of him. Gallant to me as bridesmaid, took my arm with his gloved hand, walked with me the way he was supposed to. But made no remarks beyond the splendid weather and how pleased he was for the happy couple. Bland as an egg. Nothing of the Daunt who'd coaxed me to make bird noises. Whether he'd seen me outside Jack's room that other morning I couldn't tell, but one thing was plain as a pikestaff. If he ever had been interested in me, he wasn't interested now.

Ma looked at the two of us together, nudged Pa, whispered. In his best clothes Pa was never at ease for fear he'd make a blunder, but he looked at us and his face softened. Easy to see what was in their minds. No, Pa, I thought, for once you've got it wrong.

My word Archibald Campbell was pleased, walking down the aisle with Mary on his arm. Had his hand on hers and I could see how tight he was holding her fingers, as if he thought she might fly away.

I come over tears, seeing him so proud and loving. Thinking of another man, of course, that I hoped might be just as proud and loving, walking down the aisle with me and hanging on tight.

Outside the church I laughed and threw the rice, and when Mary tossed her posy I put my hand straight up and caught it. She laughed and her eyes went to Daunt beside me.

Yes, Daunt would make a fine husband for some woman. But I held the posy up to the east. You went far enough, that's where Jack was. The sky over him was the same sky that was over me, an ocean of air joining us. I sent a message up to be carried along its currents to where he was. *No other man in the world for me but you, Jack Langland. Hurry home.*

~

Weddings beget weddings, they say, and it was true of the Thornhills that year. Johnny come of age for a licence, talked Pa into giving him the cash for the freehold on the Sow and Pickle in Bridge Street. Had his eye on Judith Martin all those years, a clever loud red-headed girl, took no nonsense from anyone but cheerful and a good head for figures. Pa was pleased, Martins was emancipist stock like us, but plenty of money and Judith just the wife for a publican.

That give Bub the idea and he married Kathleen Cobb. Her pa was another *old colonist* but a big man now up the river. Him and Pa put in together and got Bub and Kathleen three hundred acres at South Creek. Mary and Archibald come down from Garlogie for the wedding, Mary with a newlywed glow about her still, and Archibald smiling all round.

Billy Cobb couldn't take his eyes off her, poor booby.

Pa togged himself up in his swallowtail coat and top hat for the weddings, one after the other, getting his money's worth out of the clothes. Ma got tight and tearful on the French champagne he made sure of. When you was an emancipist you had to work extra hard, show you knew the best and had the money for it.

Got you settled, he said, gabby with the champagne. All of you moving up in the world like I've always wanted. Just you now, Dolly. Soon have you settled with some fine gentleman. Eh? Fine gentleman not a thousand miles from here?

Gave me a great drunken wink, had to stop and think how to do it, screwed up his mouth as well as his eye.

By the end of that year I'd been a bridesmaid three times. Sophia Langland was the one reminded me, not having Will's ring on her finger yet made her catty. Wasn't going to show her I cared, but it unsettled me. Jack and me had an understanding, but only the two of us knew.

The best of every day was first thing, before anyone was up. Had the bed to myself now Mary was gone, my thoughts private. With the sun coming in between the curtains and the birds greeting the day, I'd make believe Jack was with me. The way his eyes softened just before he smiled.

Tried to picture the place where he was, so I could be there with him. But New Zealand, the trees that grew sideways and the natives that ate people, was a blank. Mrs Trevarrow had a sealskin coat, I sat behind her at church and watched the light gleam along it, but it was hard to imagine it a living creature with a pretty face.

They'd never been away so long. Ten months, then eleven. I'd go up to the cave, look for the marks we'd left on that silky sand. Surprising how quick the wind smoothed them out. The floor of the cave was as if no human had ever touched it. Only the curving line through the sand where a snake had been. I watched the light move round the honeycomb stone of the roof and told myself, Jack lay here where I'm lying. Looked up there at what I'm looking at.

It wasn't much comfort. I was counting the days.

# PART TWO

ELEVEN DAYS into the eleventh month, Jack was back. But only him. Soon as he stepped off the boat he told us, Will was drowned. Said it flat, as if he'd thought it so many times it had no feeling for him any more.

I cried out like he'd hit me. Pa's face went crooked and his mouth squared up shouting *no!*

They'd been at some little island, Jack said, name of Codfish. Storm blew up and this island was no good in that sort of weather, they pulled up the anchor and ran for some place called Easy Harbour. But the boat went on the rocks.

Tipped over like a leaf, Jack said. Scoured off that deck, the lot of us.

And Will? Pa said, with his voice cracked.

Never saw him after we went in the water, Jack said. Only

me and a man called Matthew Stone fetched up on the beach.

I was all of a muddle inside, knowing Will was gone but waiting for him to come in and shout *Dolly!* the way he always did. My favourite brother, part of my world, part of my life.

The waste and the stupidity of it. The sadness was going to drown me too, I had to be angry.

Easy Harbour, I said. How come they call it that!

The sea. I was always frightened of it. As a child I'd once been sick in the old *Hope* on a rough passage down to Sydney. The water tossing the boat about, jerking and jarring. I remembered Will laughing at me crouched in the stern calling out *Make it stop, make it stop.*

He'd gone into that cold sea, the waves hurling themselves against the boat. That hollow wooden shell no match for it. Twisting and foundering and all of them pitched off the deck. The fist of the water in your face. Did he think, *Make it stop, make it stop*, and remember his little sister in the moment before he was swallowed down?

Washed up later, beard glistening, mouth full of sand.

Pa wanted to hear it again and again. Where was it exactly? How far to this harbour, and how did you get on the rocks, and was there a town could send out boats?

Thirty miles to the harbour, Mr Thornhill, and the wind veered round sudden. No town. Just the rocks and the wind roaring and the waves coming up at you.

Pa watching Jack. As if it might come out different if he heard it one more time.

I'm sorry, Mr Thornhill, Jack said.

He couldn't look at Pa. *Sorry*, because he was thinking he should not of been the one that lived. *Sorry*, because it was not Will here telling us the story, and Jack being mourned.

Pa took hold of Ma's hand and hung on. It might have been him drowning.

~

After Jack brought the news Pa went into himself. Sat in the parlour, listening to the clock tick through time, or out on the verandah in a black brood. Too inward to pick up the telescope, but staring across the river to the bush along the cliffs. Mouth hard, face stony.

Me and Jack sat with him. The boats went up and down the river and I watched for Dick's blue cap but never saw it. I was angry at Dick for being alive, or for being gone, or for not being my brother at all, for being nothing more than a stranger whose parents had happened to call him Richard.

There wasn't enough to be angry at, to fill up the emptiness that was the place Will had been.

Word travelled quick along the river. Every day of that first week, boats stopped at our jetty and people walked up the track. Langlands and Cobbs and Fletchers, but hard to see who they were in their mourning clothes till they got close. Pa went in the parlour while Jack told it all again and Ma sniffed into her handkerchief. They'd all say, *I'm sorry for your loss, Mr Thornhill.* He'd wait for them to be gone. Then back out on the verandah, watching the bush across the river as if it could explain.

Dead Will lay between me and Jack like a log fallen across a road. We looked at each other over it, spoke a few words across it, but Jack's eyes were blank and my face had forgotten any look except a sad one. I'd catch hold of his hand and squeeze it, trying to remember something that had gone away. This was grief. *Your loss* wasn't just the person who was dead. It was the gap in the ones left behind, a hole that swallowed everything else too. I'd lost Will, and it seemed I'd lost Jack and myself as well, both of us groping in a fog of sadness.

One afternoon Jack came to where I was in the kitchen. Waited for Mrs Devlin to go in the scullery.

A word later? he said. Up the cave?

But his face was troubled. When he said *the cave*, he wasn't thinking about what it used to mean.

We sat there side by side as we'd always done, looking out. Phillip down in the yard, filing away at Valiant's hoof, the smoke rising out of the parlour chimney. Beyond that the river. The tide flowing in strong, making streaks and curls, one current sliding past the other.

Fact is, Jack said.

He had to stop and cough as if his voice had gone rusty.

Fact is, he said, Will had a wife. Native woman. On the boat, drowned along of the rest.

A wife! I said. Will? What, Will married?

Married proper way, Jack said. Went to the parson. I seen it done.

Straight off, I was glad. That Will had a bit of life before he died. Sophia and the dull small life he'd of had with her, that wasn't the end of the story. But I wished he'd told me. *You should of said, Will.*

And Jack. Jack knew, all that time, and not shared it with me, even when we'd lain together and I'd thought two human beings couldn't be closer.

Whyn't you tell me, Jack, I said. Should of told me.

He was too sad to scold, but I was hurt.

Kept it to myself, if that's what Will wanted, I said. I can keep a secret.

But that word *secret* shot through me like the white flash of a splinter under a nail.

You got a wife too! I said. Like Will!

He put an arm round me, the first time since he'd come back.

Why'd I do that, he said. When Sarah Thornhill's enough for any man.

Well thank God, Jack, I said.

Shaky in the voice, because that flash showed me life could have claws.

Have to kill you if you did, I said. Know that, don't you.

Trying to turn it into something we could laugh at, but my voice giving me away.

One of them knives you keep so sharp, I said. Be ever so sorry to have to do it, but I would.

He come to meet me, trying to make the shape of a smile.

You would, he said. I know you would.

Jack, don't go back, I said. Don't go again.

One more trip, he said. Two at the outside.

Didn't like the sound of two more trips, but two was better than five or ten.

Sullivan's after that, I said. That what you're thinking?

That's my thinking, he said. By and by.

I'd of liked to talk about Sullivan's. Was there a well, and was there a bread oven, and did the chimney draw properly?

You tell Pa about the wife? I said. Or best not?

I told him, he said. Had to, he wanted to know every little thing. Soon's I told him he asked me straight off, was there children?

Oh, I said. Children?

So I had to tell him yes, he said. A little girl. Five or six year old.

She'd be granddaughter to him, I said. And niece to me! What did he think, Jack, what did he make of it?

He wants her, Jack said. Your pa wants her.

Wants her, I said. How do you mean wants her?

Says to me, she's an orphan girl, he said. Best here with her kin. Wants me to fetch her. Not let her grow up a native, see. Thinks she'll be better off here. Grow up white.

Well and she is, I said. Half white.

Half white, that's right, Jack said. Half black too.

Half black! I thought of a little girl with Will's face, but skinny and raggy, living in a humpy, watching me ride along on Queenie.

My niece. I was her auntie.

Have a better life, wouldn't she? I said. Here with us. With her kin.

She got kin over there too, Jack said. Way they work things, everyone's kin. I doubt they got a word even, for orphan.

Turned my hand over, looked at the lines on the palm as if they'd tell him something.

Damned if I know what's best to do, he said.

What's her name? I said.

He said a word that was no name I'd ever heard, to my ear nothing but noises strung together, gone as soon as he'd said them.

Your pa wants it real bad, he said. Begged me, the tears standing in his eyes. But damned if I know. All's I can think is, should of been me went down with that boat. Should of been me.

But I wasn't having that, and at last he let me take him in my arms.

**B**ACK FROM New Zealand, him and the girl, on a night of a sudden squall, the rain throwing itself against the house. They come into the parlour, Jack carrying the girl. Brought the night in with them. He gave me a smile, but his heart not in it. Put her down and she hung onto his coat like she'd never let go.

She was little, five or six like Jack said, and dirty as you'd expect, coming all that way in the boat. A brown pinny on, and another kind of brown down the front where food or sick had been wiped at. Barefoot in spite of the wet and cold. Black hair hanging all over her face and her dark child's hand fisted round the edge of Jack's coat.

Nothing of William about her that I could see.

This the girl? Pa asked. You vouch, do you man? This the girl?

Jack put his hand under the child's chin, pushed her head up.

Look Mr Thornhill, he said, see that face, that's from your Will. Vouch or no vouch, this is the girl.

He does not know *vouch*, I thought. But too proud to ask.

It was true, she had a look of Will in the shape of her face. When he let go she looked down. You'd of thought she wasn't breathing, she was that still. Like someone with the toothache hoping for the pain to ease.

Glad to see you back safe, Pa said. And bringing her. I thank you for that. Will you take a glass with me now?

Jack went to the chair and the girl stuck to him like a tick, four fingers and a dirty thumb latched round that edge of coat, head down as she shuffled with him.

Going to fetch the girl had aged Jack, thinning him out in the face. And brought some kind of doubt over him.

Now Dolly, Ma said, this is a poor orphan New Zealand girl. Will, dear soul that he was, he wanted us to take care of her.

No, Meg, Pa said. Best we all know where we stand.

Pulled the girl over to him in the armchair. She stood between his knees looking at the floor.

This girl is Will's child, he said.

He was going to say something else. His fingers pressing the girl's shoulder. His hands on her so big, I thought she'd be frightened, but she didn't seem to be.

Will's child, he said again, as if the words gave him comfort. Mother a New Zealander, name of, what was her name again now Jack?

Rugig, Jack said. Name of Rugig, Mr Thornhill.

The girl heard her mother's name in among all the talk she didn't understand and her small dirty face lit up. But of course her mother was not here. Never would be. In this room her mother was just a word. I saw her understand that, saw the light go out of her.

Our Will married this Rugig fair and square, Pa said.

But a heathen woman! Ma said. A black!

What Will done over there, he done right by his own lights, Pa said. Won't have it said otherwise, Meg.

She made a noise, *huh*! But Pa touched the girl's head, smoothed the black hair.

This girl is Will's own flesh and blood, he said. My granddaughter. Never mind where she come from or what went on or the rights and wrongs of it all.

What's her name, Jack, I said.

He said the word again, and I caught the start of it, Ra something.

Rachel, Ma said. That's what we'll call her.

No, Mrs Thornhill, Jack said.

He started to say the name again.

She'll be Rachel, she said. Good Christian name.

Pa smoothed the girl's hair again, looked away over her head into the fire. Him and Ma must of had words about the girl coming. He'd won out on that. What she was called was something Pa wouldn't fight. And poor thing, what did she care what we called her.

She could do with a bite to eat, Jack said. Been a long hard time for her.

Pa woke up out of wherever he'd gone.

Meg, bring the victuals in here for them, he said. Stand by the fire with her Jack, the two of you wet as fish.

I knelt beside the girl, went to undo her pinny. She pulled away, nearly in the fire she was so determined.

Best leave her, Jack said. Till she gets used to you.

I saw a flicker of the Jack I knew in the way he looked down at me. He put his hand on the girl's shoulder and I put mine over it, felt the coldness of his skin.

Strange for her yet awhile, Jack said. Best take it slow.

Then Ma was coming in with the tray, wanting to put it on the table and have them sit up and eat.

Here by the fire, Mrs Thornhill, Jack said. Be best, I believe.

Took the tray and set it on the hearthrug.

More what she's used to, he said.

They sat on the hearthrug, Jack spooning up the stew as best he could with her on his lap. The girl stuck her fingers in and fished the bits of meat out of her bowl.

That's the way! Pa said. Look at her tuck in! Look at that, Meg!

It was the first life in him since Will died. Almost laughing with the pleasure of watching the girl eat.

Yes, Ma said. All right for tonight, but I can see we got a long road ahead of us.

Yes, well, he said. Time enough, Meg. She's here now. That's the thing. Here among us.

But the girl was asleep, leaning back on Jack, a piece of meat still in her fingers. He stood up with her, and her arms went round his neck and clung, even fast asleep as she was.

Her room's the one next to Mr Thornhill and myself, Ma said. Let her go to bed dirty this once.

Held the door open for Jack, but he didn't go.

Happiest in with me, he said. Couple of cushions on the floor.

No, Jack, she said. I won't have that.

She'll wake up feared, Jack said. Never slept on her own.

Begin as we mean to go on, Ma said. Lay her on the bed, Jack, cover her up, she'll be all right.

They stared at each other, will against will.

Jack pushed past her with the girl and Ma followed. I went after them, watching the lamplight make Jack's shadow big, then small, up the stairs and along the hall to the room that Ma had got ready for the girl. He lay her on the bed, pulled the quilt up. She didn't wake.

Give her a good scrubbing in the morning, Ma said. Won't we, Dolly?

Best go a bit slow, Mrs Thornhill, Jack said. Not used to our ways.

Nonsense, Jack, Ma said. The girl's got to be clean. She'll love it, won't she Dolly, a good hot tub!

Go by what Jack says, I said. Start off just a wipe with the flannel.

That's the idea, Jack said. Take it slow.

~

I waited for the house to be quiet, crept along the hall to Jack's room. Not for what we'd got up to there before, Jack was too worn and faraway for that. Just to let him know I was there. That I'd keep him company in his wornness and farawayness.

The door was open. He knew I'd be coming along, I thought.

The rain had stopped, the moon was out, enough to see a long sleeping mound in the bed. That was Jack, but there was another mound at his feet that was the girl, coiled up in herself. Blanket on the floor from where he must of covered her up and it slid off. She was awake. Eyes gleaming at me.

Poor thing, I thought. Everything foreign, Jack the only thing you know. But canny enough to creep round till you found him.

Longed to get in with Jack, but the bed too small for three, and I couldn't turn her off, poor thing.

Auntie Dolly look after you, I whispered.

Picked up the blanket from the floor, tucked it round her, kissed the top of her head. She watched me. But never moved, never made a sign. I went back to my bed.

~

When I come down to the parlour in the morning, she was with Jack by the fire. Still in the dirty pinny. The air in the room unsettled.

Yes, well, you should of taken her back to her own bed, Ma was saying. Not wrapped her up snug like it was her proper place.

Never slept on her own before, Mrs Thornhill, Jack said.

Not one night in her life. Not the way they do things there.

Well, this is the way we do things here, Jack, she said. Sooner she learns that the better.

Only a little thing, Jack said. Bit of kindness don't go astray.

All right, Ma said. I can see what I'm going to have to do. She'll go to her bed tonight and I'll turn the key.

Lock her in! I said. That's too hard, Ma!

She wheeled around at me.

I won't have this, Dolly, she said. This answering back. And as for you, Jack Langland, you been with the savages so long you're getting to be one.

Anne rang the bell for breakfast. The girl jumped at the sound, burrowed into Jack.

Rachel! Ma said. Come in to breakfast now! Come along dear, into the dining room! Rachel!

Took her by the wrist, tried to pull her out of the room. The girl was stronger than she looked.

I'll tell her, Mrs Thornhill, Jack said. Let me tell her, in her tongue. She'll go with you then.

Got down on his haunches, made the sounds of that other language, smooth runny words. With those words in his mouth he was a man from another place.

That's enough Jack! Ma said. I'll have no more of that jabber! She's got to learn to talk proper.

Better if Jack tells her, Ma, I said. Till she gets used to us.

I was too old to be spanked, but that was the thought on Ma's face. Pale, she was that cranky.

Then Pa was in the doorway. Went straight to the girl. Put his hand under her chin, looked into her face.

How's my poppet, he said. How's my little girl.

The warmth in his voice the only good thing in that room.

Tell her, will you lad, he said. Tell her how much she means to her Grandpa.

No, William! Ma said. Got to get her in the way of English. Longer we leave it, harder it'll be.

That's well and good, Meg, Pa said. But I want her to hear a kind word.

Jack spoke to the girl. Her eyes went from him to Pa but her face was a mask. Pa leaned down, kissed the top of her head.

Thank you, lad, he said. You're as good a feller as ever drew breath.

But Jack didn't want thanks. He was watching the girl.

What's done is done, Pa said. But you get a chance, do things different, you're a lucky man.

Do what different, Pa, I said. What chance?

Pray God you never have to know, he said.

Come along, quick now William, Ma said. Bring the girl in, we'll get the breakfast done.

I let them go out into the hall, hoping for a word alone with Jack at last. Had the room to ourselves, just the girl stuck to his side. Got our arms round each other. One person again, just for a few heartbeats.

Sarah Thornhill, Jack whispered. Thank God for you.

Don't go again, I said. Not ever.

Not ever again, he said.

Then Ma was at the door.

Come along now Jack, she said. We'll have some food, then I'll get her cleaned up.

In the dining room Jack lifted the girl onto the chair but she slid back down.

Put her on your lap, lad, Pa said. That'll be all right, Meg, the first day.

A stiff silent breakfast. Ma kept pushing a plate under the girl's food where she had it on the cloth. Picked up her hand and closed it round a spoon. The girl pushed the plate away. Let the spoon fall on the floor. Whispered something to Jack but he didn't answer, just gave her another rasher.

After breakfast Ma got the tub ready in front of the fire in the parlour, the hot water, the soap, the white towel. But the girl wouldn't let anyone undo her clothes. Shied away from the steaming water. When Ma waved the soap under her nose, *see, pretty smell, Rachel*, she lashed out, it flew across the room.

Jack lad, you best do it on your own, Pa said at last. Come along Meg, leave them be. This first time.

Held the door open and she went out. But her face tight. Trouble on the way.

I got myself in the corner where the girl didn't have to see me, listened while Jack spoke to her. Her hands went to the buttons of her dress and finally she let him stand her in the tub and swab her down with the flannel. Got the clean clothes on her, a shift and a dress that had been mine and before that Mary's. Ma had put out stockings too, and soft slippers, but he left them. Sat her on the floor between his knees, the two of them watching the fire. I crept over, bit at a time, till I was beside them. Put my hand on the girl's, she let me leave it there.

Wondering if I done right, Jack said. Soon's I got her on the boat, I wondered.

The girl turned her face up to watch him speak.

Early days, I said. Ma going a bit quick, that's all.

Work itself out, that what you think? he said. That she'll settle?

Pa loves her, I said. Do anything to make her happy. And me her auntie. First niece Thornhills ever had, she'll get such a cosseting.

We sat peaceable for a time. But Ma and Pa might of been listening for the washing noises to stop, they was back too soon for my liking. The girl closed herself up. Jack and me stood with her between us.

Now, Jack, Ma said, we been thinking, Mr Thornhill and myself. Happy to welcome you. You know that. But it'll make it hard for poor Rachel. You being here. That right, William?

Always welcome here, lad, Pa said.

Yes, but not making it easy for Rachel, Ma said. Is it, William? Jack talking in language and all that. Best make a clean break of it. Not cling to what she knows.

So what you're saying, Jack said.

He left the thought hanging.

Yes, lad, just a short time, Pa said. Say a fortnight. Till she settles.

You sending him away? I said. Sending Jack away!

A fortnight, that's all, Pa said. Give her a chance to settle.

For Rachel's sake, Ma said. Wouldn't want to make it harder for her, would you Dolly? And Jack, you can see the sense in that.

Jack stared at Ma like a man struck a blow from behind.

I'll not use the language, Mrs Thornhill, he said. Guarantee it. Not another word.

Not just the language, Jack, Ma said. While you're here she won't settle. That's clear by now.

You could hear it in her voice. Knew she'd won.

Take the skiff, Pa said. See your ma and pa, Jack. Tell the girl you're going for a time, tell her you'll be back, that'll be an end of it. And, Dolly, that's enough, lass, your ma and me made up our minds.

I was starting to argue, but Jack put out his hand to stop me.

Yes, Mr Thornhill, he said. Two weeks. I'll tell her, two weeks. Then I'll be back.

He only got a few words out to the girl and her eyes widened. She cried out, the room rang with her voice. All the time in that silent body there'd been these huge hard cries waiting to get out. Ma and Pa bundled her out of the room between them.

Off you go, lad, Pa called over his shoulder. Look sharp now!

I made to go after them. Could hear them getting the girl upstairs. Ready to wrestle with them, but Jack held me back.

Fetched her all this way, he said. With good reasons, in my own mind. Best give it a fair trial. Your ma might be right. Make a clean break.

But a fortnight! I said. When you're just this minute back!

It'll fly, he said. No time at all. You and me, Sarah Thornhill, we know how to wait.

From upstairs we could hear the girl crying out and Ma's voice shrill and sharp.

Look out for her like I would, Jack said. Help her settle. Quicker she settles the better. For all of us.

Pa was on the stairs, we could hear his boots. I grabbed Jack's hand, how could I let him go?

No other way, he said quickly. Got to play the long game. Trust me on this, Sarah Thornhill.

Pa opened the door, held it wide.

You still here, Jack? he said. Look sharp, lad!

On my way, Mr Thornhill, Jack said.

And was gone, Pa in the doorway to stop me going after.

No, Dolly, he said. Best he goes. None of those sulks, God's sake only a fortnight, not for ever and a day!

*Trust me on this, Sarah Thornhill.*

I would. I'd trust Jack to hell's fire and back.

FIRST DAY the girl wouldn't let any of us touch her. Only place she'd be was the parlour. That's where she'd seen Jack last. Sat squashed into herself on the hearthrug as if he'd be there if she sat hard enough.

Middle of the day, Ma tried to get her to go across the hall to the dining room. Took an arm and pulled, couldn't shift her.

She'll come round, Ma said. See what she thinks when she's hungry.

Sure enough, at the end of the day the girl followed the smell of food to the dining room. Pa patted the chair next to him, heaped a bowl, she sat and ate.

See how good she's getting on now, Ma said. Make her use the spoon tomorrow. Get her civilised in no time.

I was thinking, how could I look out for the girl. Wanted

to meet Jack at the end of the fortnight with her hand in mine, auntie and niece close and loving. If she was settled by the time he got back there'd be no more talk of sending him away.

Next morning after breakfast I took the girl by her hard little hand.

Come and see the horses, I said. We got good horses. Give them some apple, look, I got it here in my pinny pocket.

She wouldn't understand the words, but I thought she'd hear the coaxing tone. She come with me easy enough.

Queenie was sticking her nose out the half-door hoping for something tasty. Got the bit of apple on my palm, showing the girl. Put it on hers, held it out. Queenie ducked her head, snuffled through her nose, lifted her lip, getting ready to take it. The girl saw those big yellow teeth and she screamed.

Don't be a goose, I said. Queenie won't hurt!

I pushed her hand up, but Queenie took fright at the girl screaming, backed away with her eyes rolling, whinnying and trampling. The more the girl screamed, the more poor Queenie tried to get away, banging up against the sides of the stall. Then the dogs were running out barking and snarling and the girl screaming and slapping me away.

Phillip ran out, shouted at the dogs, one word and they stopped. Got his arms round the girl, carried her away like a sack of meal. I could hear her gasping and gulping in the tack room like she couldn't catch her breath. When I put my head round the doorway Phillip had her on his lap, smoothing the hair back from her forehead. She was hiccupping, face sticky with tears, mouth trembling.

Not to worry, miss, he said. Never seen a horse, is all.

I put my hand out thinking to touch the girl, let her know I was sorry. But she cringed away, so the kindest I could do was leave the two of them together.

~

Every night Ma put the girl in her room, turned the key. I'd hear the child rattling the door. Begged Ma to let her sleep in with me but she wouldn't have a bar of it. She didn't let the girl have anything to eat till she did what Ma wanted. Then she had to eat it the right way, fork and spoon, or Ma took it away again.

Something in the girl broke. By the end of the first week she let herself be washed, let her hair be brushed and tied up with red ribbons, sat at the meal table and used the spoon. Ate, but no appetite or pleasure in it.

After the time with Queenie she didn't trust me. I'd come in the parlour, she'd be on the hearthrug, I'd see her fear of me. I'd get cake from Mrs Devlin but she wouldn't take it from my hand. Only if I put it down and went away, when I come back it'd be gone.

Pa was soft with her. Sit in his armchair with her between his knees. Smooth her hair, stare in the fire. Seemed she got some comfort from him. Saw something of her father in his face, perhaps.

He was more at peace than he'd been since Will died. More than I'd ever known him. Those sudden hot rages, always near the surface, they seemed to have burned themselves out.

Mealtimes, he gave her titbits off his own plate. The juicy

first slice off the leg of mutton. The best potato. Cut it up small, get it on the point of his knife, hold it out for her to take.

On the plate if you please, William! Ma would say.

So he'd put the meat on the girl's plate for her to eat with the fork.

There you are little missy, he'd say. Get yourself on the outside of that.

She's Rachel, remember, Ma said. Call her by her name so she learns.

Rachel, he said, and ruffled her hair. Good-day to you Miss Rachel.

A week went by, the second week wore away. The girl didn't settle. Shrank into herself, face drawn, skin sallow. Looked at no one and nothing. We never saw her smile. Her misery was like a dark ugly creature with us in the house night and day.

~

Ma won out on most things, but one thing she didn't. That child wasn't going to have anything on her feet. Twisting and biting at Ma when she came at her with a slipper, grabbing it out of Ma's hand, throwing it so hard the stitching broke.

Ma wouldn't be bested. The girl loved bread and honey so Ma got a slab of it, put it on the hearthrug next to her. Had a big loose stocking ready. Her idea was, start with a stocking, get to slippers by degrees. The girl was quick, knew what Ma wanted. Let her pull the stocking on, but the second the bread was in her mouth she ripped the stocking off, threw it in the fire. Ma had to snatch it out, you could smell the scorched wool.

I can wait, she said. Wait as long as I have to. She'll learn this about me, I won't give up.

The day before the fortnight was up, Ma called me into the girl's room. She was on the bed beside the girl with the slippers in her hand.

Soon's we get them on her she'll see they don't hurt, Ma said. Thank us for it in the end.

Plenty of folk go barefoot, I said. Matthews, Maunders, never had a shoe on their foot.

Matthews and Maunders not the same as Thornhills, Ma said. I won't have her a barefoot savage. Want you to hold her arms for me, Dolly.

No! I said. Won't be part of that. Let her be!

Ma took the girl by surprise, pushed her back on the mattress. She couldn't get a purchase, struck out in a panic, I could feel her fear, an animal cornered. She was wild but she was only a child and Ma got the better of her in the end. Forced a slipper onto one of her feet.

Then Pa was in the doorway.

Meg, he said. You stop that now this minute.

Ma let go and the girl ran over to him, threw herself into him. Not a sound. Never a tear, never a sound.

Makes no odds if she goes barefoot for a time, Pa said. But Meg, I won't have her forced.

I'd heard Pa angry, heard his voice crack with how angry he was. Never heard this metal in it.

Give me them shoes, he said. Give them here. Put them by till she's ready.

Longer we leave it, harder it'll be for her, Ma said. Got to be cruel to be kind.

That's all right, Pa said.

Took the shoes, crushed them up in his hand.

Come to it by and by, he said. When she's ready, Meg, and not before.

I counted every day of that fortnight. Sullivan's was a thought I brought out to warm my hands at when I was alone.

ON THE dot of the fortnight I was dressed and ready by dawn. Wanted to be sitting out the front when Jack walked through the gate, no matter how early he was. But when I went downstairs he was already on the steps as if he might of been there all night.

Ma and Pa were just over our heads in their room, so we said nothing. Just leaned in and found each other.

Thought you was gone for good, Jack, I whispered. Won't let you go again. Not for anything.

We sat for a long sweet time. So still, a little brown bird hopped up the steps one by one, cocked its head at us as if the two people wrapped together had turned into a new kind of tree.

Then Ma and Pa come out the front door behind us. Pa had the girl by the hand. She stopped dead when she saw Jack.

Went towards him, but slow, as if he was just a picture of Jack, or a statue.

None of the language, mind, Jack, Ma said.

All right, Mrs Thornhill, he said.

Stood up, went to the girl.

Rachel, don't you know your old friend Jack, he said. Forgot me already?

Took her hand and the touch freed something in her. She leaned against him, her arms round his legs. Not a sound, only held on like she'd never let go.

He picked her up, her arms went round his neck, legs round his waist. She was whispering in his ear. I could see her lips stiff as if she'd near forgotten how to speak.

Remember, Jack, Ma called. What I told you! Not a word now!

He took no notice. Listening to the girl. His face darkened. Reached around for her foot and held it, and I thought, she's telling him about the slippers. He met my eye.

*Look out for her like I would.* I hoped she wouldn't say about Queenie.

That's enough, Ma said. Come in now, Jack, we'll have some breakfast, you can see how nice she eats.

She and Pa went into the house and from her place in Jack's arms, the girl turned her head round to me. Her eyes so brown they looked black, and in the sunlight the marks of the tears clear on her cheeks.

This poor mite, Jack said. What's been done to her?

Not been how we hoped, I said.

Not settling, is she, he said. More like pining away.

You couldn't say she was settling, I said. No sign of settling.

Been thinking I made a mistake, he said. Soon's I got her on the boat, saw the light go out of her, I doubted. Now my mind's made up. I'm taking her back.

Taking her back! Getting on that boat again! Going away again, out on that ocean where men got drowned. But I'd never forgotten how the girl's face lit up that first night when she heard her mother's name. Be worth one more goodbye to see that light in her again.

Don't drown, I said. For God's sake don't drown!

Take her, come back, do it in a month, he said. Got no plans to drown. Better things to do with the time ahead than drown.

He made an effort to smile.

Dolly! Jack! Ma called from the house. Keeping us waiting! Put Rachel down, Jack, come here Rachel dear, come along to me!

Ma tried to make the girl show her manners at breakfast. It was true, she sat up on her chair, used her spoon. The ribbons in her hair and the pinny fresh on that morning. But no life in her. Didn't take her eyes off Jack but there was no hope in them. She was gone into herself like a sick cat.

Langlands all right? Pa said.

Yes, Mr Thornhill, Jack said. They're all right.

Your ma's foot any better? Ma said.

No, Mrs Thornhill, Jack said. Still the same.

When Ma went out to the kitchen there was a silence. Pa cleared his throat.

See you watching, lad, Pa said. Wanting to see her settled.

She's in a bad way, Jack said.

See you smarting for her, Pa said. Honour you for that, your kindly heart. But she'll come good. Meg's good with her. See them pretty ribbons she's got in her hair? That's Meg, she done that.

Yes, Jack said. Pretty ribbons all right.

Taking her time, I know, lad, Pa said. But she'll come good. By and by.

There was a silence where Jack might of said, *Yes, Mr Thornhill. She'll come good.*

The girl was watching from face to face. I wondered what I hadn't before, if she knew some English.

I'm thinking I done wrong to bring her, Mr Thornhill, Jack said. Made a mistake.

You're wrong there, Pa said. Never done a better deed.

First thing she said to me was, can we get on the boat and go home? Jack said.

A child says all manner of things, Pa said. Wouldn't want to set too much store by that.

Mr Thornhill, I know you love her, Jack said. But it's best I take her back.

Pa blinked at that, his jaw tightened. I wanted to say, Have a care, Jack!

No need for that, lad, Pa said. No call to think that way.

I heard the edge in his voice, that Jack didn't, so I got in quick.

We all of us want what's best for her, I said. Her grandpa,

you got her best interests at heart. Wouldn't want to see her sad.

I thought he softened. Jack might of thought the same, he tried again.

She got her kin there, Mr Thornhill, he said. Best I take her back to them.

That got Pa blazed up.

This is her kin! he said. Us! Here!

*Leave it, Jack,* I urged him in my mind. *Leave him burn himself out.*

But Jack was catching some of the heat off Pa.

Got kin there too, Jack said. Got a granny. Aunties and uncles.

Not like her grandpa! Pa said. And Dolly there, her auntie too!

Shouting, his eyes gone sharp.

Could take her today, Jack said.

The anger in him was turning to stone.

Trevarrow's got a boat going to Sydney, he said.

By God you won't! Pa said. You'll not take her!

Standing, the chair tipped over behind him. Hit the table so hard the cruet bounced. The girl slid off her chair, made herself small behind Jack. He stood up, the girl stuck to him.

Mr Thornhill, he said, you begged me and I fetched her. I see now I done the wrong thing. I'm sorry Mr Thornhill but I'm taking her back.

No you won't! Pa said. By God you won't!

Come round the table, nose to nose with Jack, his hands up in fists. Jack didn't flinch. Didn't get his hands up.

There was a long turning moment.

All right Jack, Pa said. No need to come to blows.

Stepped back and I thought, Thank God.

Thing is, you got no rights in law, Pa said.

The rage gone. He was half smiling now.

You're no kin to her, he said. You're nothing to her. It's me that's kin. Me that's got the rights. You take her, lad, you'll be in breach.

In breach, Jack said. What, of the law.

That's right, lad, Pa said. Law's on my side on this.

Picked up the chair. Straightened the things in the cruet as if they mattered.

Jack's face went chalky. The girl saw it, pressed against his legs. A little sound at last, a whimper.

None of this about rights in law, Pa, I said. Not about law, this business.

Making myself sound calm, like this was any reasonable kind of conversation.

We none of us want to see her eating her heart out for home, I said. Do we, Pa?

Laying out words like paving stones to cover over the glistening black thing that had opened up at our feet. *In breach.* Whether the girl should go back or not, that was one thing. A difference of opinion, one man against another. *In breach* was another kind of thing. *In breach* was inhuman, something all iron and wood that had no anger or grief, just its own cold workings.

This is her home, Pa said. I'm her grandpa. She's stopping here. That's my last word on the matter.

I could see he was not as sure as he sounded. *In breach* was another man's weapon. But he'd set his hand to it. The more he doubted, the more he'd hold his line.

Welcome to stop along of us, Jack, he said. But we got to have that understood. She's staying here. You want the skiff, welcome to it. No call to hurry back.

He turned and went out, we heard him call to Anne for his hat, he was going down the punt, quick about it lass, a man hasn't got all day!

Jack picked the girl up, folded his arms round her, their two black heads together.

Jack, I said, but he was staring at the floor, paid no heed.

I won't have you go, I said, but I could hear Pa's bluster in my voice.

How can we work it, Jack, I said. What can we do?

Only one thing to do, he said. That's me go. Like they want.

I'd never seen him bleak. Didn't know Jack Langland could look beaten.

No! I said, was trying to call up words, reasons, appeals, to throw at his bowed head.

I'll go, he said. Only not as far as they think.

Oh, Sullivan's! I said. You mean Sullivan's!

I was leaping ahead, the corn in the paddock and the kettle on the fire, me and Jack every night and every day.

Rather take her back, he said. Sullivan's the best I can do. Be close by there. She knows I'm close, poor thing be eased a little in her heart.

I went to put my arms round him but the girl was leaning

132

back in his arms to see his face and he bent to her to listen. She whispered to him, a question, and he answered, something soothing.

Got her heart set on me taking her back, he said. God knows how to tell her I can't.

Put the girl down, held her close to him.

Bide my time, all I can do, he said. See my chance. Help her one way or another.

The flatness in his voice gave me a pang, that he was thinking of the girl when all I could do was think of myself, the joys ahead of me.

But Jack, aunties got rights in law too, I said. I'll be the one keeps the door open for the two of you. He can't stop me.

A little of the colour starting to come back into his face.

And Jack, I said, think of this, when we're husband and wife you'll be her uncle-in-law. Have rights on your own account.

No doubt about you, he said, and was nearly smiling. Always a step ahead of the pack.

Here with you, Jack, I said. Every step of the way.

Got my arms round him, the girl between us.

You and me together, I said.

Sarah Thornhill, he whispered. You beside me, I'll take on anything.

The kiss we gave each other tied everything up, the past and the future, the days ahead of us, and the days ahead of the girl, too. All bound into a knot that would never undo.

Didn't know Ma was at the door till she flung the words at us.

You get off her, Jack Langland! she shouted. Get off her now this minute! William! Come quick! William!

It's all right, Ma, I said.

Holding Jack's hand, smiling at the idea of him needing to be got off me.

Jack and me had our hearts set on each other a long time now, I said. Getting married, Ma, got it all worked out.

Ma took a step back like I'd hit her. Her face went slack and I thought, this is what people mean when they say *her jaw dropped*.

Would of told you before, Mrs Thornhill, Jack started, but Ma wasn't hearing.

Over my dead body, she shouted. Over my dead body you'll marry that black!

It knocked me back like a blast of wind. Jack's hand went dead in mine.

How dare you, Jack Langland! she shouted. Pushing your way in here!

The rage boiled off her. She seemed twice her size, puffed up with it.

When you're nothing! she said. Nothing but a black never going to amount to a pinch of dirt! Sneaking round sucking up to Mr Thornhill's daughter!

No! I said. No!

That was all the words I had in me.

Don't you stand there and say no to me, Dolly Thornhill, she said. How dare you!

What do you mean dare, I said.

I warned your pa, she said. Get that black buck away before

it's too late, I told him!

It was like turning over a stone and having a snake come out at you. Your blood gone watery.

Forgotten, Dolly, have you? she said. That his mother was a black gin? The father good enough stock but you said it yourself, Dolly, it's the mother's blood he's got.

Come up close to me, touched me at the front of my dress.

Too late, is it Dolly? she said. That why you're here talking weddings? You'll always have the throwbacks, you know. Did you know that? Where you've got the dark blood. Want to look out, Dolly, or you'll have something even blacker than him.

Jack could be black white or brindle, I said. Damned if I care!

Jack moved, I thought he was going to hit her. But leaned away from her and a great laugh burst out of him.

Blacker even than me, he said. Yes Mrs Thornhill, that's damn right, blacker even than Mr Thornhill's granddaughter here that he loves so much.

What Mr Thornhill does or doesn't do, it's no business of yours, Ma shouted. You're nothing but a black buck got your eye on a white girl.

We won't stand here, Jack, I said. Hear you being insulted. We'll find Pa.

Find your pa if you want, Dolly, Ma said. But I wouldn't count on him if I was you.

I was pulling at Jack's hand, but when she said that I wondered. If not for Pa tipping that chair over, getting his fists up, I'd of taken no heed. But looked at Jack and saw the same doubt in him.

Ma saw us hesitate, stepped into our doubt with a different tone.

Your mind made up then, is it Dolly? she said.

That's right, I said, tucked my arm into Jack's. Never been so sure of anything in my life.

All those years I knew her, I never once saw her yield. But now I thought she was yielding. The rage gone back in to wherever it lived.

You might think you're sure, Dolly, she said. But you haven't thought.

Oh yes we have! I cried. Jack's giving away the sealing, we got it planned out, take up that old place, Sullivan's, make a go of it.

Sullivan's! she said, and I thought I'd persuaded her. Should of seen the grease in that smile.

Well, Dolly, she said. All I can say is, you're making a mistake. A big mistake. But you were a wilful little thing from the word go. I'm not going to be the one tries to stop you.

Meaning, I thought, that she'd leave that to Pa.

Your pa will need some talking round, she said. You want things working out, you best let me do that, Dolly. Jack and me have a chat. What he's got in mind, where the money's coming from, all that. So I can go to your pa with it.

Me and Jack looked at each other. Not sure. But knew we had to have Ma on side.

The girl hadn't moved, pressed up to Jack. In the moment we wavered, she looked up, her face all over tears.

All right, Mrs Thornhill, Jack said. We'll have a chat then.

Just you and me, Jack, Ma said. You get on up to your room, Dolly.

Saw I was going to argue.

For once in your life just do as I say, she said. Me and Jack sort it out, then we'll get your pa. Won't take long, Dolly. To say what we've got to say.

So I went. Lay on the bed waiting for them to call me. Had us in Sullivan's, the hut patched snug. I could do without a fine stone house, servants and horses. All the things Pa set such store by. He'd be pleased in the end, Jack for a son-in-law near as good as having Will back. He'd let the girl come for visits. A day to start with, then a week, then a month. *Play the long game.*

I'd learn some words of her tongue. If I knew how to say a few soft things she'd trust me again. She'd come to be glad she had me for an auntie.

Time went by, I started to think they must be done. Tiptoed down the stairs, leaned my ear in at the parlour door. Heard Ma say something, couldn't make out what. There was a noise from the room, a thud like furniture going over and something like a cough or a cry. Then the door banged open and Jack was running into me. His face was strange. Swollen. As if from one minute to the next he'd got a mortal illness. Lashed out with his arm, pushed me away. Not a word spoken. Then he was wrenching open the front door, down the steps two at a time.

Jack, I called. Hoy, Jack!

Laughing, because I was frightened.

Jack, I said, will you stop!

He must of heard but he didn't turn. Brushed past Pa, walking up from the river, and ran to the jetty, too fast for me. Untied the skiff, jumped in. Pulled back on the oars hard enough to break them. Facing me as he rowed but with his head turned away.

Then the skiff was gone behind the reeds up the Branch, and only the lap of the water against the pilings.

**M**A WAS at the gate when I got back to the house, had the girl by the hand. The girl pulling at her, trying to bend Ma's fingers back so she could get away.

What did you say to him, I said. You said something.

Dolly dear, all I done was point out one or two things, she said. Dolly's got opportunities, I told him. Better opportunities than a feller half darkie with nothing behind him. Only fair to her to think about that, I told him.

He's gone, I said. Gone off in the boat.

Left it up to him entirely, she said. Left it to his judgment. Set the facts out before him and what he done, that's up to him.

Something in my head was being stretched, or squashed. Trying to follow what was going on. Ma bent down to snap off the dead flower from a bush as if nothing was out of the ordinary. A long stripe of sun lit up the gravel. Down in the paddock a dog barked and someone called out *Get away back!*

Mild usual things, they couldn't be set in the same world as the horror on Jack's face. The spurt of the oars in the water, getting away from me. I'd been lying on my bed coddling dreams, and while I'd been doing that the joins between things had ripped apart.

Pa was in his usual place on the verandah. Had the telescope in his hand, but not looking through it. Watching me, and like a child I had the thought *Pa will put it right!*

Think you'll find your pa and I see eye to eye on this, Dolly, Ma said from behind me.

I could see from his face, Ma had already got to him. He took a drink of his rum-and-water, set the glass down.

Never been anything to you who his Ma was, I said. That he was half darkie.

Jack's as good a feller as ever drew breath, Pa said. You think he's a grand feller and he is. But not to marry, Dolly.

Not about the throwbacks! I said. Don't tell me about the throwbacks!

Pet, Pa said, you're not much more than a child. Not old enough to see your way all round a thing. No, let me say my piece, Dolly.

We'll wait, I said. Wait till I'm of age.

He took no notice of that.

You know I worked up from nothing, he said.

I thought he was going to tell me about the oranges. For a

flash I felt the bubble of a silly laugh.

Worked my way up, Pa said. Want to see you children get the good of it. Not throw it all away, slip back to where I come from.

Turned his hands up, looked at the palms as if his life was written on them. Ma coming to stand beside him, he smiled at her.

You'll have opportunities, pet, he said. Get up in the world. Marrying Jack Langland be a step down. You think none of that matters. But Dolly, I'm telling you as your father I can't let you turn your back on your opportunities.

Opportunities! I wished John Daunt dead, wished him fallen dead off his saddle. Along with any other gentleman Pa might like the look of for his daughter.

Jack's the best of men, Pa said. What he done, going off, that's to his credit.

To his credit, I said. What credit, Pa? What's to his damn credit? Put his money aside, got the place at Sullivan's! That's to his credit!

But knew whatever words I might find, they'd never be the right ones. Me and Pa was two people having separate conversations. Between us somewhere was the poison that made Jack heave on the oars to get away from me, but I couldn't see where it had lodged.

Oh yes, Sullivan's. Pa said. Of all the places on God's earth, he picked out Sullivan's.

We know it's no great place, I said. Don't have to tell us that. Make a start, that's all.

Look, Dolly, Jack wants the best for you, Pa said. The way we do. Your ma laid it all out to him, just the same way I'd of done if I'd of been there. He saw the sense of it when she put it in front of him. Told her he wouldn't want to stand in your way. That right, Meg? That what he said?

His very words, Ma said. I wouldn't want to stand in her way. She's a dear girl and I wouldn't want to stand in her way. His words exactly.

Stand in my way! I said. How's that, stand in my way?

He could see it, Dolly, Ma said. How it would look. People thinking, Jack Langland, come from nothing, seeing a chance to get up in the world.

What's it matter what people think, I said.

But my blood had stopped because I knew, before she said.

He's too proud a man, Ma said. Wouldn't lay himself open to people talking. You know he's proud, Dolly. Don't you.

I couldn't deny it. I'd seen that pride. It was something I loved in him. And yet, the look on his face as he pushed me aside and went off. Was that pride? Could pride make a man look as if he'd been stabbed?

You're not happy, pet, I know, Pa said. Think the world's come to an end with Jack gone. We can see further than you. Thank us in the end.

He spoke so kindly I knew I was beaten. His rage I could fight. But this kindliness, like someone talking to a sick person, you could no more fight that than cut water with a knife.

Got away from them and their smiles, up to my room, locked the door. Tried to think the thing through. *He wouldn't stand in my way*. That was because Dolly Thornhill was rich and Jack Langland was poor. A poor man who married a rich woman would always be scorned. It was a clever snare. The harder you pulled, the tighter it caught.

But there was one way to undo it. If Dolly Thornhill was equal to Jack Langland, the snare would lose its grip. I couldn't make Jack Langland rich but I could make Dolly Thornhill poor.

Jack would come back. He'd have to say goodbye to the girl. Wouldn't leave without talking to her. His things still here, too, in his room. When he got back I'd be waiting on the jetty. Nothing in my hands, not a thing but the clothes I stood up in. Nothing could *stand in my way*, because I'd take nothing from Pa. Not a penny, not a dish, not a wedding with French champagne and top hats. Not even a father's blessing.

When Pa knocked at the door and rattled the knob I told him, Go away.

Got my warm shawl, put my hairbrush in the pocket of my skirt. Put a ribbon through the slip of green stone, hung it round my neck. That was all the dowry I'd need.

This is the last night I spend in this house, I thought. This time tomorrow, it'll be me and Jack at Sullivan's. Lucky it's warm weather. But cold or hungry as we might be at the start, there'd be all the years of the rest of our lives to be happy.

I'd be Sarah Langland, with or without the parson. As if I'd never been a Thornhill.

Jack would explain to the girl. That it was only for a time. That him and Auntie Dolly were only a mile away, and waiting the chance to help her. I pictured her slipping out of the house one night, walking barefoot in her nightdress through the paddocks and over the rocks, past Payne's Mill, through the mangroves and the bush, till she got to Sullivan's. She had that kind of will. Once she was with us, that'd be half the battle. When Pa saw her smile he'd let her stay.

I sat up and listened all night in case Jack come back. Soon as the stars faded I stepped out into the hall. There was the door to Jack's room, that I'd opened so cunningly and gone in to find bliss. And here was the door where John Daunt might or might not of seen me.

My life till now. It all seemed a childish thing, nothing of any importance to the woman walking away from it empty-handed.

Down at the jetty the river was black, the bush dark, too early even for the birds. But Pa was there. Dressed: hat, boots, everything. Like he'd been standing on the jetty all night. The speckled dog beside him, sitting watching up the river with Pa.

Well Dolly, he said. We're of a like mind, I see.

I had nothing to say to him. This was the last time I'd stand beside my Pa.

Then the dog yipped. Just one yip. The skiff was coming towards us in the grey light. Why from the Branch, I thought, but what did it matter.

What mattered was, he was coming towards me, his shoulders bunching and stretching, bunching and stretching, pushing the boat against the tide in spurts. Turned around and saw us. Stopped rowing and the boat slid away upstream so I thought he'd changed his mind. Pushed my shawl off my shoulders, went right to the edge of the jetty. Ready to jump in, splash in that silky black water till he'd be obliged to come and fish me out.

He turned his back, bent to the oars again. Something dogged and reluctant in the set of his shoulders. Then he was alongside, shipping the oars, making fast. All I could see was the top of his head, that thick black hair.

Gone up the Branch then were you, lad, Pa said.

Jack stepped up on the jetty. His face, what I could see of it, set hard.

Right up? Pa said. Away aways up?

Jack gave Pa one heavy look. The muscle in his jaw moved. Something stirred in the space between them. Jack started up to the house. I went to take his arm.

Coming with you, Jack, I said. Here and now. Not bringing a single damn thing with me, not even the name I got from Pa. Langland from now, and proud to be.

That was the start of the speech I'd got ready, and then I'd pictured us rowing off down the river, leaving Thornhill's behind.

But he jerked away from my hand, started fast up the track. I chased him but the faster I followed, the faster he walked, long strides in his boots.

Turned in at the gate, up the front steps. Ma was there, put a hand out to stop him but he brushed past. When I followed she took hold of my arm. Stronger than you'd of thought. Turned around and around together on the verandah like two people doing an angry dance.

I got out of her grip at last and ran up to Jack's room. He had a few things in his hand, bits of clothing and a pouch with the chink of coins. Putting them together into a bundle, fumbling with them, going so fast. The girl was with him, he was talking to her. Her face opened, there was that light I'd wanted to see. He was taking her away.

Jack, I said, for God's sake what's up!

Went to touch him but he twitched away as if I was red-hot.

Forget your damn pride, Jack, I said, panting still from the run up the hill.

Then Pa was in the room, and behind him Jemmy Katter and Bob Dodd, what were they doing here in the house?

By God you'll not take her! Pa shouted.

I will, Jack shouted back. Won't leave her here with you!

The girl hanging onto Jack, brown fingers white at the knuckles, holding his coat so hard. Pa pulling at her and Jack trying to get her away. Seemed the three of them would be knotted up forever in the small room.

Jem! Pa shouted. Jem, quick now man! God's sake Bob, get hold of this feller!

Jemmy and Bob got themselves either side of Jack, got an arm each and dragged him backwards so he stumbled, nearly fell. Kicked out, twisted himself round in their grip, it took all the strength Jemmy and Bob had to hold him.

Listen to me, lad, Pa said, his arms pinning the girl. Only say it the once. I see you here again, I get the law on you. You make a move to this girl, I see you behind bars. Guarantee you that, lad. Lock you up, throw away the key. Do it, not a second thought, don't you ever doubt!

Jack went slack in the men's grip, the girl stopped struggling.

Pa stared at Jack with a face of stone. It seemed nothing would ever move again.

Take him out, Jemmy, Pa said. Turn him away. Bob, take his bundle there, see him gone out the gate and away.

The men jostled Jack out the door between them and I went to follow, but there was Ma in my way, holding me and shouting into my face. I felt the spit land on my cheek. By the time I wrenched away from her and got out to the gate, Jack was gone, Jemmy and Bob standing looking sheepish. Jemmy jerked his head sideways and there was Jack already well up the hill, long fierce strides.

I hoisted up my skirt, ran like I'd never run before. Got up to him, grabbed at him. Had no breath for words but hung onto his hand so he swung half round.

He stopped. Didn't look at me, pulled his arm away.

Look out for her, for God's sake, he said. The one thing you can do. Just look out for her.

We'll get her to Sullivan's, I said. With us. Like we said.

Forget Sullivan's, he said. That's gone. This whole rotten dirty place. Never set foot here again.

I grabbed at him again, but he was too quick. Stood a yard away and looked at me at last. His face dark, boiling, bent out of shape. The scald of that look.

None of your doing, he said. But get this straight in your mind. I'll not have any part of you. Never want to see your face again. Not now, not ever.

Turned his back on me and stepped out, driving himself up the hill, putting the yards between us. I tucked my elbows in and ran. The breath rasped in and out of my throat but I couldn't get enough air. Forced my feet on, one step after the other. The breath came ragged, tearing in and out of me, the sunlight turned black. I sprawled in the dust with no voice left to cry out after him. Lifted my head in time to see him reach the turn in the road. Saw him take the last step. The bundle giving a bounce, his boot pushing back against the ground and his elbow driving him on.

I watched the yellow dust where his foot had been. As if he'd come back if I watched long enough. Held my breath, waiting. A puff of breeze shook the bushes, coiled on the ground, rose up carrying dust and leaves. Whirled like something alive, then fell back into itself, dust lying on dust.

Jack was gone but my body would not let it be so. Refusal turned me inside out, a vomit of cries and tears ripped out of me in long bleeding wails I had no power to stop. I squatted on the dust rocking backwards and forwards to push away the thing that I would not allow. Snatched at my hair, tore it out in strands, wanting a pain in my body that would shut out the pain in my heart.

Everything was an enemy. The dirt under my hands, my clothes strangling me, the sun stabbing at me, the breeze grating at my skin. Myself was the worst enemy. I wanted to walk away, leave myself behind. Would of been pleased to stop being, then and there.

I SAT for a long time. There was no point in going anywhere. That patch of dust was the only place I could be, because that was the last place Jack had been. Leaving it was like leaving him.

The sun was high overhead when I got up at last, went down the hill. The hair sticking to my face, clothes screwed round where I'd thrown myself about.

Ma was waiting in the parlour like a spider. Put her sewing to one side, she was going to try to hug me. I got away, running up the stairs, though where was I running to?

In Jack's room the girl was standing by the bed. Touching it as if he might be hiding under the blanket. Took no notice of me. Got up on the pillow end of the bed and sat cross-legged, her face a blank. I sat on the other end, where she'd curled up at his feet that first night. Between us the idea of Jack.

He'll be back, I said. By and by. Turn round, there he'll be to fetch us away.

Anne clattered the plates in the kitchen below. Something rang like a gong. The tin dish, that would be, being hung up on its hook. Then everything went quiet, the afternoon pressing into every room around us.

I moved down the bed towards the girl, reached out towards her across the emptiness that was Jack gone. Let her see my eyes swollen with all the crying I'd done. She stared as if crying was some kind of animal she'd never seen before.

I had her fingers, cool and thin, for a touch, then she pulled her hand away, got down off the bed, slipped out of the room. I was left with the dent in the bedclothes where she'd been.

I could hear Ma calling, *Rachel? Where are you Rachel?* and her feet up the stairs.

In this house from now on the girl would always be Rachel. Her New Zealand name was gone for good. However long she'd be remembered, she'd be Rachel. Her own true name, whatever it was, gone from the world.

It was a chilly thought. How easy for a name to be lost. A kind of death. It could happen from one moment to the next, and there was no going back.

I stretched out on the bed. Up on the ceiling was a branching crack I'd never seen before. Just a crack in the ceiling, but precious because Jack would of known it. He'd of lain here just where I was, hands under his head, tracking that crack from where it started in the corner to where it ended at the opposite wall.

For a blazing second he was there with me, his head on the pillow beside mine, breathing along with me.

I let myself feel the stab. How much I longed for him. Buried my face in the pillow. I'd of picked up the scent of him, like a dog. But there was nothing. Starch and feathers, that was all.

~

Jack was gone, but I wasn't having it. Every morning I woke up with a new way to push it back. Got dressed, put on my boots, walked up the road as far as where he'd left me. Or turned the other way, down to the jetty. Anywhere he'd been. Walked there fast, sat as if he'd said, *I'll soon be back* instead of, *Never want to see your face again.*

Pa watched me go. Said nothing. Ma pestered me to help in the kitchen or turn out the linen cupboard but Pa said, leave her be, Meg. Far as the girl went, I might as well of not been there. After that day on the bed she never looked at me again. She'd find a wall, with Pa out on the verandah, or in the parlour. Sit with her back to it, make a dark place for her face behind her knees.

I knew Jack wouldn't be at Sullivan's. No point going there. But one day I took the skiff, went down the river. It was a still morning with no sun, no direction, no time, the river slimy in the dull light. The tide was with me, I hardly had to touch the oars. Past our orchard, past our corn, past Payne's Mill.

Till I got past the spur I was in sight of the house. It was too far for me to see, but I felt Pa watching me through the telescope. I wasn't going to give him a thing. Not even the look on my face.

Put my head down and if he was looking, all he'd of seen was the top of my head.

Sullivan's looked the same as it always did. A dirty-looking strip of sand with dead oyster shells all over it, a paddock overgrown with scrub, a crooked hut sliding into the long grass, the bark of the roof splitting and falling away. No man with a sharp axe had done any patching of that roof.

To be disappointed you had to of hoped.

Inside, the place struck chill. It was a box with no windows, damp and dark. There'd been no fire warming that hearth, not for years. No one had sat at that broken table or slept on the bed in the corner, all cobwebs and dust. There was a heaviness to the air. Humans had given up on the place, and it felt nature had too. It would never be a shelter for man or woman again.

I stood there in the grey light, the only sound the river lapping at the broken oysters down on the sand. I laboured to feel any ghost of Jack here, but there was none. He might of been here once or twice, stood where I was standing and tried to picture it a home, the way I was doing. But no more than that. He hadn't made it his. He'd never be here again.

Still, it was hard to leave the place that I'd had so many daydreams about. It seemed an insult to the hopes we'd had. I took off my shawl, spread it out on the bed. Tucked the corners in neat, so it looked welcoming. I knew the shawl would lie on that empty bed till it crumbled away to dust, but I did it anyway. It was a gesture, something to bring warmth to the cursed feeling the place had.

By the time I left the hut and got into the skiff again, the tide had turned and the river was murkier. Currents met in the hidden depths and sent up swirls that formed and smoothed, formed and smoothed. I let the tide take me up the river again and watched the hut till it was out of sight. I'd never go there again.

Pa was on our jetty, I saw him soon as the boat cleared that last spur. He didn't wave, didn't move. I steered to the far bank, let the river carry me past. Kept my face turned away. I thought he might call out or come after me. But he watched me and did nothing.

Up at Langland's everyone was out except for old Mr Langland. He didn't say much. Just that Jack was gone off to New Zealand.

There was a coldness to his eye.

Jack's Ma was a black gin, he said. Knew that, did you?

Yes, I said. Made no odds to me.

Well, Dolly, he said, three cheers for you.

Gave me a smirk full of yellow teeth.

There's plenty feel different, Dolly, he said. As you've found out for yourself. If you was mine, I'd of said the same. Good enough feller, but not to marry.

I wished I hadn't of come. Knew it would be no good, but had to see it for myself. Jack wasn't here. Wouldn't be again.

Best cheer yourself up, Dolly, Mr Langland said. Wouldn't bet on Jack coming back this way.

If he does, I said, tell him Sarah Thornhill wants to see him.

But Jack already knew Sarah Thornhill wanted to see him. There was no message to send him that would make any difference.

Mr Langland said nothing. Drew the air through his empty pipe with a whistling noise.

~

Mrs Herring was on her jetty, waved me over as I rowed back down the river.

Dolly, she said. You're nearly dead, lass.

Got me in front of the fire, her shawl round me, food and drink inside me. My blood started to move again and with it my feelings. I thought I'd cried every tear I had in me, but they kept coming. Mrs Herring sat puffing at her pipe. When the tears stopped she put a hand on my arm.

You know, Dolly, she said. Once upon a time I had a sweetheart.

Took the pipe out so she could have a good laugh.

Believe it or not, I did, she said. Name of Joe Giddings. Tall sturdy feller and my word I fancied him. Often think, where would I be today if I'd of married Joe Giddings.

Puffed away as if she was waiting for me to say, Why didn't you?

Well, why, that's the question, she said. He went off. Went off one day to the next, never ever did know why. Oh I was sad. Cried myself dry.

Don't tell me it's for the best, I said. Don't say that.

I hated her, sitting pleased with her story about this Joe Giddings that I didn't believe in. She started poking round in the bowl of the pipe with the knife, flicking bits of ash into the fire.

I won't, Dolly, she said. Wouldn't insult you. All I can say is, Jack would of had his reasons. Not something he'd of done lightly.

Where is he, I said. Where's he gone to.

Dolly dear, she said, I don't know, no more than you do. But Jack knows what he's about. That I'm sure of. He'd of had good reasons. You best trust him on that.

I watched the knife scraping round the rim of the bowl and wanted the old clay to break into bits. Wanted the knife to slip and slice into her.

Known you since you was born, dear, she said. If I could help you I would. But nothing I can do. Not me, not anyone.

But she wouldn't meet my eye. I knew then how much I was on my own. It had been me and Jack. Now it was just me.

Pa was on the jetty as if he'd never moved. Leaned down and got hold of the rope, held out his hand for me to step up. Even after all those years he still had a hard boatman's hand. He went on holding mine even after I was on the jetty.

I know you mourn for him, Dolly, he said. I see how you hanker. But pet, he won't be back. You know that, don't you.

He had some mercy. Didn't make me say it. *Yes, he won't be back.*

~

It was a sad house with Jack gone, the silence solid as darkness. The grief sucked everything away, every feeling except itself. Even the sun was dull.

I didn't cry again. I was cold as a stone inside, like someone with a leg chopped off. Waited for the days to pass, me and my body cut off from each other, no way to knit them up again.

All sights, every sound, led to the same place. When the wind blew and the rain fell I thought of the night Jack brought the girl, how the wet made his hair gleam. When the river sparkled it was mockery. When a bird flicked on a twig and cocked its head sideways at me all I could think was how lucky it was to be a bird.

In the mornings I got up and put clothes on, at night I took them off and lay down. Sat at the table and put pieces of food in my mouth and chewed and swallowed. Could hear Ma and Pa talking, but a long way off. Heard them calling. *Dolly! Dolly!* Their voices like a fly against the window.

I'd thought Pa loved me in his own way. But he'd let Ma do the dirty work for him. When push came to shove, he wouldn't stand up to her. Didn't say, *Dolly's my daughter, I'll see her happy*. Didn't go to Jack and say, *Pride be damned, Jack lad*.

I went over those few hours where everything had warped out of shape. No matter how many times I did, it wasn't quite right. *Not stand in her way* didn't fit alongside *Never want to see your face again*. The thing felt like a trick.

~

The girl wandered the house, into every room. Opened the cupboards, looked in. If she heard a noise from the yard she'd run out to see what it was. After she'd looked in every room she'd start again. When Ma pulled her into the parlour she'd wedge herself into the window seat watching the patch of water that was the first place you saw a boat coming up the river.

*Look out for her,* he'd said. But how did you look out for a girl who didn't want you near?

Just the once I saw her different. Walked down the track towards the river one afternoon and saw her slipping between the trees. I let her go ahead to watch where she was going.

When she got to the sandy spit on the point I saw what she'd come for. Phillip, with Belle on a halter, the two of them splashing about in the shallow water. Him drawing the mare along, little coaxing noises, and Belle pretending she didn't know what water was, pawing at it, putting her nose down to taste it.

It was something they'd done before, Phillip and the girl. You could see that. She sat on the bank, knees up to her chin, back against a tree, watching the man and the horse as if they were putting on a show for her.

He clicked his tongue at Belle and she walked forward. Hooves stepping high, you could see the power in her, and the pleasure she was taking. The water got deeper, Phillip running and splashing with the rope loose in his hand.

He turned to the girl and smiled. Not the flashing smile he put on to charm, but a quieter, privater sort of thing. From where I was hidden I could see the girl's face go soft. Almost a smile. It was the first time I'd glimpsed the person behind the sad mask.

Thank God, I thought, she's found some comfort.

~

Those endless silent days. The cliffs across the river rearing over us, making everything else small. The long afternoons of sun lit them up, yellow, then brassy, then gold. The light shifting, hour after hour. Nothing in the world would ever happen again except the light changing on the stone.

# PART THREE

A SECRET part of me must of been keeping count, because eleven months and eleven days after Jack left, I woke up different. Lay listening to the rustle of wind in the trees and felt something stir in me too.

I was going to get away.

News had come, Mary was expecting. That gave me reason for a visit, and I was going on eighteen, old enough to be out in the world now. When I put it to Ma and Pa I saw a little look go between them. See, Dolly's taking an interest again. Didn't we know it would all come right?

It was nearly enough to make me change my mind.

The morning I left, I went to find the girl. She was in her usual place, the parlour window where she could see down the river. I had Jack's stone in my hand, ready to give it to her. So silky against my skin, I had second thoughts. She'd never know. Never miss what she'd never had.

But I could ride away. Had a horse, and a sister I could visit. She had nothing, only now and then watching Phillip with the horses, and even that she'd lose if Ma ever caught her at it.

When I went to take her hand, she tried to pull away but I got the stone into her palm. She looked at it for a long time. When she closed her hand round it I saw the sinew tight in her thin wrist and a shine on her cheek.

Wanted to touch her, but she'd never wanted my touch. Wanted to say something, but words were no good to either of us. All I could do was lean in behind her, watching the same patch of bright water.

~

It was good to be on Queenie, out the gates and away. The speckled dog raced along with us down the track to the punt, grinning up at me.

Save your legs, I could of told him.

It was me and Pa and Jemmy Katter, they'd go with me to Garlogie, stay a few days then come back.

Oh, to be away from everyone, in a new place! Queenie caught how impatient I was, trotted smartly onto the punt, tossing her head and mouthing at her bit. The dog had to be stopped from running on after us and when the punt started it stood up to its chest in the water, I couldn't bear to see the longing on its face.

Over the punt we turned the horses up the road that climbed

beside the cliffs. At the top we got down to give the horses a spell.

There below us was the river, a band of green water curving round the point. There was the jetty and the fleck of grey that was the dog. The house behind the wall, Ma at the rose garden, beside her a sketchy shape that must be the girl. She'd of been ten or eleven now, but this far away you could near see through her.

Behind the house the line of the road up the other side of the valley was like a mirror to the one we were on. I could see the bend where I'd watched Jack walk away. More than a year, but it didn't seem that long. If I could of walked on air I could of gone straight across to that stretch of dust and pebbles. The strands of hair I'd pulled out must still be there, blowing about among the bushes.

We trundled along the dry miles over the top of the range, the road a pair of ruts twisting through the bush. This was what Pa watched through the glass, the country on top of the cliffs where you saw no sign of anything human. It was a long day's ride, but late in the afternoon the road tilted down and as it was coming on dark we got to Garlogie, a green place in a broad kind-faced valley.

Mary and Archibald lived in a big way. A fine stone house with a circular drive at the front, every bedroom with a fireplace and a Turkey rug and a marble washstand, plenty of maids to bring the hot water. The silver on the mahogany table was Campbell's from home, heavy in your hand, the chasing soft with wear. Would of been handed down from Campbell to Campbell, not bought last year at Abercrombie's in George

Street like the Thornhills' silver.

The way Archibald Campbell said his words was still a problem for me. He'd say something down the table and I'd try the sounds over to myself, making out I was having trouble with a bit of gristle. Archibald always the gentleman, his tidy beard with not a hair out of place and his cheeks rosy as a child's, waiting for his silly sister-in-law to work out what he'd said.

Mary was used to it. She'd see me in difficulties, make a remark that would give me an idea what he'd said.

Pa was ill at ease at Garlogie. Archibald Campbell never anything but courteous, and poor old Pa doing his best, trying to remember the manners he ought to have. Away from Ma he was a different man. Less sure of himself. It made me see how much of Pa was the wife he'd chosen and the fine land and grand house he'd put round himself. Take all that away and you could see what he'd been before. So poor, a knife with a broken tip was the best he could buy. Wearing the broad arrow, doing another man's bidding, marked with the shame of it.

He was almost shy of his own daughter, now that she was Mrs Archibald Campbell. When Archibald said something one day about a tutor for the child when the time came, Pa went quiet. You can wish for too much, I thought. You can want so much, you lose your own children and grandchildren.

He wandered about, never sure where he should be. Sat with Archibald making himself pleasant, but you could hear in his voice he was ashamed of the blunt words that were all he had. They soon ran out of things to talk about, only so many times you can say what a wonderful season, and how thick the wool. Pa would find his way down to the stables, pass the time with the men there, rough fellers like he was himself. Knew it wasn't what he was supposed to do, Mr Campbell's father-in-law sitting on a bale of straw with the stableman, puffing away on his old white pipe.

Me and Mary was in between. Not rough like Pa, not smooth like Archibald. Both of us protecting Pa from the worst of himself, the way Ma did. If we saw him go to do the wrong thing, one of us would give him a glance and he'd remember.

He stayed a week. When he and Jemmy left, it was a load off for all of us. From the verandah Mary and I watched them canter up the track. That's the finish of it, I thought. The finish of the life I'd had, being a daughter. What was next I didn't know, but it wasn't going to be that house by the river.

Mary wanted the news from home, so I told her about the girl, how sad she still was. Told her about Jack, and Sullivan's, all the rosy future we'd planned. The bust-up with Pa, Jack bundled out of the house. How he was too proud to marry money.

Couldn't bear to tell her the words that still cut me when I remembered them. *Never want to see your face again.* That last terrible look he gave me.

Always knew you two was close, she said. Good feller, Jack, none better. Shame he gone off. But you know, Dolly, might turn out for the best.

I didn't bother to answer. Jack was an ache in my chest. With me when I woke up and with me when I went to bed. There'd never be any *best* in that.

Mary had a sickly time of it that first confinement. Pasty and yellow and not keeping anything down beyond a bit of bread toasted crisp and a cup of black tea. For once Dolly was the one bustling about, getting things ready, the napkins hemmed and the tiny clothes stitched. Even got into the way of knitting. Made five pair of pilchers and five of bootees, ran the ribbons through at the end, thought I was pretty clever.

When the baby started it was a frightening time, I'd had nothing to do with babies. Luckily the cook knew what to do, and a midwife rode over from the Wollombi. I didn't see much, only a glimpse of Mary on the bed with her face screwed up, but at last the midwife come out with the baby, ugly as a prune but everyone smiling as if he looked like an angel, and of course he did once his head went back to its proper shape.

In the afternoons Mary nursed the baby on the sheltered back verandah. Smiling down at him, his hand lying on her breast as if to say thank you, ankles crossed, chubby feet moving round as he sucked.

You know, Dolly, she said one afternoon, I never been better off or more happier than what I am now with Archibald.

Even a sister wouldn't of said Mary was beautiful, but she had a serenity about her now that was a kind of loveliness.

Oh and by the by, Dolly dear, she said, John Daunt might be paying us a visit. Archibald said to me, I'd like to see John Daunt, what say we send word, ask John down to see us? Men, you know, they like a talk together.

Dear Mary, she was like a pane of glass.

I'd wished Daunt dead at one time, but had nothing against him now. Jack would always have my heart, but Jack was gone and life was long. Daunt had seemed a man with not too much starch about him. Hadn't got the vapours to see me wearing my brother's trousers, and had a bit of fun with the What Bird.

Now Mary, I said, no need to tie yourself in knots. Be glad to see John Daunt.

I wasn't sure, she said. What you felt, you know. The business about Jack.

Not a day passes that I don't think about Jack, I said. But he's gone. He's the past.

Well dear, she said, Archibald told me, John Daunt was very struck by your sister Dolly.

That was well and good. But what Archibald didn't know, and Mary didn't know either, was that moment in the hall, that far-off morning at home. If Daunt had seen me, I was pretty sure I'd be out of the running as far as he was concerned.

And if he hadn't, and things went the way those two were hoping, he'd be buying second-hand goods without knowing. He was an honest man. I couldn't be false with him.

Mary had it all mapped out in her mind, she'd probably already decided on the pattern of the china she'd give us. I wasn't so sure. When he came I'd have to feel my way, find how things stood.

John Daunt or some other man. If it wasn't Jack, it didn't make much odds.

~

I'd forgotten what a big awkward plain man Daunt was. Like a navvy in the shoulders. You'd never pick those shoulders for a gentleman's. He'd lost more hair since I'd seen him but his black eyebrows sprouting thicker than ever. Nothing to make a woman's heart beat fast.

He had something for me, six pair of kid gloves in a box with a gold edge. Different colours, best quality. He wasn't to know I never liked the feel of a glove on my hand, no matter if they were the best kid. Didn't tell him, smiled and thanked. Should of done him the courtesy of saying, Thank you, John Daunt, but I got no use for gloves.

Him and Campbell could talk for an hour together about what a bale of extra fine was worth. But Daunt hadn't come to talk about the price of wool. The night he arrived he was already remarking on what fine country it was for riding, and would Miss Thornhill care to join him on a mount in the morning?

We went quietly along one of the tracks, stopped in a shady clearing by a creek, let the horses walk into the water and twitch their whiskery lips at their reflections. Sat on some rocks that went down into the creek, regular as a set of steps. The water so clear and shining over the stones of its bed, like a moving jewel. I took my boots off to watch my feet pale and wavery under the current.

That eyebrow going off at an angle made you think Daunt was on the edge of some wry remark. Made it hard to tell when he really was. I wondered if he was thinking about that other ride, the way I was. Oh, I'd been full of sauce that day. So full of what was starting between me and Jack, so sure nothing could go wrong.

I haven't ever lost the memory of the ride we had at your father's house, Daunt said. The four of us, a grand day. I was new to it, Miss Thornhill, and relished it then, but three years more has confirmed it to me, New South Wales is the finest country in the world.

I'm glad to hear that, Mr Daunt, I said. Never known any place but this, so of course I think the same.

I have to say this, though, Miss Thornhill, Daunt said. That it's a place requires a man to share, whether he wish it or not. Such as I was recently, a man well-known in my district, goes by the name of the Jewboy, thought I must have enough for him as well as myself.

Held up! I said. That what you mean, Mr Daunt?

Sitting down to our meal, myself and the men, Daunt said. Had a couple of nice young fowl, and some new peas, we'd coaxed them up, carried the water to them, our first few peas. I'm telling you our mouths were watering. Hardly sat down when one of the men looks out the doorway and says, 'There is a drunken constable' but it was no constable, it was this feller with a pistol in each hand and another feller with a damn great musket. They sat down and ate the lot, every bit of fowl and every last pea. Gathered up our watches and coin, such as we had, then as the final insult went to the pantry and took possession of a cheese. A sad bad day, Miss Thornhill, when a man can't defend his own cheese!

I laughed, glad to be able to like him, if only for telling a good tale.

You'd be well set up on your place by now, I said. It's slipped my mind what you've called it.

Glenmire, he said. You'd remember, perhaps, that's the place in Ireland I come from. I'm a sentimental fellow you know, Miss Thornhill. Contrary to appearances.

It was true, he looked about as sentimental as a block of wood. I thought of how he must shave every morning and see that heavy-browed thick-jawed face and wish he looked more like the man he knew he was.

It's as lovely a place as you could ever hope to see, he said. The grass as thick as the hairs on a cat's back, the sheep as fat as a suet pudding and the soil in such good heart.

That blarney! As he talked I found myself wondering what it would be like in bed with him. Would he do? If he asked, would he do?

The house a solid place, he said. And remarkable fine ventilation, owing to the fact that the rogue of a carpenter has left me in the lurch with the windows. Full of promises to come back, mark you, then it will be the snuggest of places.

No need to charm me, John Daunt, I thought. Got my reasons for being here with you, and they're nothing to do with your grand place or your winning Irish ways.

I was very sorry to hear the terrible news of your brother, Miss Thornhill, he said. Quite some time ago now, I know. But please accept my deepest sympathy.

A chilly formal sort of phrase but he said it with feeling.

Thank you, Mr Daunt, I said. It was a sad loss.

I should not of made use of poor Will, but I was impatient to get things clear with Daunt before they went any further.

You might remember Jack Langland? I said. That was with Will when he died?

I felt the blood rise, saying *Jack Langland*.

Oh yes, he said.

Vague as a cloud, but I felt him paying attention.

I do remember Mr Langland, he said. Very well indeed. Although Campbell and I had only the one night at your father's house and as I remember we had to get away early. Still quite dark when we rose. Not a soul stirring anywhere in the house.

Met my eye for longer than was quite natural. If I'd ever wondered had he seen me come out of Jack's room, there was my answer. He had.

Jack went away, I said. Back to New Zealand.

I did hear so, he said. I heard he had gone.

We saw a lot of him at one time, I said. When Will was alive. But I wouldn't expect to see him again ever. Gone our different ways, you could say.

There was something shocking in putting it into words. I saw how you could know something and believe it but still in some pocket of yourself not know and not believe.

It's a painful thing, to say goodbye, Daunt said. But you and I have seen enough of the world to know there are times when a farewell has to be made. I'm glad to know about Mr Langland. I wondered what had become of him.

Bent forward, held his hand in the water, watching the flow change shape as he turned his palm, first one way, then the other.

We made our farewells at your father's, all that time ago,

he said. You and I. But I always had in my mind that it was not farewell so much as *au revoir*.

I saw him wonder if I knew the word.

I thought we might meet again, too, Mr Daunt, I said, and smiled at him so there could be no doubt what I wanted him to know.

I'd had my chance. Known what it was like to be so close to another person you were cut in half without them. That only happened once in your life. Daunt was a good enough feller. Many was the woman had to settle for worse.

If he asked, I was going to say yes.

~

By the end of the week Daunt was fretting about being away from his own place. We rode most days and he'd tell me about his government men, what a poor lot they were, not bad in themselves, but had to be stood over to get the work out of them. I could feel his impatience to be back.

I had no need of a long courtship, was impatient myself. Not that I was afraid I'd change my mind, or that Daunt would change his. But wanted to get the thing over with. If this man was my future, why wait?

I did all I could by way of smiles and looks, and let Mary fuss about my hair in a new way that she said was more becoming. When she asked, I told her yes, I liked John Daunt, he was a fine man, knowing she would tell Archibald, and Archibald would tell Daunt.

So when he joined me one morning in the summer-house

I had a pretty good idea why. He sat down opposite me, on the edge of the seat. A little pale, and his hands, I saw, a little unsteady. I had a pang for him and for all men, risking the smart of a knock-back. Even Jack, wondering if *a certain person* might of seen *something she liked better*. Being a woman and having to wait was enough to drive you dilly, but being the feller was hard too.

Miss Thornhill, he said. There's a thing I'd like to have a talk with you about. If you'd be willing.

Yes, Mr Daunt, I said. More than willing.

I've told you about Glenmire, he said. The grandest place it will be. As I've said.

Yes, I said. Glenmire sounds to be a grand place.

In short words I've everything a man could ask for, he said. Nothing is troubling me but for one thing.

What woman wouldn't know what was coming? *Out with it, Daunt, for God's sake!* I urged in my mind. What was the obstacle that stopped him from saying he had *everything except a wife to share his blessings?*

The fact is, he said, I'm duty bound, Miss Thornhill, to warn you that I am not yet in as settled a way as Archibald is here. In a pecuniary point of view, you understand me. The house not finished, and the present miserable price of wool keeping me from any large improvements as yet.

Ah, it's just the money he's worrying about, I thought. When, if he only knew, I'd once been glad to go into married life with nothing but a shawl and a hairbrush.

My situation can only improve, he said. The price of wool will come back, how can it not, and then there'll be nothing lacking that any person might desire. Only patience called for at the start, and the turning of a blind eye to some of the present shortcomings.

Poor man, he could not seem to make himself stop talking, as if afraid of my answer.

You're an honourable man, Mr Daunt, I said. Being so frank with me.

Oh, honourable! he said. If honours were pounds, Miss Thornhill, I'd never need to do a hand's turn. I'll not beat around the bush, it's a laborious life at the present time. Leisure not yet much known at Glenmire, and that's a fact.

I know about labour, Mr Daunt, I said. Never been afraid of hard work. Be surprised what I can turn my hand to.

Of all the words I might of chosen, it was that echo of Jack!

Ah no, Miss Thornhill, he said. That's where you're wrong, if you don't mind me saying so. Nothing whatever you could do could surprise me. You're a woman of many parts, from my knowledge of you. And every part much to my liking, if I might say.

He quirked his eyebrow at me, and I thought, what heavy weather a gentleman has to make of saying *I fancy you*! Smiled at him and he took heart.

Now what I want to ask is this, Miss Thornhill, he said. It would make me the happiest of men. But should you not wish, please have the candour to say so. What I have to say is, would you do me the honour to become my wife?

Thank you Mr Daunt, I said. Yes, I do wish.

He jumped up, went to kiss my hand. Must of been the Irish

way. But it took me by surprise and I flinched. We laughed and that sealed the bargain, but neither one of us laughed from joy. It was that we both saw the same thing, that we were as different as fish from possum.

PA AND Ma and the girl travelled up to Garlogie for the wedding. Pa jumped down out of the cart beaming so his face crinkled up like old leather. Hugged me, not often he did that.

Well done, Dolly, he said into my ear. Done real good for yourself. And Mr Daunt, here we all are again and what a fine thing it is!

I'd never seen him so buoyed up. As if he'd been holding himself tight all these years, his grip hard round all the things that stood between him and his hungry past. Now he could ease that grip.

Ma pulled the girl down out of the cart. Sullen but limp. No fight left in her.

I went to kiss her but Ma got between us.

Dolly dearest, she said. Such a happy time! So pleased for you!

Her eyes flicking between Archibald and Daunt, her fine sons-in-law, as proud as if she'd made them with her own hands.

The gentlemen laid themselves out to charm Pa and Ma. Archibald settled them in the armchairs, fussed about giving Ma a cushion for her back and a bolster for her feet. Her eyes everywhere, on the big black piano in the corner, the velvet curtains, the silver candlesticks.

Leaned over to whisper to me.

You see, Dolly, sometimes the clouds look black, don't they, she said. And then the sun comes out. Aren't you glad you waited, Dolly?

I was almost sorry for having said yes to Daunt.

There's the baby crying, I said. No, Mary, I'll go.

I waited out in the hall looking at the pattern on the heavy embossed wallpaper, wishing the baby really would cry.

When I went back in, Campbell was at the drinks trolley.

Mrs Thornhill, he was saying. Will you try a wee drop of this madeira, I think you'll find it satisfactory. And Mr Thornhill, I had a fine madeira at your house, I remember, I'd value your opinion of this particular one.

Then the parlourmaid was at the door holding the girl by the wrist.

Pardon me, Mrs Thornhill, she said, I found your lass wandering about, she had the linen press open, Lord knows what she wanted in there.

Ma had her glass in her hand, comfortable in the armchair. It was Pa that got up and put his arm round the girl.

My granddaughter, he said, as if the maid needed to know. From New Zealand.

And how is she getting along, Daunt said. Is she settling, now?

Middling, Pa said. A great one for wandering. Can't go past a cupboard, not without she has a look inside. Can you, Rachel?

Restless as a cat, Ma said.

She'll come good, Pa said. Won't you, pet? Talk the leg off a chair once you get started.

She stood with him the way she did at home, between his knees while he sat in the chair. Looked into every one of the faces of this place, and when she saw none of them was the one she wanted she didn't look again.

I was glad I'd given her Jack's stone. It was the one thing I'd done for her, little enough as it was. Would Daunt have her with us at Glenmire, I wondered. Could I *look out for her* that way?

Daunt came over, sat beside me.

Your niece, he said, quiet enough that Ma wouldn't hear. A shy little lass.

Should of been taken back where her home is, I said. Never stopped pining. There was a chance to send her back. But things went cockeyed.

When I said the word *cockeyed* I knew there was something not right with my voice.

I'm sorry to hear that, Daunt said. Things do go cockeyed in this world. But could it not be attempted again?

Pa won't hear of it, I said. He's got the rights in law. Made that very clear.

My voice was getting husky going over ground I didn't want to go over.

But I'd be glad if we could do something for her, I said. When a chance comes.

That would be a pleasure to do, Daunt said. She might visit her Aunt Sarah and her Uncle John. We might get her talking the leg off a chair.

Tried to picture the girl with me and Daunt, in that place, Glenmire, whatever it might turn out to be. Auntie and uncle being good to her. But it was a sad used-up sort of thought. My heart wasn't in it, the way it had been the first time around.

~

We were wed in the parlour, all flowers and sunlight through the French doors, the Reverend pleased to have a marriage done proper in a land where so many didn't bother.

Bub and Kathleen's second was due any day so they couldn't come, but Johnny and Judith travelled all the way up from Sydney, that was good of them. Johnny had on a new yellow waistcoat, the last word in smart. But alongside the gentlemen in their dark clothes, the waistcoat was a bit too much of a good thing.

Pa tucked my arm up against him for the walk across the room to where Daunt was waiting.

That's my girl, he whispered.

I had to smile, because smile was what brides did. But I

thought, No, Pa, I'm not your girl. Not since that day.

Wanted it all to be over, Ma and Pa gone. Couldn't look at them without remembering, couldn't remember without aching. Wanted to be wed and gone.

Daunt said the words a bit rushed, and he stumbled at *for richer, for poorer*. I'd thought it might be me stumbling, the words bringing up too many thoughts, but when it was my turn I was cool as glass. *Forsaking all others*, I said, firm as if there'd never been an other. *Till death us do part*, I said, and wondered at the woman I was listening to, who had no fear of forever.

When the ring went on, it felt big and cumbersome. I wanted to get it off.

~

Mary gave us the bedroom at the end of the verandah. A lovely room, and on the bed the counterpane I'd admired on her own, grey silk with a flamingo embroidered in scarlet. Daunt made himself scarce while I got into my nightdress, opened the bed, got in.

I'd feared Jack would be with me in the room. Feared I couldn't come at Daunt if Jack was there with us.

I'd feared Jack being there, but it was worse to know he wasn't. The only person in this bed was someone called Sarah Daunt, new to the world since that afternoon at half past two, and in a minute her husband would be there to love and cherish her.

Daunt come in and I did my best to smile.

The shock of me in the altogether not something I'll subject you to all at once, Sarah, he said. Work up to it in stages, I'd say, wouldn't you agree now.

While he was talking he blew out the lamp, for which I was grateful. I lay listening to the sounds of him getting out of his clothes and into his nightshirt. Had only one hope, that he'd come at me polite and do the deed quick and quiet and go to sleep.

I had a picture of all the nights of my life, every one of them with John Daunt in bed with me.

He got in. The mattress dipped in the middle and I held myself up to stop rolling against him. We lay for a time. I couldn't hear him breathing.

I thought he'd start by kissing me. That was the part I dreaded most. More private somehow than the other thing. And knowing I was no virgin he might be a bit rough with me, to show me what he thought of that. Whatever it was, I'd have to put up with it the best way I could.

Well, Sarah, he asked the ceiling. How will we go about this now?

I thought, Oh my Lord, this feller's not done it before! That put a different light on it. I was shaping a smile in the dark that I have to say was a little superior.

He moved over next to me and I felt the warmth and the weight of him against me. He made a small enquiring *Hmn?* and began to touch me, and it was clear straight away that he knew what he was doing. Not the least bit rough but very sure of himself. Sure of me too. Seemed he knew my body better than I did myself.

Didn't make to kiss me. Only his hands moving around my body, a kind of conversation.

There was no tender melting of one person into another. Not the swooning bliss I'd had with Jack. This was a different animal entirely. Two animals, you might say. Taken over by such a hard force it made both of them cry out.

It was an education. Thank God it was dark. The look on my face could only of been astonishment.

~

We had a week at Garlogie under the scarlet flamingo. I'd get into the bed first but after the first night he didn't blow the lamp out straight off. He'd get into his nightshirt and out of the corner of my eye I'd have a glimpse of him. Not a bad-looking feller with his shirt off, though pale as milk in the lamplight where Jack had been that brown of a well-cooked loaf.

With the lamp out we got to know our way around each other. Daunt required no love-talk, I came to discover. Asked nothing of me by way of declarations and gave none either. We took our pleasure from each other so we sang out with the strength of it, but it was bodies coming together, not souls. The world of the bed in the dark was a solitary one for me. It seemed to be the same for him.

I wondered sometimes, who are the other women he's known, that he's so practised?

In daylight we spoke to each other of this and that, small remarks exchanged, *making ourselves pleasant*. That morning in the summer-house was the closest we'd ever got to saying what was in our hearts.

He asked me nothing about my life. Might of thought asking would open that door marked *Jack*. I asked him nothing about his, not wanting to make the distance between us any greater than it already was. I felt that distance. Feared as time went on it might matter more, not less, that Daunt was from one kind of world and I was from another. In the end my charms might not make up for being an unlettered girl with a father who had worn the stripes, and a heart that did not belong to her husband.

IF A MAN on a good horse rode hard he could get to Glenmire in a day, two at most. But there was me and Daunt, plus two of Campbell's men in case of bushrangers, and we couldn't go any faster than the cart with all my things that Pa had brought up from the Point. It would be three days, Daunt said, and rough.

Straight after Garlogie's soft valley we went into high dark hills that the road wound up and down among. Now and then we'd come out to a high place. Ahead, nothing but ridges and valleys, a tangle of bulges, like a lamb's brain ready for the pan.

It was a poor road. More than a bridle track, but much worse than between Thornhill's and Garlogie. Clay gone to dust, corduroy on the creeks, the horses had to be walked over the logs. A crow flying might make short work of it but a human had to follow the track in and out of every wrinkle of the country.

All day I watched Daunt riding up ahead. John David Daunt. My husband. That would be it for the rest of my days, him on top of his horse, jogging on and not looking back at me. With every wild mile I was more alone.

Even in that rough country people had put down roots. Nine Mile Creek was a cattleyard and a muddy creek and the nastiest low hut I've ever been in. The man there, just the smell of him enough to knock you down. I was glad of his tea and mutton after the long day on the horse and he would of been happy to make a shakedown for us on the floor, but the fleas in that hut was so thick, Daunt thanked him kindly and said we'd sleep in the tent.

I lay in the dark smelling the oil in the canvas, hearing the frogs and the crickets close by. Weary, but couldn't sleep. Felt we'd fall off the edge of the earth if we went much further. I'd been to Windsor and to Sydney. Those places were a fair step if you took the road, but in the end you got there. Never thought you could travel so far as we had today without arriving somewhere. There wouldn't be a lot of going backwards and forwards to Mary's. I was starting to see that. Not a journey you'd take on lightly.

I thought Daunt was asleep but he spoke out of the dark.

That's the worst of it, he said. Tomorrow not so bad.

Frogs so loud they near drowned him out. Never heard such frogs.

Through the range by noon, he said. In the valley then,

easier going I'm glad to be able to say.

The village you told me, I said, what was the name again?

Gammaroy, he said. Though village, to be honest with you, that would be gilding the lily. Be there by dark tomorrow, God and the horses willing.

And your place the day after, I said.

Our place, he said. Your place too, you know, Mrs Daunt.

*For richer or poorer, in sickness and in health.* They'd thought of everything, those words. Locked you in, coming and going, backwards and forwards, up and down. *Sarah Daunt her mark.* I'd put my hand to them.

Didn't know if I could manage it, being the wife of John David Daunt. Coming into whatever kind of household he had, no other company, and no way to get on a horse and leave. By and by children would come along, and that was a fear and a mystery. I was frightened of having a child, what it might ask of me by way of medicines I didn't have, fits and fevers I wouldn't know what to do about. Not to mention the act of birth. Pain and the danger of death, that was all I knew.

I had another fear, too deep to look at. That I might not love a child not Jack's.

~

By the middle of the second day, I was sick of being on the horse. Hot in the sun, and grit all over. But as Daunt promised, during the afternoon we wound down out of the range into a great broad valley. The road no better made, but flatter, running beside a quick clear river. From a distance, Gammaroy was a dozen buildings lined up along something that resembled a street. I was glad, thinking of an inn, a cheerful woman like Judith, human society after the empty bush.

We'll sleep at the inn tonight? I asked Daunt.

Well now, inn would be putting too fine a point on it, he said. Not a house of accommodation of the kind you and I might know. A bullocky's camp, Gammaroy. Got the fenced place by the creek, see there, where they spell the beasts.

Not afraid of a few bullocks, nor yet bullockies. Didn't have a high regard for Daunt for being so squeamish.

You'll get the measure of it when you see it close, he said. What it is I'm trying to say.

As we rode through the place I saw what he hadn't wanted to say clear. Gammaroy was a dirty low place, the huts small and lopsided, not a one standing straight. Flies round the doors, dogs snapping at each other, dark-skinned children bare-bottomed on the dust. There was a blacksmith's and a saddlery and a grain mill, and a hut with a sign swinging crooked, a rising sun. As we rode past it a man lurched out, hatless, in his braces, trousers gaping open at the front, arm round a black woman wearing nothing but a man's vest, naked from the waist down. Both staggering, and the man bellowing out what he must of thought was a song.

We made camp a half-mile further on. A poor night's rest. I was itching with the dust and the heat and the tiredness, and the mosquitoes big as birds. Lay stifling under the sheet, but better that than the mosquitoes.

Gammaroy was nearly enough to do what seventy miles of

forest and two days on a rough road had not. I'd had hopes of it, that was my mistake. Lay choking down the tears, not to let Daunt know how near I was to giving up.

The third and last day on the road the country opened out. Off to the south, on our left, was the dark pile of the range we'd come through, a great corner in the earth pushed up, blunt as the side of a box. In there somewhere was Garlogie. Further again, way off beyond, was Thornhill's Point. But to the north the country smoothed out into a gentle up-and-down, all grass, no scrub, the shadow of one tree not touching the shadow of the next. It folded away as far as the eye could see, dark lines of trees in the creases showing where the creeks ran.

I'd never been in such open-faced country.

Off to the northwest was a range of sharp mountains, a faded faraway blue. Peak after peak falling away fainter and fainter till the blue joined the sky. Government called that range Limit of Location, drew the line on the map, *no one past here*, but it was only a mark on paper. Out there was where the wild blacks was supposed to be, the ones that cut out white folk's hearts, but men greedy for pasture took their chances.

The sun was low when I saw smoke rising from somewhere up ahead, a kink in the land like the fold in a piece of taffeta. Every line of hill and shadow and track funnelled towards that crease. I knew, before Daunt took off his hat and flapped it to tell me, *this is the place*. Soon I'd see it, the place I'd come to know down to the last pebble and twig. It would be new to me just this one time.

He reined in for me to catch up.

See now, he said. Where the trees are. Where we've got the brook.

Yes, I said. I see.

It's a good brook, he said. No end of water.

Tried to give him some sort of smile from under my bonnet.

Not so very far now, he said. Not more than a step.

Wondered was he going to reach over, take my hand. Wed a fortnight, sharing our breathing in the dark every one of those nights, but hadn't found a way to say how we felt. More private, somehow, than what our bodies did in the bed.

~

The house was on a sweet piece of rising ground. Long and low, sawn boards, shingle roof, three rooms wide. Looked all right, but closer up I saw what Daunt meant by *the present shortcomings*. Verandah not flagged, just dirt. No windows, just the holes for them. Sheets of bark for shutters.

That rogue of a carpenter, Daunt said. Promised me windows this six months gone. The shutters a temporary expedient, keep out the wind till the fellow sees fit to grace us with his presence.

More long words than I needed to get the gist.

At the door I felt him thinking *should I be carrying her over the threshold*. Glanced at me and decided no. Just stood back, made a bit of a bow. Might of thought I was looking stony because of the windows. It wasn't that. It was thinking about the other place I'd pictured walking into with a husband. Not this place, not this husband.

He was looking a little stony himself.

Inside it was clean enough, if a bit on the bare side. No rugs, no curtains, the walls not lined, only the boards whitewashed.

The old Irish woman, Daunt's housekeeper, made me a cup of tea and a scone, Maeve her name was. Spoke her few words of English with such a brogue she might of been speaking Irish for all I could follow, and with a whistle through a mouth that had only a few teeth left. But made a good dark cup of tea. Daunt spoke a few words of Irish with her. What an up-and-down sort of language it was, and with a coaxing music to it. I saw how his way of talking got its flavour, rubbing up against that other language. Watched his mouth shaping words I couldn't follow and remembered the way Jack became someone else when he spoke to the girl.

Was there any road in my thoughts that didn't lead to Jack?

Maeve was obliging enough, wrinkled up like an old apple but her cheeks pink, her eyes blue and bright. We'd manage together, but I was cast down that the one woman I might of shared a chat with was out of reach.

She brought me hot water and I blessed her for it after being so dusty along those weary miles. Lay down with my ears ringing and my muscles twitching as if I was still bending against every step of the horse.

Oh, the bliss of lying still and quiet and washed.

After a while I walked out into the dusk, the air holding the light. Followed the sound of water down to the creek, or brook. Watched it stream over the stones. Every stone washed, night and day, day and night, since the world began.

On the other side of the creek a bush was alive with some kind of tiny round green bird with a silvery eye. Every single one hopping and twittering, a hundred cheerful creatures all talking at once. That bush was full of birds, the way a cake left out overnight is full of ants in the morning.

I had a pang for their lively society. Grieved for that place I'd left, boats drawing up at the jetty, people coming to the house, always someone calling out, or sneezing, or whistling. I'd lost a life that would never come again.

Jack had travelled along the road with me every day, but fainter with every mile. Everywhere else I'd been, he'd been there too and left some hair or flake of skin. Now I was in a place where he'd never drawn the air into himself and breathed it out again. Never would.

The dust, I had it all ready to say if Daunt came out and found me crying. Had the feeling he might be watching me from up at the house. But if he was, he left me to it.

IT WAS the four of us in the house—me and Daunt, and Maeve and an old feller Paddy Riley—plus the four government men out on the sheepwalk.

Daunt was lucky to have Maeve, a good worker and an honest woman although a thief. Both of them from the same part of the country, though Daunt from the English type of Irish and Maeve a poor woman and of course a Papist. Back in Cork she'd lifted the watch out of some feller's pocket and would of been all right, she said, only a shopkeeper saw. Showed me one day how it was done. I put a stone in my pocket and she got it out slick as you please, didn't feel a blessed thing.

The government men were out on the sheepwalk a week at a time, I didn't have much to do with them. Londoners, never seen a sheep in their lives before. Come back, couldn't stop talking from the loneliness out there.

Paddy Riley was a different sort of feller. Been a shepherd back in the old country but too old for that now. Did the work round the yard. Milk the cow, split the kindling, bring the hay for the horses. A weather-beaten old feller, so shy he couldn't meet your eye. One pointy yellow tooth showing in his bottom jaw, and a felt hat worn to splits along the folds. Stand for an hour yarning through his lopsided mouth. Sent out years before, left behind a wife and little ones. Told me once about his son. Kept putting his hand down level with his leg, showing me how tall he'd been, as if the boy might appear under his hand.

Showed me his fiddle, hanging on a hook in a green felt bag in his lean-to. The wood black with use, and shiny where his chin rested and his fingers slid up and down. He handled it tenderly as a baby.

Play for you one of these nights, he said. Mr Daunt likes a tune.

I was pleased to hear that, pictured us jigging round on the boards of the parlour or singing along, something rousing and cheerful.

~

Gentleman and all as he was, Daunt was a hard worker. One of the government men did the heavy digging but Daunt was the one got the vegetables watered and weeded and into the kitchen. Looked after the fruit trees and the horses. Didn't do the killing of the sheep or the lamb, one of the men did that, but did the butchering of it. Could joint up a beast as neat as

Campbell cut up those fowls that day. Rode out to see the men on the sheepwalk, took them their victuals, saw to everything. When it was time for the shearing he rolled up his sleeves with the rest. In his shabby work-trousers and the check shirt all pale down the back from being so worn out, you wouldn't of picked him from the others.

He might of looked like one of the men, but of course he wasn't. Told them what he wanted, very mild, never raised his voice, made a bit of a joke of it if he could. They hopped to it. If they didn't, he didn't mind getting the steel in his voice. But never lost his courtesy or his temper that I ever saw.

Couldn't think why he'd be pleased to be mucking in with the men. Pa would never of been seen in a shirt like that, or with a spade in his hand. But something in Daunt rose to it with pleasure. He'd come back to the house after a day in the paddocks, caught by the sun across his nose and cheeks, could hardly speak he was that tired. Hands torn, nails full of dirt. But a happy man.

Me and Mary wasn't brought up to sit on a sofa not doing a hand's turn. We'd done our fair share at home. But my word I worked harder that first year at Glenmire than ever I had in my life. The food had to be kept up to the men, and only me and Maeve to do it all. Separate the milk, churn the butter, and always the worry how to keep it all cool. Mutton chops and mutton stew and leg of mutton, mutton pies and cold mutton to be sent out the men on the sheepwalk. Onions and carrots, turnip and potato, peel and chop, peel and chop. Set the yeast bottle last thing at night, don't forget or there'd be no bread the next day, and that would be the end of the world.

I was glad of Maeve, every kind of work less trying with another to share it. She'd sing away in Irish while she pounded the dough or scrubbed out the pots. I'd ask her, what's that song about, Maeve, but beyond that it was sad, she didn't have the words to tell me. In behind Maeve's worn smiling face and mild ways, another woman lived in her that you only knew about when she lifted her voice in song. No sweet small voice as you might expect, but rich and strong, so that while she sang she was like a queen, her words something you had to listen to.

Daunt's place was as he'd said, plenty of water and the soil in good heart. Deep, the colour of rust, plant anything and it grew. Good sheep country, hard frosts to make the wool thick. Still only sixpence the pound, but it was as Daunt said, it had to come up again by and by. Until then we wouldn't go hungry. Any amount of lamb and mutton, milk and butter. Bushels of potatoes and cabbages. A paddock of corn and the fruit trees coming on. I made the coarse soap for the laundry myself, the tallow candles for everyday.

But for things you needed cash down for, we had to go pretty steady. Every few months the carter come through, we'd give him the order for what we couldn't make ourselves. Daunt told me what we could run to, never more than the bare essentials. Two bags of the good wheaten flour. A small sack of black sugar. Box of tea, but just post-and-rails. A bolt of calico, the cheap kind, so loose in the weave you could shoot peas through it.

The good flour was the main thing I missed. Always plenty

of cornmeal from the mill at Gammaroy, but without the wheat to stick it together and puff it up, the bread fell apart in your hand, the scones turned out hard as stones. But as long as you knew it wasn't for ever, you could get a kind of pride out of doing the best you could with what you had.

Me and Daunt was on the go from morning till night. Then a sit in front of the fire of an evening in the room we called the parlour, even though it was parlour and dining room and office all at once. I'd be doing the mending or hemming some calico for curtains, and he'd be reading or doing the accounts, scratching away into the ledger. The *Gazette* come up on the dray with the other things, he'd put them all in order and read them one by one, as if he'd stepped back into February when where I was sitting with my mending it was already May.

One night Maeve come into the parlour with us, and Paddy after her with his fiddle under his arm.

An hour of music, Sarah, if you don't object, Daunt said. Three Irish in a house together, can't go long without some of the old songs.

I might of thought I had the measure of these people I shared my life with, but that night showed me a different face to each one of them. Paddy looked taller with his fiddle tucked under his chin. Didn't play a jig you might dance to, or the songs I'd thought, thump out the beat with your hand and shout out the chorus. Stood in the corner with his eyes closed and out of the fiddle came a wild keening voice, frantic you could say, a soul in a torment of sadness. He swayed with the music, the fiddle part of his body, his hand on the bow quick as a ferret. Taken away into some other place, some other self.

After a time Maeve lifted up her voice and sang along with the fiddle, the words caressing the music as it went up and down. Her face wet with tears, but lit up with the joy of her sadness, I could see the joy and I could see the sadness both. Of course I didn't know what words she was saying, but I heard the refrain, a woman's name, Eileen Aroon, so I thought it must be some sad tale of lost love.

And there was Daunt, sitting in the armchair watching and listening, and whatever the words might of been, and however few of them he might of known, they made the tears stand glittering in his eyes and his mouth go tender with feeling.

I was the only one dry-eyed.

That was what it was to belong to a place. To be brought undone by the music of the land where you'd been born. The loss as sharp a pain as mourning a lover.

Us currency lads and lasses had no feeling like that about the land we called ours. It had no voice that we could hear, no song we could sing. Nothing but a blank where the past was. Emptiness, like a closed room, at our backs.

~

Most nights it was just me and Daunt in the parlour. I'd of liked to talk over the day then, but Daunt would have his hand up to his forehead against the glare of the lamp, and might as well of been back in County Cork. Gone away into reading like another country where I could never follow.

Now and then he'd get a letter from Archibald Campbell, or from Ireland.

Your sister sends her fondest love, he might say and glance towards me for a moment. Or, my mother extends her warmest respects to Mrs Daunt and hopes to have the pleasure of meeting her before too long.

It crossed my mind that his mother had said no such thing. Just Daunt, knowing he was safe telling me whatever he thought fit.

It was a surprise to me that you could be more lonely, sitting with another person who didn't speak to you, than out in an empty paddock. There could be lonelier things than empty.

What's that you're reading, I said one night. That's got you so interested?

He read me a piece out of the *Gazette*, some feller called Boland thought you could grow grapes round our way and make wine. Got to the end, turned the page, something else caught his eye. He forgot me, reading in his head again.

You know I don't read, Daunt, I said. Don't you.

He looked up startled, closed the pages.

Life is long, Sarah, he said. You can't read *yet*. Could teach you your letters if you wanted. Fact is, you'd pick it up in no time.

Daunt was still a stranger to me in many ways but I knew him well enough to know that when he started something with *fact is*, it meant he was feeling awkward.

Where I was from, no one had their letters other than poor pickled Loveday. No shame in it. But now I wished I knew how to turn marks on paper into words. Would of liked to take up a pen and soften my loneliness with a letter to Mary. Have one back from her. It would be some kind of conversation.

I should of said, *Thank you, yes*. But Daunt being so awkward pricked my pride. Instead it was, *Oh no, I'm all right the way I am*. Haughty, so he didn't insist.

Some nights he'd get out the ledger and the pen.

How's it coming out? I'd say. Just the two bags of flour next order, or could we stretch to three?

Oh well, he'd say. I can't altogether tell you at this minute. What will be the return on the clip, you see, that's not known as yet.

It started to feel as if he'd as soon tell the horse anything that mattered as tell me. Not ladylike to go into the money side of things, I supposed. That would be vulgar.

Come along Daunt! I said. Not asking for chapter and verse, just are we getting ahead or behind? Two bags or three?

Oh well, he said. Best stay with the two bags for the time being.

You can't force a man to talk, if he's not of a mind to. I had to go back to my mending, but bleak inside. This was the life I had ahead of me. Me and Daunt, together, but strangers. Till death parted us.

~

Along from the house was a piece of rising ground, grass and scattered trees, and at the top a cluster of boulders, one just the right shape for your backside. When the day's work was done

I'd walk up and take a breather.

It was a lovely spot in the last of the sunlight, every rock and tree a long straight shadow. The trees up to their knees in grass, the trunks with streaks like watered silk, lemon-yellow and dove-grey, leaves a soft green that was halfway to blue. The hills all velvety folds, the mountains changing shape as the light faded.

A bigger sky than ever there was at Thornhill's Point. Such a lot of sky, it made my life seem small, nothing but a tiny bud of light. It was so important to me, but it was lost in the greatness of a world that went about its own mysterious business with no thought to the young wife sitting on a hill with the dusk around her.

How high would you have to go, to see New Zealand? A bird might do it. Rise up into this soft light, turn its head east, start flying, not stop till it got to Jack. Did he ever climb a hill in New Zealand, wonder how high he'd have to go to see me?

I tried to picture him. Jack on a sloping wet deck, or stepping out of a boat onto a beach. He'd turn and see me, on the deck or the beach, and smile.

Sometimes I could only see the other picture. Jack flinging off my hand like a spider. Striding up the hill, his bundle hanging off his shoulder. Then gone, gone, gone.

He could of been dead. But I didn't think he was.

I thought of the girl sometimes. She'd of surely settled by now. A person couldn't go on locked in on themselves for ever. But oh, that house by the river must be lonely. No one but Ma and Pa, and nothing for that poor child to hope for.

I'd like to have her here with us. A fresh start, her and me.

In this open place, under this broad sky, she'd come to life. Couldn't see how she might come to us, but it was as Daunt said, life was long.

From up on the hill you could watch the weather coming in. The far-off mountains fading away into grey, one peak after the other, and a wall of cloud creeping towards me across the valley.

I'd go back down to the house and wait for the sound of the first drops on the shingles. They were like old friends. I'd watched them make their journey all that way across the country.

Daunt never asked what I did on the hill. He might of understood it was the same as him going away into his books. He had his way and I had mine.

~

There was blacks round about. More than on the Hawkesbury. Had a camp further down the creek, in among thick trees. You saw the smoke. Stand at the front of the house, look out, you'd see a darkness above the trees in the valley.

I'd been at Glenmire a day or two when I saw two black fellers walking up the hill. One in a pair of trousers all tatters round the ankles, the other with a woollen undershirt more hole than shirt and trousers gone at the knees. Their square feet coming down soft on the dirt. Walked round to the back of the house. When I went to see, Daunt was trundling a barrow with an axe in it out of the shed.

You'll be seeing a bit of these fellers, he said. This one is Wednesday, the Lord alone knows why. Gets the wood. Skipper fetches the water.

Skipper was already heading off down to the creek, a pail in each hand.

Now they'll be coming to the kitchen later, he said. For what they're owed. Maeve's inclined to stint, I'm afraid to say. Be glad if you'd keep an eye out. Plenty of meat and potatoes, and baccy enough for the week.

The man called Wednesday took the barrow, wheeled it away. Daunt looked at me rather intent.

Not frightened of them, are you, he said. Because I know there's a lot are frightened of a black.

Never seen any cause to be frightened, I said. Poor things, no harm in any of them.

Told him about the blacks coming to the kitchen at home, Mrs Devlin grumbling but giving. The camp where Pa took victuals.

Took it down himself, I said. Took it down, give it to them from his own hand, except they wouldn't take.

Did he now, Daunt said. Did he indeed. Mr Thornhill down at the camp. Glad to hear that, because you'd know not everyone would agree. Beresford, you'll meet Beresford by and by. Got a down on any black face. Coulters along the road not so hard on them. But pay them scraps. Leavings, what we'd give the fowls.

He watched Skipper walk up from the creek, his arms straining with the full pails. Over in the paddock Wednesday was starting on a dead tree, the axe blade shining as he brought it down, the noise of it coming along after.

Good workers when they turn their hand to it, Daunt said. Any one of them worth two of the government men. Worthy of their hire in my view and agreeable with it.

This was a way of looking at the thing that was new to me. Not *cadging* and not *Christian duty*. Not even *because your mother took their part*.

All the rest of the afternoon Wednesday worked on the tree. Brought the wood up to the yard in barrowloads, Skipper stacking it when he'd filled the water barrels.

Late in the day I was in the kitchen and there was a noise on the doorframe, Wednesday scratching his fingernails at the wood. When he saw I'd heard he stood back. Waiting with Skipper, heads down, faces in shadow.

Blacks, Mrs Daunt! Maeve said. The blacks!

Spoke something in Irish, a prayer it might of been.

Yes, Maeve, I said, that's all right. Get that loaf, and the forequarter. Bag of taters. The baccy Mr Daunt left for them.

She put the things down on the doorstep. Wouldn't go near the men.

Now Maeve, what's this about, I said. Been listening to nonsense about the blacks, have you.

Maeve could be stupid when she chose. Make out like she'd forgotten her few words of English.

Good lot of wood you done, Wednesday, I said.

He was an ugly feller, nose took up half his face and his eyes buried under his brows. But smiled in among his beard and by heaven you never saw such fine teeth, and his frowning face warmed by that smile.

Yellerjack, missus, he said. Damn good.

Yellerjack, I said. That the name of it?

Split him, wood's yeller as a guinea, he said. Ever see a guinea, Missus?

I have not, I said. Sad to say. You?

He didn't answer, chuckling away inside his beard.

Cheeky ones, Maeve said behind me. Come off, Mrs Daunt!

I never saw any men other than Wednesday and Skipper, but now and then women appeared at the kitchen door. Always two or three together, their bits of clothing the same colour as the dirt, little ones with them naked as Adam, an old woman with bad eyes led along by a girl. Half of them marked with the smallpox, and all of them knobs and bones like the ones at home.

Never looked at me. One of them might hold up a billy and shake it, that was as near as they'd come to asking.

I gave them what I thought was right. Eggs when we had them. Always a piece of meat. Cornmeal. A billy of milk. I'd hear one of them say, Thank you missus, then they'd be gone.

One week it come round to wash day and when I went to get the water the barrel was empty. Hadn't seen Wednesday and Skipper for a time. Went out the front, looked down the hill, sure enough the smoke was gone.

Daunt walked up from the orchard for his midday meal and I was waiting for him at the door.

Where have those damn blacks gone, I said. Leave me in the lurch, all the wash to do and no damn water!

I'd caught him on the hop, he was all over dust and sweat.

Well, he said. That's the thing about the blacks. Grand workers. But not reliable, more's the pity. Come and go as it suits them, not as it might suit us.

Then it'll have to suit you to have nothing clean, I said.

Crankier than was reasonable. Seemed to of made up my mind to have a barney with him.

We'll get you your water, he said. Give us our meal, Paddy and I will get the water up for you.

I went out to the kitchen, set to chopping at the potatoes, hacking the meat, throwing wood in the firebox.

Mrs Daunt, Maeve said.

Pushed the chair at me, took the pan out of my hand, fixed the fire where I'd spoiled it. So gracious about it, and Daunt so uncomplaining, I was ashamed.

I knew why I'd taken such a little thing so hard. I wanted a reason to feel hard done by. I'd promised to forsake all others, and I had, but nothing could stop me wanting.

I dished up, put Daunt's plate in front of him.

No call to get the water today, I said. Out of sorts, that's all. Wash can wait.

Ah, well now, he said, caught on the hop all over again.

Get the water first thing, he said. They'll be back by and by, you know. But no joy asking the whys and wherefores of it.

A week later, the smoke was hanging over the trees again, Wednesday and Skipper walking up to the house like they'd never been gone.

WE HAD a couple of neighbours, if you can call a person who lives an hour's ride away a neighbour. On the west we shared a boundary with Beresford. Huge horse of a man, a drinker's nose and no doubt as to his opinions. No wife, just him and his men. He'd ride over to see us now and then, take a glass with Daunt. Something about the way he looked past me made me think he was one of those men had no time for women. Educated, been to a grand school back in England, spoke very nice, but from all accounts lived rough out on his place. Didn't encourage visitors.

To our east it was Major and Mrs Coulter. From the same part of Ireland as Daunt, he told me. They'd come out here in the early days with three children and a couple of cousins and a maiden aunt and seven servants. Had an in with the governor, got a big spread. As far as a bit of company went, Coulters sounded like my best bet.

The first time Lucy Coulter came to visit, she was on the loveliest pony, the servant coming along behind on a sad old nag. She jumped down off the pony light and bouncing as you please, just dropped the reins, knew the man would get hold of them.

In that one thing I could see the world she was from.

She knew Daunt, and I suppose thought Mrs John Daunt would be out of the same box. But first up I saw her notice my pinny, patched in the middle and ragged along the hem, and my boots, strong men's boots you could walk anywhere in and not worry about, and my rough hands that told her I did my own washing. In one glance she saw all that and her thought was plain as the nose on your face: poor John Daunt, such a shortage of women in the Colony, he'd had to *marry down*.

Why Mrs Daunt, she said, and took me by surprise, shaking me by the hand the way men did. The hand she was shaking had been in the flour bin not long before. I wanted to pull it back, but she hung on.

I cannot express to you the pleasure of seeing another female of the species! she said.

You could hear the Irish, but refined.

Set to banging the dust off her riding habit, then she saw it was blowing into the house.

Oh I do beg your pardon Mrs Daunt, she said. A thousand apologies!

I was cross about the flour on my hands that had got onto

hers. I'd seen her wipe it off as if it was dirty, so I spoke a little sharp.

In a world of dust another pinch won't kill us, I said. Ashes to ashes and dust to dust, Mrs Coulter.

She was so startled her smile slipped. I saw her make an adjustment to her idea of me.

Daunt smiling away. Embarrassed, I thought. I didn't care. Those Lady Bountiful ways got my hackles up.

We settled ourselves in the parlour and Maeve brought us tea. Got out the good cups without me thinking to tell her. Had Lucy Coulter's measure, I could see.

And tell me Mrs Daunt, Lucy Coulter said, I wonder were you born out here?

She'd of known I was, of course, by the way I said my words. What she was really wanting to know was, did I have the taint?

Yes, I said. My father William Thornhill. An old colonist, well known on the Hawkesbury.

Ah! she said. Well. And is it a big family, Mrs Daunt?

Middling, I said. The two of us girls, and two brothers.

Had the words ready to say there'd been another brother too, but had a bust-up with my pa and brewed up rotgut now. But had mercy for Daunt.

There was three boys, I said, but my brother Will was drowned at New Zealand.

Lucy Coulter's face squeezed up to show how sorry she was and a pair of lines creased into the skin between her eyebrows, so you could see how she'd look when she was old.

Oh Mrs Daunt, she said, how terribly sad for you all and what a shock for your poor mother.

All hands lost, I said. Only one saved, man by the name of Jack Langland.

Hadn't known how much I wanted to hear that name.

She wrinkled herself up again, made an *oh dear* sort of noise.

I wanted to go on, say *Jack Langland* again, but my throat closed up. Had to find my handkerchief and make out I was coughing.

And Mrs Coulter, how are your dear children getting along? Daunt said. Such a fine flock you have.

You good feller, I thought. Knowing and forgiving in the one moment.

Lucy Coulter was one of those women could tell you all day about her blessed offspring, down to the last mouthful of porridge they had for breakfast. Charles a good head for figures, Charlotte wrote a neat hand, and little Septimus would soon settle to his studies, at his age one didn't expect miracles.

Daunt made out he was agog at it all, and I got myself together, nodded and smiled.

But would there never be an end to it, the hole in my life where Jack should of been?

Lucy Coulter finished at last with her children but had the next thing ready.

Did I tell you, Mr Daunt, she said, and Mrs Daunt you will be interested in this, I am making a study of the natives' tongue. Before they die out. Their ways and their words a curiosity worth preserving.

Spoke some words that she said meant *eel* and *wooden bowl*.

Like children, poor things, she said. Happy to exchange a small vocabulary for a blanket or some tucker.

Put *tucker* in a frame by the way she said it, inviting Daunt to share its quaintness. He didn't smile.

When first I got settled here I went down to the camp, he said. Gave them a few spades, a bag of seeds. Thought they'd be glad of the chance to grow some corn. Couple of axes, make a house better than the kennels they had.

I noticed that in company with Lucy Coulter, his Irish way of talking was stronger.

Thought to make cottiers out of them, he said, and they both laughed, the funniest thing they'd ever heard.

Well, I didn't know what a cottier was. Damned if I was going to smile and make out I did.

Thinking to make farmers of the blacks! Daunt said. Fresh from County Cork I was, green as grass.

I thought, thank you again, John Daunt.

And I wonder was your experiment a success, Mr Daunt, Lucy Coulter said. Or did you find what the Major has, that they are woefully work-shy?

It would depend, Mrs Coulter, on what you might term a success, he said. They took the spades and the seeds and the axes and they thanked me very prettily. Kept the axes but sold the rest at Gammaroy, I heard, for half a rope of tobacco and a few blankets.

Mrs Coulter gave a little gasp but Daunt looked at his hands, the skin cracked round the fingernails and a blister in the curve of his thumb from the woolshears.

I tell you what I think of it, Mrs Coulter, he said. That these are folk too clever to break their backs heaving dirt. I've come round to the view that a man shouldn't be in too much of a hurry to judge them. I'd say no more than this, that their ways are not the same as our ways.

Well, Mr Daunt, Mrs Coulter said. What a very interesting view of the matter. Not a view I think I've heard expressed until today.

Soon after that she gathered her gloves and her smart riding hat. Made her goodbyes graciously, but I had the feeling Mrs Coulter might not be paying too many visits to Mr and Mrs John Daunt.

Daunt and I stood out the front watching the glossy rump of her horse till the dust hid it.

Now I'll tell you, he said. Every time I see Lucy Coulter I think the same thing.

I steeled myself for what was coming. How charming she was. How lively. What a fine mind.

I give thanks to the Good Lord, he said. My mother told me I was within a whisker of being a Septimus myself. Imagine that now, going through life number seven.

When he was amused his big plain face lit up.

I look at Lucy Coulter, he said, and I see a woman that could saddle some innocent babe with being Septimus!

Took my hand in the manner of someone sealing a bargain.

Do I have your word now, Sarah, he said. That no child of ours will be a Septimus?

You do, I said, and had to laugh, he was putting on such a show of being in earnest.

You'd almost of thought he could read my mind. That he saw how Lucy Coulter made me feel. But married and all as we were, half a year now, somehow we'd never yet got the hang of speaking straight with each other.

It told me this, though. Daunt was thinking about children. Going so far even as to think what their names might be. Natural enough, marriage generally brought on children. But it made me know I wasn't ready.

Not that I didn't want little ones. But what kind of mother could I be to Daunt's children, when the need to hear another man's name was a hunger inside me?

OUT IN the bush it was the way of things to be hospitable when fellers came through. They'd be driving a mob of sheep north or bringing down a dray full of bales. Give them a hot feed and a shake-down for the night in with Paddy, send them on their way next morning.

Great ones for a yarn, long tales about how they near died from snakes or thirst. One feller showed us his hand, been out in the bush on his own splitting timber, reached in for the wedge, log snapped shut on two of his fingers. Had to chop them off with the axe. Lucky he could get to it, he said. Else he'd be there still, a pile of bones with its hand still in the log.

Plenty of tales about the wild blacks, the trouble they made. Huts set on fire, sheep killed. A shepherd with one old musket, the blacks waiting all day till he fired it, rushing him while he reloaded.

Then there was what the white men did. Nothing said straight out. *Teach them a lesson*, they might say. C*lear them off the place*. A gesture along with the words, a gun to the shoulder.

It was always about places past Limit of Location. There was no one to say what went on that far out. I'd never seen the bush blacks that was supposed to be doing all these things. Took the tales with a pinch of salt. The odd sheep killed and eaten I could believe. Trouble over women now and then. But shepherds speared to death, I couldn't see it. The blacks I knew, Wednesday and Skipper and the others, would no more of speared a man than fly.

True, there was some ugly characters about and I supposed there might have been some went after the blacks with guns. But not as a common thing, the way these fellers would have you believe. Had to sing for their supper, that was what I thought. Yarns one way of doing it. Scrabblers all of them, dreaming about getting a lot of land and a lot of sheep and dying rich. All this about the blacks just big-noting themselves.

Three fellers come through late one day with a mob of sheep. Been through once before, me and Daunt not too pleased to see them again. Two of them hard-drinking fellers couldn't keep a clean tongue in their heads for any money. But the old feller with them, Billy Undercliff, no harm in him. Billy didn't come in. The others said he'd stay out with the sheep. You could tell from the way they said it they thought he was nothing but an old fool. I thought the better of him for wanting to keep clear of those two.

They lined up bottles on the table as if the place was a public house. I could see Daunt wanted them gone, but it was cold and near dark. I had a pot of stew and luckily three loaves baked that morning. Get plenty of food into them, I thought, mop up the liquor.

They ate all right, but it didn't stop them knocking back the drink like water and getting loud. Even busy in the kitchen I couldn't get away from their talk.

A story started to come out, something gone on somewhere up past Limit of Location. These fellers were cagey at the start, but the liquor loosed their tongues.

They'd been out in a hut miles from anywhere, these two fellers and old Billy Undercliff and a few others. A mob of blacks along with them, the men working with the sheep, the rest camped close by.

There'd been a spearing. Of man or sheep, that wasn't clear. These fellers took it into their heads to teach the blacks a lesson. Sent the men away with the sheep. Got the women and children and old men into the hut. Tied them up neck to neck. All bar two girls of the right age to seem like a good idea for these dirty fellers to keep. And one little boy that Billy Undercliff hid behind a barrel.

Drove the rest up the hill behind the hut and shot them.

Every damn one of them! one of the fellers shouted. Clean sweep!

Didn't know if I believed them or not, but I wasn't going to stay in the house to listen to any more of their nasty boasting.

Made up a billy of stew and a pannikin of grog, took it out to old Billy. Had the sheep bedded down in the folds, had his little fire but pleased to see me coming along with the stew.

He got out two tin plates, shared out the stew between them, tore the bread in half.

I already eaten, Billy, I said. This is for you.

Thinking he was a man of more heart than I'd of guessed, sharing his meal with me.

Oh no, Mrs Daunt, he said. It's for my boy. Got my boy here.

He got up and took the plate over to the side. There was a boy there I hadn't seen. A young black boy. Still as a stone, crunched up small against a tree, only his knees and feet and the top of his head showing.

Best leave him, Billy said. Won't never eat with anyone near. Come away Mrs Daunt.

After a while you could hear the little noises of the boy's plate.

Where's the lad from, Billy, I said.

He didn't give me an answer, just worked on the stew. When he'd finished he wiped his beard with his hand, looked over at the boy.

Never speaks a word, he said. Not a word, not ever.

The boy was folded up into himself, the plate empty beside him, bread gone.

He'll come good, Billy said. Come good by and by.

I didn't say anything, just took the plate and went back to the house. But I was feeling a little cold thing somewhere inside, because the boy being there made it seem the story might of had some truth in it after all.

But not wanting to think it. Telling myself there could be all sorts of ways an old feller might end up having a black boy along with him.

Daunt had got the men into the lean-to. From our bed we could hear their voices through the wall, then after a while snoring. They'd stop breathing, then suck the air in sudden with a great snort.

Billy Undercliff's got a boy with him, I said. Young black lad.

Has he now, Daunt said. Has he indeed.

Reckon they was skiting? I said. Reckon that's all there is to it?

Well now, he said. To be honest I'm not sure. There's the devil of a lot of bad about. But what the truth of it might be, hard to say for a certainty.

Think it's true then, I said. Not just a yarn.

There's a lot of nonsense talked, he said. But men killed, you know, that's true enough. Black and white both.

Never heard that, I said. Not that I'd believe.

Yes, well, Daunt said.

I could hear the thought. You don't read. And a woman never hears how men really talk among themselves.

I didn't know what to make of it. How to go about thinking the thing through. Men pushing out with their sheep, they had to make a living, same as we did. Easy to see that. But then on the other side you had the blacks, sent away from where they'd always been. Sent off and sent off, and ending up narrowed down to a camp along from the white man's house, having to go to him cap in hand for their tucker. Or worse, somewhere like Gammaroy. Those women with not too much choice in the matter, and the little ones growing up in the dirt with a mother black and a father God knew which bullocky.

What do you make of it, I said. The rights and wrongs of it.

I couldn't tell you, he said. I think about it and I don't know. But it does put me in mind of the tenants back home. The Irish. Once upon a time they owned the whole of Ireland. Then the English came. My lot. Took it away, one acre at a time. Now there's not an Irishman left hardly that owns his own land.

No doubt about him, Daunt was never a man to jump the way you thought he would.

It made me think about things I'd never thought about before. Once upon a time Thornhill's Point would have been like the country past Limit of Location, wild and empty but for the blacks wandering over it. Somewhere along the line someone took it over. One acre at a time.

My lot was like Daunt's, English. If Pa hadn't been sent out, I'd of grown up in London. *Oranges and Lemons, say the bells of St Clement's.* Pa was still English. The way he spoke, the memories in his head. Pa could go back, take up life again in the place he'd always known, let the blacks have Thornhill's Point again. New South Wales was nothing to him but the place where he'd made his pile.

But I wasn't English. I had no other place in my bones

than this one. The ones like me, currency—we had no *back* to go back to.

Ireland's a small place, I said.

To myself as much as Daunt, thought he'd gone to sleep while I'd been trying to work the thing out.

We got all the room in the world here, I said. Don't we.

Enough for all of us, Daunt said. That your thinking?

It was, I supposed. But I wasn't satisfied. Fell asleep trying to balance the thing out. Blacks on the one side, us on the other. How could you make it right?

NATURE TOOK its course, and late my first year as a married woman I knew I was in the family way.

When I told Daunt his face frightened me. Joy, but something like fear too, and a wildness I'd never seen in him. Put his arms round me, started to hug me, then jumped back as if he thought he might squash the baby. Jumped back so fast he knocked up against a chair and sent it crashing and Maeve come in to see what was wrong.

A baby, by God, he said. A baby, Maeve!

As if a baby had never happened before in the history of the world.

He was thoughtful in those ways a woman values. Got up even before Maeve, had the fire going and the porridge on. Would come to me while I was still in bed, saying, Will you not have a good hot cup of tea now. Took over all the heavy work, I'd never thought to see a man wringing out sheets. Saw me carrying a bucket of water one day and was the nearest I'd ever seen him to angry.

Promise me, Sarah dear, he said. Want you to promise me you won't be doing that again.

Heaven's sakes, I said, not a piece of fine china going to break!

But did as he wanted.

As the time went on I ached everywhere, legs, feet, back. Told Daunt and he took to one of the chairs with the hand-saw. The low chair eased the aches and I sat for everything I could, peeling potatoes, mixing up a pudding. Touched, that he cared enough to think of it, and not mind cutting into one of the good chairs.

He'd always kept himself clean-shaved but now he grew out his beard. Like letting go the picture of himself that he'd made every morning in front of the mirror. Now he was just himself, a man hairy like any other.

I'm a great ugly lump of a feller, he said. Pity that poor child if it takes after me.

You're a fine-looking man, I said, and as I said the words was surprised at myself, because I told no lie. Handsome you'd never say of Daunt, but I seemed to of come to another way of seeing things, where a man needn't be handsome to be a fine-looking man.

Daunt had the idea that a woman carrying ought to have a lie-down of an afternoon. He was not to be shaken in that view.

But I'd never been one for lying down in the daytime. Tried, but had to say to him, thank you, Daunt, for your care, but I'll scream if I have to lie in that room once more.

We worked out a middle way, which was that I could go over to the hill and sit there, take it easy that way. But only on condition I went slow and careful on the track, and took the little bell from the kitchen in case I got in trouble and couldn't call out.

Jack had always been with me in that private place on the hill. But the woman who sat there feeling the little flickerings of the baby stirring was not the same one who'd sat in the dust and tore at her hair. Not the one who'd said yes to the first man who asked, because what did it matter? Not the one who'd feared she could only love Jack Langland's child.

Here I was with a bub I knew I would lay down my life for, but he or she had no part of Jack Langland.

Those pictures of Jack I'd gone over so often were stale from so much remembering. Shrunken like an apple at the end of winter. Still the shape of an apple, the colour of an apple, but no life left in it.

I'd gone on and I was someone else now. It was a shock to see one day that Jack would of gone on, too. When he'd taken that last stride out of sight it felt as if he'd stepped out of the world. But it was only my world he'd stepped out of. He'd of gone on walking, unseen by me. Somewhere in the world now was the Jack he'd become. Not just the man in the pictures in my head, those dried-up memories, but a living man going about his unknown life.

He'd of got some lucky other woman by now. A New Zealander most likely. He'd watch her tenderly, the way he'd watched me. He'd have little ones that he'd love. They'd be like the girl, a foot in the black world and a foot in the white. He wouldn't of forgotten her. He'd think about her and he might think about me now and then, too. I hoped so. But I'd be growing distant and faded, the way he was for me.

Be happy, Jack, I said, out loud into the air of the glowing afternoon. Be happy, live long.

~

It was a cold windy season when I started to show, every gust blowing in at the empty places in the walls. Of an afternoon I'd sit beside those window-holes to get the last of the light, stitching away at the things I had to get ready for the baby.

Daunt found me there one day, my skirt blowing around me.

Sarah dear, you're frozen, he said. Look at you. Come away from that damn window!

Got me settled in the armchair, lit the lamp and brought it over, piled wood on the fire till it roared.

Instead of going back outside like I'd expected, he sat in the other chair, his heavy eyebrows drawn into one troubled bar of black.

The wool will come up, he said. Never been so low. Everyone feeling the pinch.

Yes, I said, it will come up.

Thought we'd be doing better by this, he said. I promised you. For better or worse.

That was true enough, but poor man, how could he help the price of wool?

Well, there's this about it, I said and looked over to one of the holes where a square piece of hill was bright in the late sunlight. No need for any pictures of scenery on the walls, we got the thing itself.

I hoped my poor joke might cheer him up but he put his face in his hands.

I brought you here, so far away, he said. Let you down. That's the fact of it. That damn *Gazette* comes, I go straight to the wool price. Still sixpence the pound! Do they not need their socks and blankets? Has the damned equator shifted and made County Cork as warm as paradise?

I knew what I was getting into, I said. Made my choice. Never wanted or needed a palace. Just a good man to go through life with.

A good man! he said. I made you those promises! Can't look you in the eye, thinking of them.

Ah, now I understood. All those nights gone away into the *Gazette*, giving me no answers when I asked about the money. I'd thought it was shame of me, his ignorant wife. When all the time it was his own shame. The fact was, John David Daunt didn't have a feather to fly with.

Any fool could of seen it, but I'd been so wrapped up in thinking about myself and my sad lost love that I hadn't seen what was under my nose.

I laid aside the sewing, come round behind him, my hands on his shoulders.

Well, John, I said.

The word was a little stiff in my mouth, it was the first time I'd called him by his name.

What a lucky thing you don't have to, I said.

He put a hand on mine and we stayed like that a long time. I watched the fire and thought, how easy it is to get the wrong end of the stick. A man won't talk to you, won't share his thoughts, you jump to the idea he's got no regard for you. When all the time it might be the very opposite.

I sat down and leaned over towards him. John, it's when you won't talk to me, that's what I mind, I said. More than glass in the windows I'd value a bit of talk. Ireland, say. What's the place like, where you're from? Wish you was back there?

Oh no, he said.

Come along now, I said. Have to say more than that to make me happy!

The words light, but I heard the tone of a real plea in my voice and he must of caught it too.

Well, he said, shifted his chair round so he was more facing me. It's a narrow place. You know at home, we're in that valley at Glenmire. Only ever two ways to go. Ahead, or behind. But I was forever wanting something else. Not what I could see ahead and not what I could see behind.

I knew what he meant. Those cliffs at home, closing in.

Mind you, he said, it's a sweet place. Fields so green, hedgerows green enough to eat, the woods on the hills bursting out of themselves with leaves. A place you might say of vegetable excess.

Vegetable excess, I said.

Then I saw he meant to amuse.

You do have the gift of the gab, I said. Go on.

A smaller sky, he said, but snorted, scorning himself. How can that be, a smaller sky. Yet it's so. A fierce low sky the greater part of the time. And rain, day in day out. Might wake with the sun but turn to scratch yourself and the rain will be coming down again.

Wasn't sure if he was having a lend of me. That much rain?

A lot of brightness in the sky, he said. But not a lot of the sun shining. The air so wet to start with, the rain nothing more than the air dropping on you.

Staring into the fire, back in that other place.

Maeve was crying that night, I said. When Paddy got out his fiddle. Even you. Tears in your eyes.

We're a sentimental lot, us Irish, he said. Those tunes, they pluck at you. But this place does get under your skin. A fine country, not a finer in the world.

But your family, I said. You'd have to miss your ma and pa? You'd have brothers and sisters?

Ashamed that I'd never thought to ask.

To be frank, the Daunts aren't a great one for family, he said. Not like you Thornhills, what a solid family there.

*Only if you didn't know it from the inside*, I thought.

My brothers and I sent away to school at five years old, Daunt said. They thought that was the proper way of doing things.

He leaned forward, elbows on his knees. *They* must be his

Ma and Pa and it did shock me, a lad so young sent away.

Five years old, he said. Can you imagine. Soon as I could write home I did, every week it was the same, take me away, come and fetch me away.

Gave me a sour smile.

Reading and writing not such a grand thing, you see, he said. Did me not a damn bit of good, they never came for me.

One thing I'd wanted to ask since that first night, and now I took the risk.

Was there someone, I said. You know. Back in Ireland?

He was silent and I'd taken the breath to say, None of my business, John, forget I asked.

There was, he said. Janey Davis was her name. The ringlets and the blue eyes, and the charm and the wit, and money with it. The princess of Glenmire. We all panted after her. She took a shine to me. You know, I had my hair then, was not such a bad-looking feller.

I thought how it might be, watching your hair fall out, week by week, and nothing to be done about it. It might make you mistrust yourself.

Janey had not come down in the last shower, he said. Knew what she wanted, and how to teach a lad. Lost my heart completely, green as I was. But when I went to propose, oh, that was the best joke she'd ever heard. There I was, a lad with no means and few prospects, wanting to make an honest woman of her!

Like Lucy Coulter, I thought, all tinkling charm and witty ways, but cold at her heart.

I was crushed, I can tell you, he said. But it made me ask what I wanted in life. What sort of a person I might choose to make it with me.

He put out his hand and cupped it over my knee. I could feel the warmth of it through my skirt.

I wouldn't go back to any of it, he said. Not the place, not the people. Everything and everyone I want, I've found here.

I watched the coals glow and sparkle. If wool was a pound a pound and the windows stopped with the best glass in the colony, I'd still be sitting here with a silent husband, stitching up all my disappointment into a smock instead of counting the lucky hand life had dealt me.

And you yourself, he said. I wonder now. If you think about what's gone, at all.

I do, I said. You know that. Heard me turn a conversation to say his name.

*Jack Langland*. I tried it over to myself, but felt nothing.

He was a good man, such as you are yourself, I said. No Janey Davis, toying with a person's life. But long gone, and me a lucky woman. Janey Davis was a fool, John. Not to know the best of men when she saw one.

He leaned over, touched the hair back from my forehead.

We had but a weak beginning, Sarah dear, he said. But might be happy enough yet.

I was wiser than I knew, I said. Saying yes that day.

That night, the first time since we'd been husband and wife, we lay together. Not just our bodies, but our spirits too, trusting each other at last.

AS MY TIME grew near I was frightened. Had no idea in the wide world what to expect, only that it would hurt. And that you could die of it. How exactly I didn't know. For the first time I could remember I wanted my mother. Why did you have to die and leave me, I thought, to meet this thing on my own?

Would of liked Mary to help me, but she was far gone with her second. Lucy Coulter might of helped, having got as far as Septimus she'd of had to know a few things. But she was in Sydney with the children, not expected back for another month.

I was lucky, it turned out Maeve had had a child, once upon a time. Perhaps more than one, she didn't want to say. Tried to get me ready for what was ahead of me.

It does pain, Mrs Daunt, she said. Oh, sad pain.

But that was all she could say, and when it started I knew why she couldn't be clearer. It was nothing like when you fell and hurt yourself, or had the toothache. A griping pain with no word for it that I knew. Closest I could come was, it was cousin to the worst pain from your monthly that you could ever imagine. Got into every particle of you, along your blood, every muscle and bone crying out. Great dreadful swells and surges of it.

In one of the clear moments I thought, men are the ones in charge of the words, that's why there isn't one for this pain that only a woman can feel.

I told myself, this is only my body. Not me myself. Stood at the foot of the bed gripping the iron rail. There was the crocheted bedcover, there was the hole in it I must darn, do it quick or it would get worse, and did I have the right colour of wool. But try as I might, the pain wouldn't let me have any other thoughts. It was too big a thing. It filled the air in the room. There was nothing to breathe but pain and nothing to think but pain.

Look Mrs Daunt, Maeve said. This way.

Took heaving breaths, ducked her head as if under a curtain. I breathed the way she was showing me, found I could in a manner of speaking become the pain, by diving into it.

That did the trick for a time. But the pain went on. It didn't need to rest, but I did.

The me that I knew got smaller every time the pain came back. I tried to tell myself who I was. Sarah Thornhill, I said over and over, crouching under the thing twisting in my belly. Sarah Thornhill, Sarah Thornhill. But I shrank smaller and weaker. In the end I forgot who I was. Forgot I was a person at all. There was no me-here and pain-over-there, there was nothing but the pain. I was nothing more than a pebble rolled around in the pouring of that terrible white tide.

Maeve got the hot cloths for my back, sponged my face with cold water. A rag to suck when I couldn't swallow. Walked me up and down the room. Talked to me, I suppose, but I was past hearing.

Daunt stood at the doorway once, I remember that. Stricken as if he'd made a terrible mistake. Twisted his hat in his hands, couldn't look at me straight. I had to laugh, the poor man, tried to tell him not to be so mournful, it was no more than the ewes did out in the paddock. But before I could work out the words the pain was roaring over me again, nothing with me but Maeve's hand squeezing mine.

After God only knows how long, the pain shifted into another kind of thing, smaller and more ordinary. Something you could put your hand to and say, the pain is here. My head cleared, I was myself again.

Push Mrs Daunt, Maeve kept saying. Push!

Never worked so hard in all my life as getting that baby out. Remember thinking, labour, this is why they call it labour.

~

I could not believe that this small person had been produced by me. Carrying her was one thing, feeling her foot through the wall of my belly, the way she shuffled and stretched in her nest. New and odd, but part of me. Now she was in the world she was completely herself. Like any other stranger, that you'd learn to know as time went on.

Daunt so proud and tender, standing by the bed with the babe in his arms.

You bring me all them gloves, remember, I said. Six pair of kid gloves. Still got them. In the drawer there.

Tell the truth, I hardly knew what I was saying, my head not quite my own and my body emptied like a bag.

Well, Sarah dear, he said, I must have thought you were worth every last one.

The morning after she was born the baby woke me up before dawn, just a little cry from her cradle beside our bed. Slept like a top, poor thing, after that last long effort we'd both made to bring her into the world. I took her out to the verandah, where Daunt had put the cut-down chair, to show her the place she'd come into.

As the sky grew paler the place grew larger. Darkness had made it seem small. A bird balanced on a branch, you could see its beak glint, then it threw its head back and warbled.

The baby looked round in a wise sort of way. Like she'd been here before and was glad to see it again but not in the least surprised. I could see Pa in her features, and Daunt as well, something about the eyes.

My mother would be there too. Having a daughter was the nearest I'd ever come to knowing her. I knew now the pain she'd been through to bring me into the world. The pain, and the joy too.

My mother's mother must be in there too. Her father. And

Pa's mother and father. Never thought till this moment of Pa having his own pa and ma. Further back even, a pa and a ma beyond him again. All the people that had gone into her making were part of her. The dead ones and the live ones, all packed into this parcel of brand-new person.

Love made me skinless. She slept in my arms and I watched her blue-veined eyelids flickering with dreams. A swell of feeling rose up inside me, like a yawn or a sneeze. Something your body decided to do of its own accord.

Of its own accord, too, a thought floating up as the sun rose. About another mother and another daughter. Somewhere in that place I couldn't picture, New Zealand, a woman would of sat the same way I was doing now, feeling her daughter's sweet weight against her. Just the same way I was doing, she'd of called down every god she had, to keep her daughter from harm.

But that daughter was the child I'd known. That sad silent poor thing. Not kept from harm.

The baby woke and opened her eyes. Such wise old eyes. Put out her starfish fingers to my face and made a little wondering sound. A tear fell from my cheek and made its way down hers. I watched her taste it, that little mouth shaping its first surprise.

~

I hesitated to ask Daunt if we could name the baby Sarah, since it was my own name, but I wanted to draw my mother, that other Sarah, into this new life. Daunt was more than happy, he said, to have not one Sarah but two, and the baby could be Sadie in case anyone should mistake the mother for the child.

Celia was for his own mother. He was surprised when I suggested it, but it seemed a courtesy to have both the grandmothers named.

When the dray brought the *Gazette*, Daunt showed me the piece that told the world that Mr and Mrs John David Daunt had been blessed with a daughter Sarah Celia Daunt. He cut the piece out, wedged it up on the wall above the cradle.

Sarah Celia Daunt, he said. Ah Sarah dear, this is the happiest time of my life, I tell you that for nothing.

I'd never until that moment wished I could read, but looked at the scrap of paper now and saw how words written down made something last. Written down, it was there for all time, never forgotten.

Daunt was a doting father, would come in early from the paddocks to hold the baby on his lap by the fire. Maeve was like the most indulgent granny, kissing her head and rocking her to sleep with an Irish song so sweet and lilting I was asleep myself, hearing her. The days passed in small quiet ways, everything circling round the baby. Feeding her and putting her down to sleep and playing with her when she woke up.

The hill was still my favourite place. I'd go there with Sadie of a late afternoon when the heat was gone out of the sun, spread out a rug and peel the layers of clothing off her. She kicked her fat legs and clutched at the clouds, crowing and chuckling. So tiny a thing in all that air. I held her up to let her feel the breeze on her nakedness. Let warm summer rain fall on us. She blinked at it on her skin, her body slick as a fish, and I knew life could offer no greater happiness than to watch your child greet the world.

MA AND PA sent word they wanted to meet the baby and see how everything was at Glenmire. They'd stop with Mary and Archibald and then come on to us, that was the plan. But Ma fell on the front steps and hurt her leg, so they couldn't come for a time. I was in no great hurry to see them, but would of liked them to bring the girl.

It was a hard weather that year, roads washed away and the creeks running a banker, so it was over the twelvemonth, Sadie sitting up and feeding herself, by the time they planned to travel. We expected them, but weeks passed.

One day I was out on the verandah with Sadie and saw in the distance a man on a horse coming along. Thought it would be word that Ma and Pa wasn't far behind. Daunt saw the horse too, waited with me. As it got closer we could see how fast it was going. A man on a horse coming that fast could only mean bad news.

Mary! I said. Oh God, it's Mary!

Knowing in that instant how I loved that bossy sister of mine. The dust came closer and when I saw the horse I knew it for Star. That meant it was word from Thornhill's.

I ran down to the road, Daunt along with me, and when the rider pulled up and jumped off, it was Jemmy Katter.

Rattled off his piece like he was afraid he might forget.

The New Zealand lass died, Mrs Daunt, he said. Dead this fortnight past.

Dead! I said. Dead how?

Got with child, he said. And died at Mr Scott's.

But she was a child herself, I said. And what's Mr Scott's?

Thought he must of got the message mixed up.

Don't know, Mrs Daunt, Jemmy said. With child, I know that, they say it was the darkie in the stables, the lad Phillip.

I knew then it must be true. But had no time to take it in, because Jemmy had more to say.

Mrs Daunt there's something else, he said. When the news come about the girl dead, Mr Thornhill took some kind of a fit.

A fit, I said. Dead! Not dead!

Not yet, Mrs Daunt, Jemmy said. But the doctor given up on him. Lying like a stone. You want to see him, you best come quick.

Sadie stood clinging to my knees and crying, too little to know what was wrong, only that something was. The girl dead. Oh, the cut of *too late, too late*. All those good intentions I'd had.

Had for a moment, then forgotten. That poor sad child, beyond any good intentions now.

And Pa dying. Might already be dead. That man I'd thought would be forever. My father, a man like a force of nature, shaping our lives, mine and the girl's both.

I'm sorry, Mrs Daunt, Jemmy said. To be the one has to tell you. Very sorry. But Mrs Daunt, you got to be quick.

Quick, I said. Got to be quick. Yes.

But I could not begin to think how to be quick. How to deal with this thing that had fallen like a boulder into my quiet day.

Go to the house now, Sarah, and sit a moment, Daunt said. He put an arm round me and turned me up the path.

Thank you for your speed, Jemmy, he said. Go through to the kitchen now, Maeve will give you something.

He sat me down in the parlour, took Sadie up on his arm.

I'm very sorry for that news, he said. Sad news of the girl, poor thing. But not too late to see your father. You can be on the road in an hour.

Pa and Ma and the world of the Hawkesbury were removed from me now in so much more than distance. Getting myself there seemed as impossible as a tree pulling its roots out of the dirt and walking.

On the road, I said. How do we, John? I can't do it.

You've got but the one father, Daunt said. You can. We'll make you up a bundle. Put the saddle on Champion. You'll kiss me goodbye and you'll kiss Sadie goodbye and you'll get up in that saddle and ride along with Jemmy.

My daughter and me had never been parted, not for a day,

hardly for an hour, since she was born.

I can't leave her, I said. Look at her, a babe still. Have to take her.

You can't take her, Daunt said. Think of it, dear, on the horse.

Of course I saw he was right. He didn't say any more, just took Sadie to the kitchen and I heard her singing along with Maeve, a song they did together, she liked to make out she knew the words. When he came back I was already feeling the lack of her.

You're torn, he said. Wouldn't be the fine loving mother you are if you weren't torn. She might cry once or twice, but it won't last. And for me, Sarah dear, it's the chance to be father and mother both. I'll rise to it, I promise you.

He was so sure, and it seemed that for once in my life I had to be told what to do.

I made up a bundle, put on my strong boots and my warm cloak, and when it was time to go I went into the kitchen and kissed the child, no more than I did a dozen times a day. Got on Champion and leaned forward on his neck. If I'd of looked back I couldn't of left. I was naked without a child in my arms, but Jemmy set a cracking pace and it was as much as I could do to keep up. The way he whipped up the horse, I could see he thought it was going to be a close call.

~

It was dark when we crossed the punt three days later and urged the horses up the hill to the house. Johnny was waiting at the gate. He'd put on flesh, was red in the face and shiny, and with another fancy waistcoat, satin with mother-o'-pearl buttons.

Dolly, he said. Good to see you, Dolly.

*Dolly* felt like another person. Someone I'd known, but long ago. Odd to walk up those front steps with Johnny and into the house over three years later. Everything as it had always been. I knew then just how far I'd travelled.

The others were in the parlour, Bub and Mary and Ma. Bub had always been like a man in his middle years, even as a boy. He'd grown into his older man's slowness and solemness, but still answered to Bub.

Mary was pale and thin, her babies coming too close together. The latest with her, only a few weeks old. She'd set out in the cart, she said, the minute she heard. A baby and a cart and a rough road, she said, never try it, Dolly.

I took the baby and snuffed up his smell, my heart yearning for Sadie. Little Charles felt strange in my arms, so tiny after my daughter. I had a pang of fear for her, stood with my cheek against Charles' downy head and sent a prayer along the miles. *Keep her from harm!*

Ma got her arms round me before I could stop her. I stood in her embrace stiff as a lobster. Wanted to go upstairs to Pa, but she held me back.

Know you want to see him, Dolly, she said. But too late now today, he's sleeping. Best let him rest.

*Rest*, the word hung in the air, none of us looking at each other. We knew he'd never be rested. Only the last rest, that was what was ahead of Pa.

I was ready to fight her.

I come all this way, I said. To see my Pa.

Now, Dolly, you listen to me, she said. I said no.

There was the steel showing in her voice.

It's me that's his nearest and dearest, she said. Not you. I'm the one decides.

His nearest and dearest! As if a man could only have one near and dear, and she'd made up her mind it'd be her. She'd got our Pa and she wasn't going to share him.

But no one should have to beg to see their own father on his deathbed and I wouldn't give her the satisfaction of denying me again. Sit tight, I said to myself. Just sit tight. Pa, hang on.

Without him the parlour seemed empty. I found myself watching the door for him to come in. He'd always taken up so much of the space in a room. His armchair empty, none of us wanting to sit in it. The bald velvet on the arm where he'd smoothed and smoothed at the nap.

How did it happen? I said. What kind of a fit?

That black girl give your pa his death blow, Ma said.

Johnny crossed one leg over the other, Mary turned her knitting. I thought, they've already heard all this.

Broke the poor old feller's heart, she said. Rutting with the black buck in the stables.

Was it Jingles, did you say, Mary said.

No, the other one, Ma said. Got rid of him quick smart. Got shot of Jingles too. Never liked him and his scowling ways.

Her eyes small with malice. She'd had to be sweetness and light in front of Pa. Now he was gone, or as near as, she could show her true colours.

Broke the poor old fellow's heart, she said again. The way she never said a word. All his kindness and never a word in return.

I knew that for a falsehood. I'd watched Pa with the girl. Enough for him that she was there. He'd never needed chit-chat.

But none of us wanting to argue with her. Johnny looked into the fireplace, Bub was picking at a bit of skin round his thumbnail.

The girl, I said, what happened with that poor child?

I was asking Johnny, but Ma jumped in.

Your pa heard the news right here in this room, she said. The man come and tell us, your pa jumped up out of his chair, I'll never forget the great shout he gave, fell straight down on the floor.

We all looked at the chair, the worn velvet. How he'd loved the feel of the nap under his hand.

I did warn him, she said. Leave her in New Zealand, I told him, she'll only bring trouble. Have them under your roof, nothing but trouble come of it. As we know, don't we.

She was waiting for me to see Jack in her words.

It's the bad blood, she said. The mixed blood.

For a moment I knew what it must of been like for the girl. Living with that hatred till she died of it.

Phillip would of been the only warmth in her days, but that warmth was what killed her. They'd of had a little time, the two of them, like Jack and me.

Then one day the girl would of been standing in a certain

way, in a certain light, and Ma would of seen. Would of guessed it was Phillip, or might of seen them together. She'd of got the constable. They'd of found a crime in it somewhere.

Then she'd of asked about. Oh, you want Mr Scott's, someone would of said. Best place for that kind of thing.

One of those places where girls in trouble went.

What lie did Ma cook up, that Pa let her go?

Ma would of taken her to Mr Scott's in the carriage and left her in the corner of some bare-boarded dirty room. They'd of done something to her, stop the baby, if Mr Scott's was that sort of place. Or kept her there till her time, if it was the other sort of place.

Whatever way it had been, in the end the girl was dead. Hardly more than a child herself. Dead, and on her own, with no one near who could speak her tongue or hold her hands.

I had to turn away so they wouldn't see the tears in my eyes. Johnny in his fancy waistcoat, jiggling his foot. Bub looking at his cracked farmer's hands, slanting them into the light. Mary with the stocking in her hands, she was halfway up the leg, head tilted to make sure every stitch went round the needle. They didn't hear the knife in Ma's words.

These people were my family, my blood kin. Brothers and sisters, but no better than strangers as far as our hearts went.

~

In the morning I didn't wait for her say-so, went up to see Pa straight after breakfast. But she was in the room with him.

Dolly dear, she whispered, you'll find he's wandering in his mind. Coming out with all sorts of nonsense. I wouldn't credit anything he told you.

What, you mean delirious? I said.

Only he's got some funny ideas, she said. None of them got any truth to them.

So it was already too late, I thought. He mightn't even recognise me. And if he did, what would I say to him? *You did wrong, but you meant well* or *Turned out all right, no thanks to you?*

Perhaps I had nothing to say to him. Other than a daughter's goodbye.

He was propped up in the bed. His mouth slack, a line of shiny dribble in one corner.

He made a sound, some kind of a mangled word, when I leaned over and kissed him. Scrabbled for my hand, held it on the coverlet.

Ma was settling into a chair, crocheting in her hand.

Need a bit of time alone with my Pa, I said. You'll have to leave us now.

The crotchet hook stopped in mid-stitch. I saw her mouth move. *How dare you*, she'd start.

I had the words ready.

He's my father, I'd say. He was my father before he was your husband.

I'd march her over to the door if I had to. As a matter of fact I was looking forward to it.

She must of seen it in my face.

I'll let you have five minutes, she said, trying for dignity.

Soon as she was gone Pa took a breath, licked his dry lips.

Dolly, he said. Want you to do something.

He could speak better than I'd feared. Hoarse and slow, but I could understand well enough.

Yes Pa, I said.

Rachel, he said, and I thought Ma might be right after all, he was mistaking me for the girl.

Felt a pang. That he was thinking about her and not me.

Thought I done right, he said.

It was no more than a whisper.

But I done wrong.

He shut his eyes then, and I wondered if it was a tear I could see shining under the lid, or the wetness of his eye. His chest heaved, gathering up the air.

Trying to put it right, he said. What I done.

Turned his head from side to side as if trying to get away from something. I squeezed his hand and we stayed like that for a time. Then he lifted his other hand in a jerky effortful way, wiped it across his face, opened his eyes.

Dick, he said. Up the Branch. Go up and fetch him back for me, there's a lass. Want to see him.

Yes, Pa, I said. Dick Blackwood, you mean?

His eye was as stern as ever it had been. Even lying like this he could still skewer you with that cold look.

Not Dick Blackwood, he said.

Slurred as it was, you could hear the scorn.

Dick Thornhill. Your brother.

Ah, after all this time. The fourth brother.

His tears brimmed over and slid down the deep furrows on

his cheeks. It was like the sun running backwards to see Pa cry. I leaned forward and tried an awkward hug. But he didn't want comforting. I felt his impatience.

Bring him here, he whispered. Here to me. Today, lass.

I could hear Ma on her way up the stairs.

Not tell your ma, he said.

I made an asking noise, wasn't sure if I'd heard him right.

Not tell your ma, he said. She don't see how a man might be sorry for what he done.

Then Ma was in the room again and he turned away, his grip slack, it was like sleep except the breathing was so heavy.

Come away now Dolly, she said. He's had enough.

She followed me down the stairs.

Hope he didn't trouble you with any nonsense, she said. Did he, Dolly?

But Anne was at the top of the stairs calling that Pa was wanting Mrs Thornhill. Nearly dead, the old feller, but he had a few tricks left in him.

IT WAS ODD seeing the skiff still tied up at the jetty as it always had been. I got in and took up the oars, shiny where you held them. Jack had held this oar, that last morning. Opened my hand to see the place his palm had been. Old grey wood, the grain opening up. That day felt as remote as Moses.

Rowed up to where the Branch angled off, stroked up past Devine's, past Matthew's, past Maunder's. The day had clouded over. The water grey, the bush still. Not a bird calling, not a cricket chirping. Only water whispering under the bow and the splash of the oars.

*Sorry for what he done.* To send a child away and not try to put it right till now! No wonder he wept.

Dick, he'd be another proud one. Laughed at me for saying he was sent off. My own free will, he'd said, but I wouldn't remind him of that hollow boast.

Leave well alone, Jack had said, but I hadn't. I was glad I'd tried, that day at Mrs Herring's. Wished I'd managed it better. Been not so blunt, gone a bit slower. Thought how it might feel from his side. Not blundering in wanting to know, just for the pleasure of curiosity met.

Jack, dear Jack, you knew, I thought. Knew about being the one pushed out of a family.

With Jack at the oars, the distance up the Branch had seemed nothing. On my own it was a long and weary way, the river adding bend on bend, surely long past where those dogs had come after us.

*You do get a man in a pickle, Sarah Thornhill!*

I'd remind Dick about that day. We'd have a good laugh about it. Late in the day for brother and sister to find each other, sad too that it took a father's death, but life was long, handed you these gifts when you least expected.

The jetty hadn't changed. Dick Blackwood's old skiff tied up and the dogs running down barking like they had before, but this time a man coming along behind. Shouted at them, they stopped barking, went back up to the house.

I got the skiff in, he leaned over and got the rope out of the bow, reached down to help me up. Kept holding my hand when I was standing beside him.

Dick Blackwood. The same black beard, overgrown dark hair, a brown face that had known plenty of weather. And his eyes. Sharp, like that other time. What I hadn't seen then, he had Pa's eyes. That sharp blue, and the same shape.

I hoped he was smiling but with the beard I couldn't tell.

Dick, I said, it's Sarah Daunt. Sarah Thornhill that was. Your sister.

Thought you might come, he said. Thought one of you'd be up to see me.

Saw you once, I said. At Mrs Herring's.

Oh yes, Dolly, he said. I remember. You and Jack Langland. Come up here, only the dogs come after you.

It's Pa, I said. He's poorly. In a bad way.

He nodded once. I wasn't telling him any news.

Wants to see you, I said. Sent me to say, will you come?

In among the beard there was some kind of a curl to his mouth.

Think he might be sorry, I said. You know. That he sent you off. Wants to make good.

Dick laughed. I could see his red tongue, his strong teeth.

Oh dearie me, Dolly, he said. Told you that other time. It weren't him sent me away. It was me went. More than willing.

He looked down the river as if he could see all the way I'd come, past the reeds and bush, to where Pa lay.

There's a lot never been said, I can see that, he said.

Up at the house I could see someone had put more wood on the fire, the smoke from the chimney faster and darker. His wife, that would be, getting the kettle boiling. Why Dolly, she'd say. Glad to have you under my roof at last.

I could of done with a dish of tea and a talk with her. Wanted us to make up for all those years.

Can't ask you in, Dolly, Dick said. Can't bring you in the house.

Why's that, Dick, I said. I got no quarrel with you. Between you and Pa, whatever it was.

He didn't rise to that, took me by surprise changing tack.

Jack Langland, he said. Think about him, do you? Still?

I was a woman married to a husband who was the best of men. But when Dick asked that, I knew some part of me would always rise to that name.

Yes, I said. Always be with me.

This Daunt feller, he said. He all right?

He's a good man, I said. I'm a lucky woman. But Dick, if you know something. About Jack. Be a kindness to tell me.

A kindness, he said. Not what I'd call it.

I remembered what I hadn't thought of till then. That last morning with Jack, watching the skiff come down out of the Branch. I'd wondered why, just for a second, but never thought about it again till now.

What is it, Dick? I said. Something you know that I don't.

You wasn't even born, he said. Nothing in it any of your doing.

Wasn't even born! I said. A silly young girl, yes, but not that much of a baby!

No, Dolly, Dick said. This goes right back. You not born, me just a lad. Not our doing, but set our lives down for us, the path we'd go on. The both of us, Dolly, you and me both, no matter it was none of our doing.

Best tell me, I said. You best tell me, Dick.

He turned towards the house. Something moved, a figure in the doorway, then another, a child that went to run out and was pulled back.

Can't have you in the house, he said. But I'll fetch us a drink of tea. Sit yourself down, Dolly.

I sat where he pointed, a fallen log by the water. The grass worn away on the river side, the wood polished from backsides. I was in her seat, that unknown person boiling the kettle.

Dick walked back down with mugs of tea and a plate of johnny-cakes.

Nothing against you, Dolly, he said. She says, make sure your sister gets one of these.

I wasn't hungry, but I took one and ate it as a greeting.

Makes a good johnny-cake, Dick said. Now I best tell you, much as I hate to say the words. There was trouble, see. With the blacks.

With the blacks? I said, when I thought he wasn't going to say any more.

I been with them since I was old enough to run about, he said. Played along with them, spoke their tongue. Closer than kin to me.

It was hard to imagine this grim man a child.

What sort of trouble, I said.

The blacks was camped up here, by the lagoon, he said. Mob of men come along. Killed them, all but five.

Speaking so low, I could only just hear.

Fact is, he said, that man was with them. Your father and mine.

With them, I said. How do you mean, Pa with them? With the blacks?

Not with the blacks, Dolly, he said. Old Tom Blackwood, he was here. Built that house. Had a wife, native way. And a little one, four or five years old.

Stared down the river as if he could see the little one there.

Them fellers didn't go for that, he said. Wanted to be rid of the blacks. Taking the corn and that. Couldn't abide that Blackwood was here with them. Come up on the tide one morning. Remember the *Hope*? Come up on that. Rushed the blacks while they was sleeping. Guns and swords. One feller had a whip. Laid about him with that whip. Got old Blackwood fair across the eyes. That was it for him, never made out light from dark, that day to this.

They needed the boat, I said. Pa got them up here. Needed the *Hope*. That's all.

He was in with the rest of them, Dick said. Never doubt that, Dolly. In with his gun along with the rest, shot one of the old fellers stone dead.

No! I said.

Dick got up, flung his tea leaves out on the grass.

You can say no if you like, Dolly, he said. Like everyone else. No, it never did happen. No, it weren't me. No, never heard a word about it. Eleven dead, Dolly, in the end. Some hurt so bad they might as well be. Two women got away in the bush, a few little ones with them and a young lad.

The doorway was empty now, but a shape in the window was someone watching. He didn't have to tell me. One of the ones got away, one of the little ones, would be the woman up there.

The old feller, I said. Lives down near us on the point.

Half his damn head gone, Dick said. Yes. You got the idea, Dolly. You got it now.

Pa holding out the bundle of food like someone begging, the man never looking his way.

I come up here after, Dick said. Threw in my lot with Blackwood and the ones that was left. Never seen that man, that day to this. Won't be seeing him now. You can tell him that, Dolly.

Jack? I said.

Hardly a whisper, because I almost knew.

You got the right to know, Dolly, he said. Jack come here one day, burning up with feeling. Your ma, she'd said some things about what happened.

He laughed, a hard *humph!*

Wise feller, Jack, he said. Knew you couldn't trust that woman far as you could throw her. She told him, You don't believe me, you ask Dick Blackwood.

Believe what, I said.

Jack's Ma was dead, Dick said. Before the killings. But she was kin to these folk here. Your ma told him the whole thing. Told him, the man you want for your father-in-law got the blood of your kin on his hands.

*Never want to see your face again.*

My word Jack loved you, Dick said. When I told him, I felt like that feller with the whip myself. Often thought, should I of done different. Told him no, it was all a story.

Why did you, I said. Why'd you have to tell him?

He looked away down the river so long I thought I wouldn't ever get an answer.

Dolly dear, he said finally, I told him because one fine day it would of come out. No water deep enough to hide a secret like that.

Said yourself, I wasn't even born! I said. Pa's secret, not mine!

That man's blood in your veins, Dolly, Dick said. Mine too. No getting away from that. That man's money putting the food in our mouths and the clothes on our backs, and the money coming out of what he done that day. I saw Jack go off, Dolly. Nothing else he could of done.

I'd been at the other end of that going off. Jack rowing to the jetty, boiling over and frozen. He'd flung my arm away like a spider.

No! I said.

My voice echoed back at me across the water.

You wanted to know, he said. Now you do. I'm glad to see you, Dolly, but best you go now.

He untied the skiff, stood with his foot on the stern waiting.

Hard thing to hear, he said. Call me a liar if you like. If it helps. Welcome to do that.

Came over to where I was still sitting, got an arm under me, got me on my feet.

In you get, he said. Got a long row ahead of you.

I tried to hang onto him, but he peeled me away, got me in the boat, pushed it into the deep water. The current caught the bow, swung it round, pulled the boat downstream. Dick lifted a hand, turned away, walked up towards the house.

The boat slid round a bend and it was all gone, Dick, jetty, house, lagoon. Bush, water, the birds with red beaks in among the reeds, everything so ordinary I wanted to pretend none of that other place was there. No Dick, no jetty, no house, no lagoon. A dragonfly hovered and darted away. A black bird swooped from one side of the river to the other. A breeze ruffled the reeds, roughened the water, was gone.

Everything as it had always been. Only the person looking at it was struck dead.

The sun was still shining, but shining darkness. Every leaf and reed and twig carried a load of strangeness. The hand on my knee was someone else's, sallow in the sunlight like a corpse. My eyes dry with staring.

Tears would of been a luxury.

The boat slewed around, nudged into a wall of reeds. A bit of dry leaf fell on my skirt and clung. Things went on obeying the rules they always had, things falling, hearts beating.

I squeezed my eyes shut and everything went to blood. It was a sickness that had hold of me from inside. It lived in my chest, my belly, in the softness behind the bone of my head. I hunched down over myself like a poisoned rat. It helped to be a rat. They took the green powder and went in circles, looping, falling, getting up, falling again. Dragged their bodies in somewhere dark.

There was no darkness here, only Dolly Thornhill bent over the thing inside her.

Such pretty pretty stories. I'd swallowed them down and smiled. My Pa, that good man, so generous to the blacks, oh, how proud of him I was. And Jack, a grand story, wasn't it sad, lost to me because he was proud and Dolly Thornhill so much higher up than him.

Those stories were turned inside out like a bag. All those years the inside was there, only I'd never thought to look.

I hadn't done it, no. Hadn't lifted the gun. But Dick was right. I'd eaten the good food off the cedar table with the double damask cloth. Slept in the soft beds. Sat in the parlour, never known a day's hunger or cold, never asked where any of it come from.

Jack was a hollowness inside me, scooped out like a hanging carcass, an empty place where life had been.

Noises came out of me, a groaning of things coming apart. I'd lived in a cosy place made out of secrets and lies. Now I was in another country, and its climate had no mercy.

I HAD NOTHING to say to Pa. No words. But I wanted him to see me. Let him die knowing that I knew the thing he'd spent his life hiding.

I went in the back door. Had a glimpse of Ma in the parlour, asleep in the armchair. Head back, mouth open, ugly as a toad. I looked at her neck where the blood ran strong in the big vein there. Knew there was a killer in me too.

At the foot of the stairs I heard Mary in the kitchen, a rumble of men's voices, someone talking about *mud up to their hocks*. Someone else laughed. A hand opened the stove door and threw in wood, the kettle clanged, the baby let out a cry and was hushed.

I'd never again be in the world where people smiled and talked, not knowing. This thing would always be with me now, stuck to me as fast as my shadow.

I crept up the stairs into Pa's room. He was asleep. I watched the bedclothes rise and fall on his chest. His face flickered, tugs of feeling.

My Pa. Always been part of myself, like my big toe. My Pa, part of the world that was always there. He was a stranger now.

The dawn with the guns and the people asleep. That hand on the coverlet, spots of black where the sun had got him, red scars, the knuckles bumpy and swollen. That was the hand that had raised the gun and pointed it at a person.

Asleep, Dick said. Dawn, all asleep. No time to run or fight. Guns and swords. And one feller with a whip.

Oh, I hoped Pa wasn't the one with the whip.

He'd kept those things with him in the eye of his memory. They'd been with us, but not seen, every time he carried me as a child, every time we met round the table and he served out the good food. With us when he sat on the verandah staring at the bush through his telescope. They were written on every line of his face if you knew how to read it.

They were with us now, in this room behind that skull. He'd made another kind of skull to keep those memories, not made of bone but silence.

He woke up. Strained upwards, a painful twist of his lips, the cords in his neck standing out. Looked at me and behind me. Looking for Dick.

His head dropped back on the pillow, his hand moved on the coverlet as if brushing something away.

You saw him, he said, but unclear. Saw Dick.

His hand fumbled towards me, but I drew back. Something rose up in my throat, like a creature in there blocking the air.

I met his eye and let him see. It was a savage kind of triumph. Here I am, your daughter who knows what kind of father she's got. What legacy he's left her. What you did, that can never be put right. Have a good look, Pa. Die uncomforted.

He was breathing as if he'd run up a flight of stairs. I thought, he'll die, here and now. I hoped so.

But his chest went on heaving. He said something, very slurred. *Bad days,* I thought it was, but I wasn't sure.

Bad days, he said. By God I wish it all different.

His tongue licked round his pale lips. He seemed to want to speak again, but closed his eyes. His breath drew hard in and out, a kind of snore. He gave a quick gasp and a jerk and woke up.

You happy, he said. You happy, Dolly, with Daunt? Are you?

Kept his eyes on me like the grip of a hand, but weakening with the effort to make the words.

By God I wish it different, he said. Wish it all different. Have it to do again. And do it different.

Waiting for me to say something. I couldn't and I wouldn't. Any word would be like forgiving him.

He stared, trying to get inside me with his eyes. Then he was asleep again, long heavy breaths.

~

He lived another week but said nothing more. We sat round the bed listening to him breathe. For gaps of time he was so still that one of us would lean forward to check. Sometimes he seemed so nearly dead that every breath was a surprise. The only sound was the click and rustle of Mary turning her knitting, or putting it down to nurse the baby. Her gaunt face tender, watching him. Bub stared out the window as if he was thinking about the weather. Johnny tapped his fingers on his knees, got the watch out of his waistcoat pocket and stared at its face.

Ma tried to touch me once, I flung up my arm to be rid of her. She was still Margaret Grant when it happened but Pa must of told her. She'd stored her knowing away, brought it out like a knife when it suited her, to slice me from Jack, slice Jack from me. The knife so cunning it couldn't be seen. Never would be now, because anyone holding a lamp up to it would be *wandering in his mind*.

Cunning as a fly, that woman.

And my mother? Did she know? She must of. That's why Pa stood begging. Could you sicken of that kind of knowing, turn to bones and yellow skin? Did she die of it?

Pa knew Dick wouldn't come. But knew he'd tell me. Sending me up to fetch him was confessing, but at a remove.

Watching my brothers and my sister, I knew why he'd done it that way, said without saying. How could you find the words? How could you drop this thing into lives where people fiddled with their watches, worried about the hay, doted on their babies? How would you ever come together with them again, the shame between you like an unwanted guest that never left?

I knew why he hadn't spoken because I couldn't either. I tried to picture Mary looking up from the baby to listen, or Bub or Johnny. *I met our brother today*, I'd say. *Found out some things.*

I couldn't do it. They wouldn't hear, wouldn't believe. Like I'd done with Dick, they'd say *no!*

That was part of it. But more it was the shame, that I couldn't bear to hold up to the light. This was how Pa must of felt, all those years. I was drawn into the same dirty secret he'd lived with for so long.

It would be with me now till the day I died. Once you knew, there was no way to not know. There was no cure for the bite of the past. When bad was done, it was like a stone rolling. You put your foot to that stone and pushed and there was no stopping it. Every roll of the stone brought more bad. You had to live with it, and your children too. And their children, down the line. Whether they knew it or not, they lived in its shadow.

I could hardly bear to touch the open wound of the idea of Jack. Somewhere tangled up in that idea was a lie. Not the lie Ma told, that he'd gone off out of pride. The bigger lie was mine. I'd lied to myself about who he was.

I'd been so proud, telling Ma that Jack's mother being a darkie made no difference. Don't care if he's black white or brindle, I'd said. But it did make a difference. Not the colour of his skin but himself, the man he was. No one called him a black, not till Ma did, but that was the truth of him, a truth no one wanted to own.

He'd tried to show me, that day he talked about his mother. Mr Langland told him he should pass for Portugee and I'd done the same, only different words. Brushed aside his darkness, proud of myself for doing it. Couldn't see what I was telling Jack, that I'd take the white part of him but not the black.

He knew better than me. Knew the colour of your skin and the colour of your mother's skin wasn't a thing you could brush aside. It was part of who you were, even if no one wanted to talk about it.

He knew, even before he knew why.

When he left me on the road that day it seemed like the end of the world, because the man I knew as well as myself had become a stranger. I saw now what I couldn't see then. If Jack looked a stranger that day, it was because he'd always been one.

The final day, you could feel Pa restless, some spark of will fighting the sluggish body. He stirred and muttered, tossed a hand up in the air, kicked a foot under the bedclothes.

His eyes flickered open, his lips shivered. But if he wanted to speak after a lifetime of silence, it was too late.

FROM THE moment I got off the horse at Glenmire, they all saw something was amiss. Sadie watched me solemnly, as if seeing a different mother. Daunt took one look at me.

Sarah dear, you're ill, he said. Straight to bed with you.

I slept, it seemed for weeks. Even when I wasn't asleep I lay under the bedclothes not able to find the will to get up. The house closed itself down round me.

Daunt looked after me every way he could. Brought me the cup of tea of a morning and the jug of hot water. The lovely sound of the water going out of the jug into the basin woke me. Then I'd remember.

The only good and simple thing in my life was Sadie. Oh, she was patient with me, knew to come halfway to meet my sadness. Curled up beside me on the bed, sucking the bit of rag she wouldn't be parted from, warm and alive. She'd lay her hand on some part of me, like a rope that might save me.

When she'd had enough of her silent mother she'd fetch her doll and tuck it in beside me under the covers and slip away. I'd hear her out in the kitchen with Maeve, her clear voice trying the tune of their song. The splash of water, she'd be helping Maeve do the potatoes, the afternoon sun slanting in the door onto the boards, the water in the bowl shining as it shifted.

Sometimes Daunt lay down beside me, but he didn't try to make me talk.

After a time I got up, but I wasn't right. There was a black knot in everything I did. It would creep up on me, a slow pain. I'd be doing the bread and the tears would start to fall into the dough, and Maeve would make me go and lie down. Or I'd find myself in front of the hearth with the poker in my hand and the fire gone out, the tears running down my face, and Daunt would come in and take the poker from me.

I'd make myself picture it: that lagoon and the people sleeping, the men coming up on the *Hope*. Pa lifting his gun and squinting along the barrel.

What happened then? Did they bury the bodies or throw them in the lagoon? Did they laugh and slap each other on the back?

No, they'd put their heads together and decided to tell nobody what had happened. Would of shaken hands all round the circle of men and promised never to tell. My own Pa there with them. Shaking hands, promising.

My thoughts were like stones. Hundred years of wearing away, they'd be still the same. The past could never be any way but the way it was.

The sun rose and set again, clouds gathered and cleared, wind blew from the east and then from the west. It would be the same when I was dead and gone. That was a comfort. I was a part of the great world. But the great world didn't need me and the darkness I carried round with me.

Me and Daunt sat by the fire of an evening as we always had, but he didn't read or scratch in the ledger. Sat staring at the fire, leaving silences between us like an invitation.

More than once I went to tell him. John, I'd say, but then I'd have to stop.

Yes? he'd say. What is it, Sarah dear?

I'd shake my head. I could see how easy something could disappear. Pa was gone and I'd be gone one day, and so would Jack. Even Ma would have to die in the end. All it took was each one of us deciding not to say. Once the story was gone, there'd be no bringing it back. All those things might as well never of happened.

Shame would keep us silent, shame and the wishing that it was different. Dick and that woman who'd sent me down a johnny-cake, they'd tell their children the story. There was no shame in it for them, only grief. But who would listen to them?

The knowing was Pa's poisonous gift to me, and I was sick with it. But I couldn't be sorry I knew. The woman who'd smiled and laughed and went about her days with a light heart was no better than a fool, or an accomplice.

I got some things one day, put them in a gunny-sack. Leg of mutton, pound of butter. A loaf. Potatoes and greens. Not all we had, of course. Just all I could carry.

I'd never been to where the blacks lived, but it was easy enough to follow the narrow track their feet had made in the grass. It was a bigger camp than the one at home. Eight or ten humpies and a couple of fires with people sitting round. They glanced at me sideways and looked away. I knew one of the women, she'd been up the house a few times, and there was a boy that I'd trusted with a billy one day and he'd brought it back shiny with the scouring it'd had. The old woman with the bad eyes. A little girl, five or six, with a blanket. When she saw me looking she pulled it up over her head.

I stood on the edge of the clearing with the gunny-sack hanging from my hand. Standing at their door, same way they stood at mine.

The woman I knew got up and moved towards me. Stopped a few yards off. I held out the bag. Held it out so long my arm started to shake. Then I put it down on the ground, got some of the food out.

The others were watching now.

The shining meat, the loaf of bread. Like stones in my hand. Like rubbish. Pa had been the beggar before. I'd be the beggar now.

*As cold as charity*. Now I knew how true that was. Cold for the one getting the charity, but dead as ice for the person giving it, when giving was a way of admitting something so bad you couldn't let yourself think it.

No use to anyone, not in the long run. The food eaten and gone, nothing changed the day after. I didn't know what else to do, so that was what I did. But the bitterness, knowing I had no better thing to offer. No way to mend what had gone so wrong.

The woman stepped forward and took the food from the ground. The boy walked over, picked up the sack. They went back to the fire and put the things down beside them.

Nothing said, no look exchanged. The clearing silent except for the whistle of the breeze. I was hardly breathing. A lizard could slow itself down, be no more than a pulse of blood ticking at its throat. That was as much as I wished for, to be a living stone.

When I got back to the house it was near dark, Daunt waiting for me on the verandah. He said nothing, took me by the hand, led me like a blind person. Sat me in the armchair. Went away, got back with a basin of water and a flannel, washed my face as if I was a child, put my hands in the water between his and smoothed them together. Had a towel over his shoulder, dabbed at my face, dried my hands.

All the while not a word.

Sat me up at the table, put a bowl of soup in front of me. Opened my hand and put the spoon in it and I ate a little. He led me into the bedroom, put me to bed, got in beside me. I lay with my back to him and separated from him by a small distance. It was a dead-dark night, me and Daunt nothing but breath and body.

There's a lot no one ever spoke of, I said. In our family.

Yes, Daunt said. Yes, Sarah dear. You've not been the same since you got back.

Having to find the words made me tired.

Thought it might be to do with your father, he said.

Yes, I said. Yes it is. To do with my Pa.

Saying *Pa* was like undoing a knot. Everything fell out, every single last twist. Out in the air in words it was a filthy thing.

When I was done it seemed nothing could ever be spoken again.

Daunt felt for my hand among the bedclothes.

Sarah my dear, he said.

He would think of what he might say to comfort me. But comfort could only be a lie.

That's a terrible thing, Sarah dear, he said. A terrible sad thing.

He was holding my hand as if to stop me falling, but if I was going to fall, his hand told me we'd fall together.

~

I didn't go to the blacks' camp again. They walked up to the house now and then, as they always had. They knew something was wrong. The woman who'd taken the food from me that day looked into my face.

Been sick missus? she said.

Yes, been sick, I said. Better now.

I went to the cupboard, got both the loaves, all the eggs, the smoked hock that was going to be our tea. Made up a package of sugar, a bag of flour. Went to the press, got a couple of blankets.

Word got round: Mrs Daunt was a soft touch.

I was ashamed every time I handed over the things. The women didn't thank, and for that I was grateful.

I WAS out on the hill late one afternoon with Sadie, she was three going on four, the girl and Pa in the ground nearly two years. Daunt had got a goat from somewhere that thought it was a dog, followed us everywhere, sat beside us now on the hill.

Sadie loved as much as I did the light and shadows the clouds made on the land, the brush of air on our skins. Every day the sky was a new thing, the feel of the air, the shapes of the clouds. The roos hopped up close. She knew to be still, they'd take us for part of the rocks, shift round on their long feet, curl their tails up like another leg behind them, twitch their ears.

I saw a movement, a man walking on the road from Gammaroy. That usually meant some feller on his beam ends, nothing in his pack, come to cadge from Mrs Daunt.

I was thinking what I had in the cupboard. Most of yesterday's loaf, could give him that, and there was a shank of mutton, if he has a dog the poor creature will be glad of the bone.

But the man coming along in a knee-high cloud of dust was alone. That was out of the ordinary. As a rule these poor old fellers had lost everything, always some sad story, but a dog where all their love and longing went.

As he got closer it seemed to me that under the hat his face was dark. That was unusual too, a darkie on his own humping a bluey.

A fold of the land hid him for a minute or two, then showed him again, first his hat, then his face, close enough to call out to, and I stood up. Could see now that his face wasn't dark of skin, but from a net of lines, patterned like a beetle's back.

At first I thought poor feller, what in God's name has happened to him, it was like no pox marks or burns I'd ever seen. Then I saw it was tattoos. But not just coloured skin. Every one of the lines on his face was a ridge of scar. A picture carved into the living flesh.

I knew two things in the same thought. They were marks made as a great work of pain. And the man who owned the face was Jack Langland.

Sadie was frightened, I felt her run into my legs and wrap her arms round them so I stumbled, caught my toe on the hem of my skirt. Jack put out his hand, caught me by the forearm, went on holding it.

It's not ever Jack, is it, I said.

He said nothing, only put back his head and laughed so all

the lines twisted into new shapes. I half expected his tongue to be tattooed.

I was trying to calm the child burrowing into my legs, too frightened of this laughing striped man even to cry, and down at the house Blackie was barking her silly head off, and that brought Daunt out to see what was going on. Looked up to the hill, at the man and the child and me all wound together, and started up towards us, Blackie straining at the leash.

Well, Jack said, Well, here we are.

Looking at me the way I was looking at him, as if my face was carved like his and had to be read slow, one bit at a time.

Jack, I said. A few things happened since you been gone.

Yes, he said.

Pa told me things, I said. Well, not Pa. I saw Dick.

You been told, then, he said. You know.

Yes, I said. Dick told me.

I moved towards him. It wasn't that he moved back exactly, but he tightened himself away from me.

Pa made sure I knew, I said. The one thing he did right.

I heard he died, Jack said.

His eyes, there were his eyes that I'd never forgot. That colour I'd never seen on any other man.

Wasn't sorry when I heard, he said. Hope he had a hard time of it.

He did, I said. Died burned up with it.

Then Daunt was striding up the last bit of the hill and Jack turning to meet him.

Jack Langland, Mr Daunt, he said and put out his hand. Met you at Mrs Daunt's father's place years ago.

It was a funny roundabout way of saying it.

I was a friend of his son Will that drowned, Jack said. You might remember.

The manners Daunt had learned at the school he'd hated stood him in good stead, even when he had to deal with a man with a carved face.

Oh yes, he said. I recollect you, Mr Langland, and I see you have been in New Zealand.

Yes, indeed, Jack said, been there this last few years, whales keeping me busy.

Both as if they'd taken a bet not to say a word about a face like nothing else on earth.

Did you come on foot, Daunt said.

He was calm, looked Jack in the eye, but I knew my husband and knew he was flustered.

Not from New Zealand! Jack said, stopped himself from laughing aloud. Walked when I had to, Mr Daunt. Kind souls give me a ride on their carts some good part of the way.

I pictured the cart pulling up behind the man trudging along. Hop in friend! some cheerful feller or other doing a kind deed would sing out, then see the face under the hat. My word that would startle the wits out of your average bullocky doing the Quirindi run.

Come to see Mrs Daunt, Jack said, though no one had asked.

*Mrs Daunt.* Did I have to call him *Mr Langland*?

He'd never called me Dolly, or Sarah. Only ever *Sarah Thornhill*. It was that name, *Thornhill*. He wouldn't say it.

Bit of old history needs sorting out, Jack said. Hoping she might see her way clear to helping me with it.

Old history, Daunt said, and I was thinking for God's sake Jack, you don't want to talk about our old history, surely to heaven, not this late in the day!

About the girl, Mr Daunt, Jack said. The girl I fetched from New Zealand, God forgive me. You would of heard she died. Bit of business needs attending to.

You're welcome among us, Mr Langland, Daunt said. Welcome as long as you care to stay.

The words were warm, but I knew all of John Daunt's tones and knew this was not a warm tone.

A kind offer, Jack said. I thank you for it, Mr Daunt.

He led the way down the hill so I could see the long hank of hair hanging down his back. He went ahead of us, even though the hill was not his but Daunt's, and in the normal way the owner of a hill would go first. It was so Daunt and I could walk together. He knew we'd need a moment to sort ourselves out. What man could be pleased to see his wife's old love on his doorstep? When I smiled, Daunt smiled back, but there was a wariness to it.

At the house he was hospitable, pouring his best Jamaica and settling Jack in his own armchair. I made myself busy in the kitchen, busier than I needed, getting the meal ready and seeing to Sadie. All the ordinary everyday things had gone strange because of Jack being in the next room. There was the glass in his hand that I'd washed and put away a hundred times, but now it was like a thing I'd never seen before.

My feelings gone foreign to me, too. I'd longed for Jack all that time, then the longing had faded into something sad but faraway, and now he was back, and how I felt I didn't know.

There was something unhinged about hearing Jack and Daunt making themselves pleasant in the next room. I heard bits of what they were talking about, the whales that had taken over where the seals left off, Daunt wanting to know how long the harpoon was that you threw at the whale, and how many yards of rope on it, and how many barrels you might get out of a whale of ordinary size, and Jack returning the favour, how many acres, and how many sheep, and how many could you shear before you had to stop and sharpen the blades?

The meal was a strain, what with Sadie fidgeting and Maeve in and out to have another stare at Jack.

I had to stop myself staring, too. Not to marvel at the lines on his face, astonishing though they were, but to see what had brought him here to my door. I could not imagine, only knew that whatever it was, it could be no light thing.

AFTER THE meal, when Sadie was finally coaxed to sleep, we settled by the fire. Daunt fussed about, making sure I was comfortable, the bolster for my feet and a cushion for my back. His way of telling me it was all right. And of reminding anyone who might be watching that I was his wife, who had forsaken all others.

I found myself shy of Jack. He sat in my husband's chair, a man contented in his own skin, no matter how extravagantly that skin was decorated. He'd chosen who to be, and to show it on his face. This Jack had travelled into a different self. Another man had been carved out of the one I'd known.

I wasn't the woman he'd known, either. Sarah Thornhill was still here, because it was Sarah Thornhill he'd come to see. Sarah Thornhill was the one who'd shared that history with him. Whispered into his ear in the dark and kissed him, pressed herself so tight up against him that she'd felt his heart beating.

But day by day Sarah Thornhill had been replaced by Sarah Daunt. Sarah Daunt had no way to speak to Jack Langland, because she didn't know him, even though she could tell you how the last hair of his eyebrow grew.

These two men I knew so well could hardly of been more different. But both were the best of men. I was a lucky woman to have two men like them in my life. Luckier than ever I deserved.

I'd never used the word *love* to John Daunt. We didn't talk like that to each other. But I watched him with Jack and knew that I loved him now, as surely as Sarah Thornhill had loved Jack Langland.

Got to go back a bit, Jack said. To get to why I'm here. Bear with me, if you please, Mr Daunt, all this old history.

Indeed, Daunt said. All the time in the world, Mr Langland.

You remember the girl, Jack said.

For a moment I thought he was going to tell me she wasn't dead, only sent away, and Ma put it about that she was dead. I had it all laid out in my mind and the smile was coming to my face.

The New Zealand girl? Daunt said. Yes. A sad thing that she died.

Indeed, Jack said.

There was a little silence where I thought about miracles. A man might appear from nowhere that you'd thought never to see again. But no amount of wishing could bring back a girl who'd died.

It was me took her away, Jack said. Me brought her to Mrs Daunt's father. Not a day goes by I don't regret it.

Leaned into the fire so the light fell on his face. You could see every chip the chisel had made. Hard to think how anyone could stand what it took to mark that picture on their face.

You know my Ma was a black native, he said. There was a time, God forgive me, when I turned my back on that. Made out to myself like I was white. Well, Mrs Daunt's father wanted the girl with him. Wanted it worse than any man I've seen want anything, and I thought it was right. Let her grow up with her father's folk, I thought. Grow up white. Like I done.

He seemed no older and no younger than when I'd seen him last. The lines on his face rode over any of that. He'd be the same for the rest of his days, beyond age.

But I could of said no, he said. I see it very clear now. I should of said no. Time I saw it was a mistake it was too late. Mrs Daunt knows I couldn't take her back. But I could of stayed close, and I didn't. Had my own troubles. Left her there.

You're here to confess, I thought. I'm the only one can hear it, because I was there too. This is why you've travelled all the way from the Southern Ocean.

All that's between me and my maker, he said. Not what I'm here to tell you. Thing is, I heard the girl was dead. Then I get word, the girl's granny wants to see me. Old lady, not long for this world.

Her granny, I said. Then she was no orphan.

No such thing as an orphan among those folk, Jack said. Think I told you that, Mrs Daunt, back then.

He glanced at me. Remembered as well as I did that day in the cave, the sweetness of being side by side. But nothing in his look invited me into that private thing we shared.

For this old lady, he said, not enough to know the girl's dead. They got their ways, see. How to do things proper way when a person dies. Send them on their way, sing their life. Who they were, how they lived, how they died. This old woman can't go to her grave with that not done for the girl.

He looked at me and I wished I could brush away the marks on his face, so I could see what he was thinking.

You're the one was there, Mrs Daunt, he said. Only one now can say how it was.

No I can't, Jack, I said. I didn't see. Just one day a man come on a horse, told us she was dead.

That was a lie. I was there, as much as anyone was.

The old lady not wanting chapter and verse, Jack said. But of every soul still living on this earth you're the one knows most. Other than that woman, and I won't be asking her.

A single half-hour: me upstairs on the bed, Ma warping the shape of our lives.

Her granny would go to her grave with her heart eased, Jack said. To hear it from someone. To know someone was willing.

The crackling of the fire was like another conversation going along beside the one we were having.

Willing, I said. You mean, go there. To New Zealand.

Yes, he said.

Go to New Zealand! Daunt said. You'd come here and ask! Sit there and ask!

Not asking, Mr Daunt, Jack said. Laying it out, that's all. Up to Mrs Daunt.

But you've come here, Daunt said. To take her! You think I'd let her go?

He was on his feet now, standing over Jack, and if Jack would of stood up, Daunt would of struck him.

John! I said. Leave it now!

I was half-laughing in my fear and confusion to see him shaping up to Jack when surely it was a muddle of some kind, surely in heaven Jack had not really meant me to go with him to New Zealand!

You'll not go! Daunt said. I'm telling you now, you'll not go!

He'd never in all the time I'd known him had that shake of rage in his voice. In the harshness of it I knew his love, as I'd never truly known it in his softness.

Think of it, he said. Those seas, the gales in that ocean. Your brother drowned in those same waters, or have you forgotten that?

I'd hardly understood what Jack was asking, but Daunt had seen the whole thing clear in an instant.

Sit down for God's sake, John, I said. There's been a stick got hold of by the wrong end here. Jack don't mean that.

But I do, Mrs Daunt, he said. That's why I come. I've said my piece. Now if you'll kindly show me, Mr Daunt, where you'd have me sleep, I'll leave you be.

Daunt sat down, stood up again.

I come to ask, Jack said. That I had to do. Up to Mrs Daunt now. And yourself.

But Mrs Daunt had something of a chill in her marrow, because now she could see what was being asked of her, and she was not equal to it.

In an awkward silence we pushed the chairs back, got the rugs to make a shakedown in front of the fire. When it was done we all looked down at it, the rugs and the pillow spread out where Jack would sleep.

The sand on the floor of that cave was like silk through your fingers.

Yes, Daunt said. Goodnight, Mr Langland.

In the bedroom every sound Daunt and I made getting into our nightclothes was as loud as the only sound in the world. In the bed we lay well apart. He blew out the lamp but neither one of us settled for sleep.

To even think of it, he said. To ask! When it might leave a child motherless! Not to mention your husband a widower! And for what?

Hoarse with wanting to shout but having to whisper, because on the other side of the wall Jack lay with the firelight flickering over his face.

A sad old woman sitting by a fire in that place I couldn't imagine, breathing slow through all the days of Jack making the journey here. Waiting for Mrs Daunt. Mrs Daunt, her lucky life that stood with its feet in other peoples' sadness. I had to go, because this was a hand held out to say, *Here is this chance. Take it.*

But surely I could not go. Leave my child! Have her grow up with a dead drowned mother who'd gone off with a man come out of the past!

The girl was gone. There was nothing of her left in the world. I could barely remember her face, wondered if I'd ever seen it clear. I'd never thought to ask myself the thing this New Zealand granny wanted to know, how it had all come about, how it had been at the end.

I didn't even know where she was buried. There'd be a headstone somewhere. *Rachel Thornhill*, it would say, and that would be a lie, but there was no one to know any better. That was another kind of shame.

I'd never known the people sleeping by the lagoon. The shame of what had happened there was mine only because of the blood I carried. But the girl was known to me. She'd withered under my eyes while my mind was somewhere else, and that shame belonged to me.

Daunt was asleep, lying apart from me, but a foot found mine in his sleep. I could feel a tremor through it now and then, as if his body was still storming inside. Sadie sighed and rustled in her cot. I slid out of bed, felt my way over to her. Picked her up, she made a little asking noise. Her hand brushed over my face, her head pillowed itself on my shoulder, she slept again.

I stood with her for a long time, feeling her breathing against me. My most precious gift, that I had not earned.

~

I woke as sudden and complete as if someone had jabbed me. Daunt was still asleep, folded into himself but with one foot still touching mine. The sun had laid a stripe along the dresser. I knew that stripe, watched it every morning as it moved across the doily, shone into the mirror, slid away along the wall. The sun would go on rising out of the hills, making that moving stripe, until the doily and the mirror and the wall were all crumbled away to dust. Even then it would go on rising and setting and shining on other walls, other women, until Sarah Thornhill was forgotten, not even a name in anyone's memory.

I could hear the birds outside, all those tiny lives not knowing they had such a short time to find a mate, make their nests, hatch the chicks.

They didn't know, but I did. Life was not for ever.

You could put a number on the sunrises I'd had. It was a big number, three hundred and sixty-five for every one of the twenty-three years I'd been alive. I was planning on having a good number more, but no one could name that number. Not yet. When I was dead someone would be able to say exactly what that number was. Big or small, it was a particular number.

Every moment that passed, while I lay and watched the sunlight move round the room, was a moment that would never come back.

I counted them. One, two, three. Every one, gone forever.

The stripe of sun got thinner, cut off by the wall. I will go, I thought. Otherwise I'll be dead and it not done.

When Daunt woke up he lay still for so long I thought he must of gone back to sleep.

Sarah dear, he said. I'm frightened to have you go. The thought of losing you to the cold sea. Can't live with that thought. It happens, you know it does. Every day of every week, somewhere on the ocean.

I'll hear him out, I thought. Then I'll tell him. There'll be no arguing. I'll make it clear, my mind's made up, I can do no other. Only go.

If I loved you less I'd forbid you, he said. Tie you to the bedhead and fight that man.

He made a grimace half smile and half wince, picturing that unequal contest.

He was a dear man. I was sorry I'd have to go against him.

But this thing, he said. I can only say to you, this is your choice to make. If you go I'll be in a fret of fear every minute and pray God every day for you to come back safe. But Sarah dear, I'll not stand in your way.

I nearly laughed or wept then, because these were the old words from out of the past. *He told me to tell you, he won't stand in your way.*

# PART FOUR

WHAT A smelly dirty thing that boat was. The first week at sea was all right, calm seas and sunshine, but then the storm came down on us. Every wave swelled up and broke at the top, the spray flying out ahead of itself, the top of the wave smashed off into foam, and when the boat upended and headed into the hollow between two waves we were so far down the wind fell silent. Didn't know what was worse, the nasty silent thing down in the trough, the water stretched and mottled like a caul, or the scream of the wind on the crest, the boat heaving and shuddering and the foam flying into our faces.

Never been one to pray but by God I prayed then. Not to be saved, I thought that was something not even God could arrange, but for a quick death. A quick death, and my daughter to forgive me.

Leaving her had been even worse than I'd feared. My last sight of her was seeing her wave from the verandah, her hand in Daunt's. I'd ridden half a mile feeling tugged. Finally had to turn the horse, gallop back, say goodbye again.

The second goodbye was worse. Daunt pale and stiff, trying to smile for the sake of the child, and I thought, what kind of fool am I, leaving this dear man and the dear child we made together, for some old woman a stranger to me? Sadie not crying, but looking at me as if she was thinking the same thing I was. *Will I ever see her again?*

Look after her, John, I cried in my mind as the boat swung and jarred, every timber creaking against every other. Keep her from harm, my beloved child!

That far-off day when *Industry* went down, another mother would of seen the same green angry ocean, would of felt a boat like this one toiling through the waves, heard that cruel whistle of the wind in the ropes. She'd of gone into it, breathing water and crying, *Keep her from harm! Keep my child from harm!*

If I die here, I thought, sinking with this pip of a boat, there'll be justice in it.

Then the sickness come down over me like a bag. There was a place under the deck with a few berths, the water not three inches from your face behind the planks. I wished to die. There was a dark patch on the wood, Lord only knows what kind of stain, and in my misery it took on the shape of a grinning horse's skull, other times a great fat beetle.

Oh my word I was sick. Make it stop, make it stop, I whispered, but this time there was no Will to laugh me out of it.

No time, no place, no me, no other. Nothing but this grey sick thing and the dark patch next to my eye. Sarah Thornhill, Sarah Thornhill, I said, as I had in the pangs of childbirth, but the sounds meant nothing.

Jack brought me water in a tin cup and a wet flannel for my face. Told me it would not last for ever. Sat with me, held my hand, and the feel of his hand told me he thought I was worth saving. Gulfs wider than oceans lay between us, the deep water of the past. But the touch of his skin was a bridge.

He was right that it would not last. One morning the heave of the water was no longer an enemy, but simply the way the world was. I was myself again, went up on deck, held the hard cold rope of a bit of rigging in my fist. The wind still hurled itself along and the waves reared up, webbed with white foam on their smooth green sides, but the boat rode steadier.

In short, this was not to be the time of my death.

It was cold on deck in the damp blast of air but I wanted never, ever, to go back down to that bunk again. Got myself in a nook between a cask and a coil of rope big as a table, sat down on the boards, watched for land. But there was nothing, only water, every heave and suck of it like every other but different too, arranging itself in a new way every time, and after a while I forgot about land and was content to watch water instead. The sky all rags of cloud and the wind pushing us along like no wind I'd ever felt. It had started on this endless open space of ocean and blown across it for God only knew how many miles and weeks, nothing in its way but the odd boat and seagull.

Up ahead where sea met sky, a line of cloud lay on the

horizon. Land, perhaps. That dim colourless shape my first glimpse of New Zealand.

For the girl it would of been her last, every up and down of the boat taking her further away. She'd of stared till her eyes ached, till the cloud became the same as the sky, the last ghost of her home gone.

What Jack had said, how he'd put it to the girl's kin, I didn't know. That it was just for a visit? Or did he talk till they agreed it would be best for the girl?

Did she leave happily? Did they promise her some adventure that would appeal to a little girl? A good life with her grandpa, a new family? But what child, if she knew it would be for ever, would leave her place and go to live among folk she didn't know? That sallow child in the lamplight of the parlour had not been someone having an adventure.

For a moment she was as present to me as if she was standing alongside. She'd of stood like I was, hanging onto wet rigging and feeling the wind stream past. She'd of seen these same waves, these racing clouds, heard the same creaks and knocks of the boat pushing itself through the hills of water. Exactly this, give or take the weather.

I was doing the journey home she'd longed to do, squeezed up in the corner of the window, hour after hour, day after day. It was why I was here. In her place. So little and so much too late. But it was all I could do.

Jack was up at the bow with a couple of the sailors, at ease on the pitching deck. He saw me, made his way along to where I was.

Best watch out now, he said. Mrs Daunt up and about. Good-day to you, Mrs Daunt, glad to see you on your feet.

Under the fierce lines on his face I saw the Jack that I knew, and who knew me.

Making good time, he said. Not far off. Be there tomorrow.

I looked ahead but no matter where you turned your eyes, there was only water heaving itself up and down.

How can you tell, I said, thinking he was saying what I wanted to hear.

See them birds, he said. Stick by the land.

I hadn't noticed them, they were so much like the dark water, skimming so close you'd think they'd scrape the tops of the waves.

Good eating bird that, he said. Like a mutton chop.

I was going where a human face could be carved like wood and a bird might taste like a mutton chop. What else was there? And was everyone carved like him? I tried to imagine it, being the only one with a naked face.

You done the right thing, he said. You're a good brave soul. Always have been.

It was the first time he'd spoken soft to me. *You're a good brave soul.* Precious, the nearest thing to forgiveness.

We folded ourselves down out of the wind and he got me ready for what was ahead.

First off, there was his wife. Her name was Hinewai.

You'd have children, I said.

Just the one, he said, our Maria, five going on six, smart as paint, never saw such a girl for catching onto a thing.

I heard the pride and love in his voice and was glad. *Be happy, live long.*

Now I best tell you this, he said. These people, they got a special way of welcoming. Sing a song for you, do a dance. Then you got to do it back. Not the dance, let you off the dance part. But you got to sing something.

Singing out in front of a whole lot of strangers! My thin little voice, and what song would I sing? Could they let me off the singing as well as the dancing?

But I thought of the girl. Her sad face. If having to sing in front of some strangers was the worst that would ever happen to me, I was a lucky woman.

Then after the singing they'll come up to you, he said. One by one. Press their nose up against your nose.

I tried to see past the marks on his face, if he was having a lend of me.

Real gentle, he said. Like we might shake hands.

Press their noses, I said. Right up to me. My nose.

I stared at the cask beside me, a knotty bit in the wood and a nick out of one of the hoops. Needed to think about something simple, something I knew about, wood and iron. The closer we got to the place that had given Jack his new shape, the more clear I saw that the things I knew about would be of no use to me. Where I was going, the person called Sarah Daunt was not as clever even as the smallest child.

One of the men shouted from the bow and Jack went back to them, the hair lying between his shoulder blades with the wind ruffling it sideways.

Next morning when I stepped out onto the deck, the cloud on the horizon had firmed into a shape. Some trick of the light made a pale line between the dark sea and the darker shape so it seemed to float on the water.

By degrees as the morning went on, with no boundary where one thing turned into another, the land made itself visible. A steep place, high and dark, all clefts and shadows. The tops of the high parts sliced off flat where they went up into cloud. Thick bush on every fold, a green so dark it was near black, smooth and thick like the nap on velvet, coming down to the water, only for a skirt of black rocks.

The boat curved past a headland, the high land fell away behind us. Ahead a wide stretch of open water, low hills all round. The water glassy, the land sheltering it from the wind. But under the smoothness, a secretive slow swell like the sea breathing, a long hump of water travelling along under the skin.

We sailed slow and calm towards a low spit of land on the far side, so pale it was hard to see against the water. From this distance it was something the shape of a lizard, flat along the water, the long nose going away to nothing, the small humps of its body. Where the head met the body, a dip in the land like a neck, and out of that neck I could see smoke rising, and dark shapes different from anything I'd seen for two weeks: houses.

People, too, little moving shapes walking down a track towards a beach. One of them the granny perhaps. All those years ago she'd of watched the boat carry her granddaughter away. She'd of waved in the beginning, no matter what she'd of been feeling, sent the girl away with a cheerful face. She'd of seen the girl wave back. Then too much air would of come between them, the girl a speck on the stern, then not even a speck. The sails would of become pale small shapes you might mistake for birds, but the granny would of gone on standing on the beach, looking, even after there was nothing to see.

We'd come close now, but not close enough to make out the faces of the people on the beach. The anchor chain clattered against the boards and the boat stopped moving, quietly riding the breathing of the water.

From the bow I heard a man calling, a long run of words sent out towards the land. It was Jack, standing up at the bowsprit, his hands cupped round his mouth, and it was no words I knew. He stopped and a call came back from the group on the beach, the voice of a woman, but strong, a rope of human sound flung out across the water.

Backwards and forwards, Jack's voice and the voice from the land, and then it seemed the exchange was finished. The sailors heaved a skiff over the side and there was Jack helping me over the rail and down the ladder. I watched the land come to meet me and for one frightened moment wished I could go back, all the way along the miles, all the way back to quiet familiar Glenmire. Then the bow crunched into the sand and I stepped out onto that unknown shore.

I'D THOUGHT New Zealanders might be in the same mould as our natives, black and skinny, with that way of not meeting your eye. But these folk were tall and strong, well covered with flesh, legs thick with muscle. One or two of the men had faces carved like Jack's, some of the women had a shape drawn round their lips and on their chin, a neat blue line like on a teacup. But no grass skirts, like Will and Jack had told us about, just trousers on the men and serge skirts on the women, and the most of the faces as unmarked as mine.

They stared at me, spoke to each other about me, laughed and called. Long ago Will and Jack said they cooked their enemies and ate them. I could believe it, but I was not here to be a meal.

They had a name for Jack, something that slipped away

when I tried to catch it. He spoke to them in their tongue, a big dark man among other big dark men, not the same as them but welcomed like kin returning.

Jack's wife reminded me of my sister. High round cheekbones, skin tight over the bone, chin like a spade, only browner in the face than Mary, and her hair black. She smiled, held my hand and spoke to me, shapes and sounds like water.

Hinewai says you are right welcome, Jack said. She thanks you for making this long journey. Says, you are a brave woman. That's the truth of it, Mrs Daunt. You are that.

Hanging back behind Jack's wife, a little girl.

Our lass Maria, Jack said. Our dear lass.

Maria reminded me of the girl. The colour of her skin, paler than the others, and the different shape of her face. I wondered if Jack saw the likeness too.

She carried so much in her, this girl. Hinewai, and Hinewai's mother and father, all the way back, the life of this place. Jack too, and through him old Mr Langland, and the woman whose kin I'd got a glimpse of at the house by the lagoon. All those men and women, coming together in this solemn big-eyed child staring at the woman her father had brought.

They took me towards the houses. On a rise of land behind them was a building bigger than the rest, with an open space in front.

They'll greet you, Jack said. Make you welcome. Women's business, I got to hang back.

I smiled and thanked and let myself be led, sat on a chair brought out for me, and all around me that other language flowing past like a creek of thick water where there was nothing for me to latch onto.

The girl had floated like this. Our life at Thornhill's Point, so crisp and real to me, had been something she'd floated and floundered in, a place where nothing had a reason, where every face was unknown and every object was without the softness of knowing what it was or what it was for, where it was from or where it was going. A place you hoped was a dream, so you could wake up from it.

The women got together in front of me. They'd changed their serge for grass skirts now. Sang a loud fierce song and twirled themselves about, doing things with their hands and shoulders and sliding their eyes sideways. I thought it must be the welcome song Jack had told me about, so I stood up and tried to look welcomed. In truth I was frightened. When they sang and danced it wasn't one woman here and then another woman next to her. It was a single creature stronger than any of them. It was warning as much as welcome.

Then they stopped with a great shout. It was my turn now. So many faces watching. Hinewai not smiling, nothing so sociable, but there was a warmth about her. *Let me see who you are*, her face said. *Show me who you are*.

I knew I had to sing. Not very much was going to be asked of me here. Nothing at all compared to what had been asked of the girl. I must not fail her. But my mind was empty of any song and my voice had dried up.

Then from behind me, Jack started. *Oranges and lemons, say the bells of Saint Clement's*.

He faded off and I heard a reedy voice take over. It trembled and stretched thin, weak as a child's. But I was singing.

*You owe me five farthings, say the bells of Saint Martin's.*

Such an odd thing, the sort of thing as happens in those fussy worried dreams when you've slept late. So strange and odd to be standing in this open space with these women smiling and watching, and my little voice. The words floated up as easy as if I'd sung them the day before. Stored like a cheese in its rind, all that time.

*When will you pay me, say the bells of Old Bailey. When I grow rich, say the bells of Shoreditch.*

But I was ashamed. What kind of world was I from, where this was all the answer I could make to a song of welcome?

When I was finished Hinewai laid her fingers on my arms and leaned in to me with a bright open look. Her face coming in to me close and the feel of her skin on mine the softest thing in the world. I'd never been so deep in another person's eyes, or had them so deep in mine. Felt the warmth of her face, her nose pressed against mine.

They all did it, the whole line, must of been twenty women, all leaned in to me with that bright face. By the end they felt like family. You might kill a person you've kissed. Kill a person you've done the other thing with. But it came to me that it would be hard to kill a person you'd joined your face with.

Hinewai took my hand again and we walked together with all the women into the building behind the open space. High like a church, but dim lit and hazy with smoke. She took me to the far end, let me go. Everyone fell back and I was on my own, facing an old woman in a cloak of a soft straw colour with dark tassels all over it. The skin of her face was creased and crumpled and on her chin a pattern, neat blue lines gone soft with age along with the skin.

She made a sign and I sat down on the mat facing her. She put her hands round mine so I could feel the warm skin of her palms. Smooth as a lady's.

She started to talk, or perhaps it was a prayer or a poem. The other women now and then murmured something, like in church when everyone says Amen.

After a time she stopped. Was that the end of it, should I get up? But behind my ear Jack spoke, quiet and low.

What she's been telling you, it's about the girl, he said. How it was when she was born, middle of summer. Trees in flower, the cod running.

We'd never marked the girl's birthday. Never as much as wondered when it was.

Born as the sun was coming up, he said.

He hesitated as if thinking how to say it.

Lovely, he said. Lovely as the sun, she says, her face like the stars and her body strong as the sea.

I wanted to turn away from the woman's gaze on me but I had to face her. Made myself look at her, listening to the way she loved the girl.

I got to say the next part now, Jack said. What I can't forgive myself for. How I took her away.

His way of speaking the New Zealand tongue was slow and careful. I could hear the sounds like beads on a string, paid out one at a time. He stopped and she said something. Not gentle. He bowed his head.

Now you got to tell her, Jack said. What happened after she got to your place.

Everywhere the broad brown faces watching, waiting for me to speak. Some of these women here might be aunties to her, like I was. That made us kin, in a roundabout way. If Pa hadn't sent for the girl, she'd be here now, among these folk, holding her granny's hand and helping her on her way.

I'd thought about what I'd say. Made myself look at those pictures. Not pretty pictures. That wasn't what I was here for, soft false comfort.

I told how the girl stood in the parlour and hung onto the edge of Jack's coat. How she heard her mother's name and looked around and the light went out of her face. How she got up on Jack's bed that first night. After that, locked in.

I stopped, thought Jack might put what I'd said into the old woman's language. I was pleased to stop. It was hard looking at those pictures.

Go on, I heard Jack say. Best go on.

I made myself say about how sad the girl was. Every minute of every day a sadness. Got out the words for the thing I most hated to think of, how I'd made her put out her hand to the horse, how frightened she was. How she never spoke. Sat all day in the window watching down the river for the boat to take her away.

Might as well of taken a knife to her heart, I said. Only we did it by inches.

The old woman's eyes were fierce as an owl's. Whatever part of my words she understood, she didn't need them in her own tongue. She was looking past the words, into the woman speaking them. My voice was thready, telling it with those eyes on me. My feet and hands cold and trembly. Wanted to stop, but there was too much silence, and stopping would be one more lie. The women pressing in around me, and not a sound, except my voice, pushing on into the quiet.

I went away to my husband, I said. To my own life. I left her there.

Wanted to say things. How I was sorry. How I should of. How I wished. But my being sorry was nothing but air.

Next I knew, word come she was dead, I said.

Everyone waiting.

I can't, Jack, I said. I don't know. How she died. None of that.

The lines round his eyes made him stern.

You got to tell it as best you can, he said. Got to say.

His voice hardly his own, it was so grave.

I turned back to the old woman. She bent forward a little, as if hearing the words I wasn't saying. I met her eyes, that looked into me, saw who I was. She knew I couldn't tell her how her granddaughter died. It wasn't the hows and the wheres and the wherefores she wanted. That wasn't what I was here for.

What she needed, what I was here for, was to watch me go through the telling of it. To hear the shake in my voice and see the twist in my mouth. To watch me see the pictures one by one and put them into words, word by sad word. To know

301

I felt it, what had been done.

They must of took her to the cemetery, I said. They'd of buried her. I don't know where.

That was the end of what I had to offer.

I had planned to ask, what was the girl's name. Her true name. But there were no more words in me, only tears.

No one moved, no one leaned to me, no arm went round me. The women watched and they listened. My tears would go on for as long as they had to. The women were not unfeeling. But they knew that there were times when tears ought to be shed, as many tears as was right, and this was one of those times.

When it was finished, I was emptied. By and by I heard the women start in to singing, a sad quiet song. At first I thought they were singing for me. But then they all moved up around the old woman, took her in among themselves. They were singing for her. I glimpsed her for a moment, then all I could see was their backs, their broad shoulders, their shining black hair, and out of the body of them came the rise and fall of their singing.

My part was finished. The shred of story I had, I'd handed it along. Paid the only price I could. These women had taken it into themselves. It was theirs now, part of what they would do to honour the girl.

Jack was gone. I waited, but he didn't come back.

I got up at last, went to the door, unsteady like someone who'd been sick in bed a long time. The sun had set, but the sky was still full of light. I went across the open space and down a path that curved over the low ridge of land towards the sea. Walked along half-blind, seeing nothing but my feet moving.

Grass and stones and sand, and a dune with threads of grass like the tassels on the old woman's cloak. Then I was on the beach, the wind in my hair, cold on my wet cheeks.

There seemed no reason to do anything. There was just this empty place, and the emptied woman in it.

The wind was cold, the sand grey with the last light. Small waves ran up the shining wet sand, pulled back. A gull, bright white against the grey sky, floated along the wind, then tilted sideways, its wings taking gulps of air, stepping down along nothing.

~

How will I ever find a way to tell everything that brought me here? How I found myself in that place where the wind never stops blowing and nothing lies between the land and the ice at the bottom of the world but an ocean full of dark water? How tell the story of me and Jack Langland and a girl who only ever had someone else's name? Of those things left undone that we ought to have done, and those things done that we ought not to have done?

Rippling away into all those lives, down along the fathers and daughters and granddaughters. Generation after generation, the things joining us and the things cutting between us. All made by something done so long ago.

I'd go back to the houses in a minute, sit with Jack and Hinewai, be a gracious guest. I'd come to know Maria, and think of my own child so far away. Go back to Glenmire by and by, live out my life alongside of John Daunt and Sadie and whatever other children life might bless me with. There'd be gladness and sadness, mistakes made and things done right. If there was anything I could do to mend things, I'd do them.

I'd grow old, I'd die. All the things I'd seen and done and felt would die along with me, carried off to where there was no bringing them back.

I'm never going to be able to tell what it was all about. Jack would be the only one now, and Jack's not here. I can only tell what I know. Cruelties and crimes, miseries on every side. But of all the crimes done, the worst would be to let the story slip away. For what it's worth, mine had best take its place, in with all the others.

# ACKNOWLEDGMENTS

As always, I could fill a chapter with a list of people who made this book possible.

It starts with my mother Isobel Russell, who in re-telling the family stories always mentioned the fact that her great-great-grandfather Solomon Wiseman (on whom William Thornhill is loosely based) was said to have had a daughter 'who got pregnant to the riding master, was thrown out of the house and died'. In the moment that I realised this story, if true at all, might be about his granddaughter rather than his daughter, *Sarah Thornhill* was born. If my mother hadn't preserved this detail I'd never have gone looking for the remarkable histories that inspired parts of this novel.

Since I wrote *The Secret River* I have learned that 'history' can be an inflammatory word, so let me say clearly: this is a work of fiction that takes the past as its starting point. (You can find more on the history/fiction demarcation dispute, and on the sources for this novel, at kategrenville.com)

Particular thanks and appreciation go to Nigel Prickett, who seemed to know before I did how important the story of Thomas Chaseland would be to this book. Without Thomas Chaseland there would be no Jack Langland. Talking with Lynette Russell and reading her paper on Chaseland enriched and broadened my sense of the man he might have been, and the larger meanings of his story. At an early stage of research Barbara Dawson generously shared her PhD thesis and its invaluable bibliography of sources I'd never have found on my own. Bill Dacker did me the very great kindness of reading the last part of the book and making important suggestions. Pat Grace opened my eyes to the possibility of a story that was not just about the past, but the present and its unfinished business.

My great thanks to all of you for your generosity.

Others whose support and assistance I'm extremely grateful for are: Paul Diamond, Laurie Edwards, Rachael Egerton, Deborah Figuera, Brian and Beryl Forbes, Lloyd Jones, Melanie Nolan, Marita and Ernie Ranclaud, Eric Rolls, Te Manu Adventures on Rakiura, Sir Tipene O'Regan, John Mackie, Patrick Matthew, Don Maunder, Roger Milliss, Jacqui Mott, Des O'Malley, Jennie Pattrick, Henry Reynolds, Michael Skerrett, Kate Stevens, Angela Wanhalla, Dean Whaanga, Lydia Wevers, Suzi Whitehead-Pope and Bellbird & Swallows, and Louella and Gerard Windsor.

As always, the greatest thanks to my family for their unfailing and essential support.

# READING GROUP QUESTIONS

1) Do you find the portrayal of Sarah Thornhill as an illiterate Australian-born woman convincing? Do you believe that such a woman would have had the insights and imagination that Sarah Thornhill has? Or do you feel Sarah is too 'modern' and too insightful for an uneducated country girl?

2) Why do you think it might be difficult to imagine the world of a person who can't read or write, and to write a convincing voice for that person?

3) Do you have family stories passed down from generation to generation? If you do, how many of them are passed down along the female line, from mother to daughter? How many of the stories are *about* women and their experiences of life?

4) Sarah is about 15 when she and Jack consummate their love. She's about 18 when she gets married, and is only about 23 at the end of the book. This is a story of a very young woman – for much of the book a teenager. Do you think this would be a useful or interesting book for today's teenagers?

5) At one level, *Sarah Thornhill* is about love. There's the 'thunderclap' passionate love that Sarah and Jack experience. Then there's the 'slow-fuse' kind of love that Sarah finds with John Daunt. Are these two different kinds of love true to your experience? Do you think that this book has a 'happy ending' in the sense that the love

Sarah finds with Daunt might be more substantial than the love she and Jack shared? What problems do you think might lie ahead for Sarah and John Daunt, given the differences in class and education between them?

6) At another level, *Sarah Thornhill* is about family secrets, and what happens when they come out. Do most families have a secret? Should they sometimes stay hidden, or is it better to bring the skeletons out of the cupboard? Was it for better or worse that Sarah discovered the secret in her father's life?

7) Did her father want the secret to be discovered, as Sarah thinks? Was sending Sarah to fetch Dick really his way of confession?

8) *Sarah Thornhill* is also about the hidden aspects of a nation's past. The secret in Sarah's family is the same secret that for generations went unspoken about in Australian history – the story of the 'frontier war' between the first Australians and the colonists, which was largely ignored or forgotten until historians brought it to light towards at the end of the twentieth century. Do you think that on this level Sarah represents present-day Australians, in that she has to decide what to do with her new-found knowledge?

9) Sarah responds to the challenges of the past by being more generous in her charity to the nearby indigenous people, and also in making sure the story isn't lost again. Do you think these responses are appropriate? Are they enough? Is there some other response she could have made? Or do you think that her sense of shame isn't appropriate, since she wasn't the person who committed the violence?

10) The story of Sarah's niece, taken away from her extended family and her language, has echoes of Australia's 'stolen generations'. Some would argue that children were removed from their indigenous families 'for their own good', as Sarah's Ma and Pa think. Jack, though of mixed descent himself, agrees. Yet the separation was a disaster for the little girl, as it was for many of the 'stolen generations'. When people do the 'wrong' thing for the 'right' reasons, what attitude might we take towards them? Do you think this book judges the characters, or does it simply explore the moral tangle they find themselves in?

11) Kate Grenville has said that she's 'not especially interested in the past for its own sake, but in how it's shaped the present'. Do you think *Sarah Thornhill* is about the present, as much as the past?

For further questions and extra material, please visit Kate Grenville's website: www.kategrenville.com.